I0613277

Anonymous

A Memorial of Charles Sumner

Anonymous

A Memorial of Charles Sumner

ISBN/EAN: 9783337093099

Printed in Europe, USA, Canada, Australia, Japan

Cover: Foto ©Andreas Hilbeck / pixelio.de

More available books at **www.hansebooks.com**

Charles Schulz

A

MEMORIAL

OF

CHARLES SUMNER.

"HIS EULOGY IS HIS LIFE; HIS EPITAPH IS THE GENERAL GRIEF;
HIS MONUMENT, BUILDED BY HIS OWN HANDS, IS THE ETERNAL
STATUTES OF FREEDOM."

Senator Anthony's Speech in the United States Senate.

BOSTON:
1874.

WRIGHT & POTTER,
PRINTERS TO THE STATE.

CHARLES SUMNER.

COMMONWEALTH OF MASSACHUSETTS.

IN SENATE, June 16, 1874.

ORDERED, That the Joint Special Committee appointed to take suitable measures to provide for the delivery of an Oration upon the life, character and public services of CHARLES SUMNER, be directed to prepare a Memorial Volume containing the proceedings in the Legislature on the receipt of the intelligence of the decease of our late Senator; the account of the Funeral and Commemorative Services, and a copy of the Eulogy delivered by GEORGE WILLIAM CURTIS, and the Poem by JOHN G. WHITTIER; and that five thousand copies of such Memorial be printed and bound for the use of the Legislature. And that each member of the Legislature, the Clerk and Chaplain of each branch, and the Sergeant-at-arms be allowed ten copies each, and the other officers of the Legislature, and the reporters to whom seats are allotted in the two branches, and each city and town in the Commonwealth, one copy each; the residue to be distributed or otherwise disposed of according to the best discretion of the Committee.

Adopted.   S. N. GIFFORD, *Clerk.*

HOUSE OF REPRESENTATIVES, June 17, 1874.
Adopted in concurrence.

GEO. A. MARDEN, *Clerk.*

REPORT OF THE COMMITTEE.

THE undersigned Joint Special Committee, acting under the preceding Order, herewith submit the MEMORIAL VOLUME which they were directed to prepare.

The Committee have asked Mr. WILLIAM HOWELL REED to give his editorial supervision to the several reports and documents, in order to insure a completeness and precision, without which the work would lose its value. They are entirely satisfied with his work, and as the volume has taken form under his direction, they may say with propriety that they believe it will fully meet the wishes of the General Court.

MOODY MERRILL.
GEORGE F. VERRY.
JOSHUA B. SMITH.
WILLARD P. PHILLIPS.
SMITH R. PHILLIPS.

CONTENTS.

DEATH OF CHARLES SUMNER.

CHARLES SUMNER died at his residence, in Washington, at thirteen minutes before three o'clock on Wednesday afternoon, the eleventh day of March, 1874.

He left his seat in the Senate Chamber for the last time on Tuesday afternoon, with a premonition of the sufferings which so soon ended in his death.

About nine o'clock in the evening, he sent for his physician, Dr. Joseph Tabor Johnson, who administered the prescription of morphia, made by Dr. Brown-Sequard, but the pain increased. At twenty minutes past ten, the doctor announced that the usual reaction had not taken place, and that his patient was in serious danger. His pulse could scarcely be felt. Powerful restoratives were at once given, external applications made, and a consultation of physicians promptly called. Through the night, stimulants were administered, but at eight o'clock on Wednesday morning, it was felt that the patient was in a hopeless condition.

About ten o'clock the stupor passed away, and Mr. SUMNER recognized his friends, with a few words of greeting. He complained of great fatigue, but of no pain, except when he moved of his own strength. He was, he said, tired in every nerve and muscle, even in his bones. He wanted rest, and begged for more morphine to allay his weariness.

He had spoken several times during the morning of the Civil Rights Bill, whose passage he had much at heart. On one occasion, recognizing Judge Hoar, who was standing at his bedside, he said, "*You must take care of the Civil Rights Bill, Judge;*" to which the reply was made, "We will take care of it."

At a later period he said, "*Judge, it is very good in you to come.*" About two hours before the Senator's death, sitting on a low chair by his bed, and chafing his hand and arm, the Judge said, "I wish we could do something to make your hands warmer." To which Mr. Sumner replied, after a pause, and looking steadily into the face of his friend, "*You never will.*"

At a still later moment, and about fifteen minutes before Mr. Sumner died, giving his hand to Judge Hoar, who was at his side, he said, "*Judge, tell Emerson how much I love and revere him.*" To which Judge Hoar replied, "He said of you, that he never knew so white a soul."

With the exception of a word or two casually spoken a few moments afterwards, this message to Mr. Emerson was the last utterance of Mr. Sumner.

After sleeping a few moments he was awakened, probably by a violent nausea, and raised himself in bed; but after the convulsive effort for relief was made, and even while his friends were bathing his face and lips, and before he could be laid back upon his pillow, the action of the heart ceased, and CHARLES SUMNER was dead.

High medical authority states the disorder to have

been Angina Pectoris, in this instance arising from an enlarged and diseased state of the right coronary artery. It is a disorder which often terminates fatally after a few paroxysms.

Twenty-three years of illustrious service to the Commonwealth and the Nation, give to Massachusetts the high privilege of a grateful recognition of their priceless value.

"No pyramids set off his memories," but those who loved him for his gracious personal qualities of heart and life, may join in the requiem:

> "And now he rests; his greatness and his sweetness
> No more shall seem at strife,
> And death has moulded into calm completeness
> The statue of his life."

Action of the Executive and Legislative Departments.

MESSAGE OF THE GOVERNOR.

COMMONWEALTH OF MASSACHUSETTS.

Executive Department, Boston, March 12, 1874.

Gentlemen of the Senate and of the House of Representatives:

It becomes my painful duty to announce to you the death of our senior member in the United States Senate. Yesterday afternoon, at ten minutes before three o'clock, in his own rooms at Washington, at the age of sixty-three years, CHARLES SUMNER departed this life.

Eighteen years ago he was struck down at his place in the vanguard of freedom, and from that terrible wound, nigh unto death, he never fully recovered, though he struggled against its effects with all the forces of his nature, and was aided by the best efforts of medical science. But he had regained such a measure of health and strength, that of late his intimate friends and associates were encouraged to hope he might be spared to us for some years longer. The shock of his death comes upon us suddenly, and when least expected. The last enemy of man has finally triumphed, and our great orator, scholar, statesman, philanthropist,—the champion of universal freedom and the equal rights of man,—after a life of labor and usefulness, has fallen under the burden of disease long and heroically borne.

Of him, as much as of any man of his time, it may be said, that he lived not for himself or his kindred. A special representative of this State, his Commonwealth was the whole country. For years one of the most prom-

3

inent and influential citizens of the United States, he was
recognized by the civilized world as one of the foremost
advocates of struggling humanity. Thus acknowledged
at home and abroad, his death will be deeply and sincerely mourned, not alone by his State and this Nation,
but by every people and country reaching out for a
higher and freer life.

Twenty-three years ago this spring he was elected to
the United States Senate, and at the time of his death he
was the senior member of that body in length of consecutive service. His devotion to the duties of his place was
an example worthy of general commendation. He rarely
allowed personal considerations of any kind to interfere
with his public obligations. Had he not been blessed
with an iron constitution, he must long ago have succumbed to the weight of his labors. Devoted to many
phases of one comprehensive cause, the advancement of
man; throwing himself with great energy and power into
whatever work he undertook; it was given him to see a
noble triumph of that for which he aspired and wrought.
Thousands and thousands of men and women find the
way of life easier and brighter because of him, and in
almost every town and village of the country, there will
be praises of honor to his name.

During his long period of service some mistakes he
doubtless made, for despite his great learning and intellectual grasp he somewhat lacked the every-day wisdom
frequently given to those much his inferiors. But this
was in no sense to his discredit as a man. His aims were
high, his purposes were pure. His voice was that of an
honest man, his endeavors were those of an upright
statesman. His moral integrity stands out as a sublime
figure in these later years. While the atmosphere around
him was foul with corruption, no stain of suspicion ever
fell upon him. However other public servants prostituted
their positions for selfish ends, we all felt sure that

CHARLES SUMNER would not be smirched by any disclosures or investigations. This single fact alone is enough to crown him with glory.

Gentlemen, you must have unspeakable satisfaction at this hour in your recent action on the matter relative to the army register and national battle-flags. It was communicated to Mr. Sumner while he was in the full possession of all his faculties, and we may well believe that he rejoiced in this vindication by the constituents whom he had so long and so faithfully served. I thank you for giving me the pleasure of transmitting to him, by the hands of one whom he honored, a representative of those for whom he had so heroically struggled, this fresh token of the regard in which he was held by the people of this Commonwealth.

It was his desire, often expressed, that he might fall, when fall he must, while at the post of duty. His wishes in this respect were gratified. The day before his death he was at the Senate Chamber attending to official business as our agent and servant: and one of his last utterances, when in the very arms of death, was a request to an intimate friend to take care of the civil rights bill, the passage of which he had much at heart. Thus he went out from among us, with his last moment of consciousness still pleading, as he had so often and so eloquently plead through many years of vigorous manhood, for the down-trodden and oppressed.

The great Senator has fallen, and we shall see him no more on earth. Being dead he yet speaketh — by the hopes he inspired, the works he accomplished and the recollection of his virtues. In a few days his mortal remains will be laid away in the grave. Be it ours to guard most tenderly the memory he hath left to us, and approve ourselves the fit constituents of CHARLES SUMNER.

W. B. WASHBURN.

COMMONWEALTH OF MASSACHUSETTS.

IN SENATE, March 12, 1874.

ORDERED, That the message of His Excellency the Governor, communicating the melancholy intelligence of the sudden death of Hon. CHARLES SUMNER, senior Senator of Massachusetts in the Congress of the United States, be referred to a Joint Special Committee of five members of the Senate with such as the House may join, with instructions to consider and report what measures it may be expedient and proper to adopt as a recognition of the important services of the late distinguished Senator, and a public acknowledgment of the grateful esteem in which his memory and character are held by the people of the Commonwealth.

And Messrs. BANKS, NORCROSS, WASHBURN, HAWES and LATHROP were appointed on the part of the Senate.

Sent down for concurrence.

S. N. GIFFORD, *Clerk.*

HOUSE OF REPRESENTATIVES, March 12, 1874.

Concurred, and Messrs. PHILLIPS of Salem, SMITH of Cambridge, CODMAN of Boston, KIMBALL of Boston, ADAMS of Quincy, DICKINSON of Amherst, NOBLE of Westfield, PHILLIPS of Springfield, BUFFUM of Lynn, BLUNT of Haverhill, SLADE of Somerset, CUMMINGS of Woburn, and ESTABROOK of Worcester, are joined.

GEO. A. MARDEN, *Clerk.*

RESOLUTIONS.

In SENATE, March 13, 1874.

THE following Resolutions were reported by Hon. NATHANIEL P. BANKS, in behalf of the Joint Special Committee on the Message of the Governor, announcing the death of Mr. SUMNER:—

COMMONWEALTH OF MASSACHUSETTS.

In the Year One Thousand Eight Hundred and Seventy-Four.

RESOLVES ON THE DEATH OF CHARLES SUMNER.

RESOLVED, That the Legislature of Massachusetts receives the sad intelligence communicated by His Excellency the Governor, of the sudden death of the Honorable CHARLES SUMNER, senior Senator of Massachusetts in the Congress of the United States, with emotions of profound and abiding grief.

RESOLVED, That, in this sudden calamity, Massachusetts mourns the loss of an inestimable public servant, whose separate qualities are sometimes found in individual citizens, but rarely united in one man. His industry was tireless, and his fidelity unlimited. In the prosecution of those great measures to which he gave his support, his energy, constancy and courage were unconquerable. In his contests for the supremacy of the principles upon which he had staked the hazard of his life, he was unmoved by assault and insensible to fear. Against the allurements of power and of corruption, in every form, he stood a tower of adamant. At every crisis in public affairs his bearing was that of one who, confident as to his own duty, was

considerate of the rights of others. His extraordinary
acquisitions as a scholar, made him eminent among able
men in every department of learning. He was an accomplished legist and jurist, and as an orator unsurpassed
by any man of his time. The vigor of his intellect ; his
great experience and capacity ; his philanthropic spirit ;
his ardent patriotism ; his irrepressible love of liberty ;
his limitless devotion to the rights of man, gave to all
classes of the people, to all sections of the country, and
to the world at large, a permanent interest in the pro-
longation of his labors and his life.

RESOLVED, That, deploring the public loss, it is yet a
consolation that the people of the Commonwealth share in
the triumphs, resulting, in great part, from the labors of
their illustrious Senator, to which in the agony of death
he gave his last and noblest thoughts, and which culmi-
nated in the destruction of an odious and sectional system
of chattel slavery ; in the enfranchisement of four million
slaves ; in their political and social elevation ; and the
incorporation of the sublime doctrines of the Declaration
of American Independence into the text and body of the
Constitution of the Republic.

RESOLVED, That in the galaxy of her illustrious children, whose colonial, revolutionary, constitutional and
military services shed an undying lustre upon her name,
MASSACHUSETTS HAS NO WORTHIER SON !

PROCEEDINGS IN THE SENATE.

Hon. HENRY S. WASHBURN, of the First Suffolk District, then spoke as follows upon these Resolutions:—

MR. PRESIDENT: There are times in the experience of most men when, overtaken by sudden bereavement, they feel the poverty of human speech to express emotions which struggle for utterance. This is as true of communities as of individuals—moments when a voice almost audible seems to say to us, "Be still, and know that I am God!" "I was dumb and opened not my mouth, because Thou didst it." We have reached such a point in our experience as a people. An event has transpired which, though not unexpected, has nevertheless come upon us as a thief in the night,—as it were, in a moment, in the twinkling of an eye,—and we labor for fitting terms in which to express the grief that oppresses us.

The portion of time occupied by the life of the illustrious dead, covers a most important period in the annals of the nation; and it is quite impossible in the hour allotted for this service for any one to present even a brief analysis of his life-work. I shall not attempt to do it. This task will, in due time, be submitted to other and abler hands. Let us rather mingle our tears and sympathies together, as we bow before the affliction which has come upon us—sorrowing most of all that the places which once knew him will know him no more forever. Given to us by Providence, as we must believe, for the accomplishment of a great mission upon the earth, he has finished the work allotted to him; oh, how worthily; and now, early in the golden afternoon of life, weary and worn from the fields of his triumphs and victories, he rests from his labors and his works they will follow him.

It is an impressive reflection that there is no home in all the Commonwealth where sorrowing kindred wait for his remains when they may be borne hither from the capital of the nation. With the exception of a sister living upon the far-off Pacific shore, he was alone in the world; and so the more, Mr. President, are we all mourners to-day. The State he has done so much to honor, will receive all that was mortal of him, and lay him tenderly to rest upon her bosom, amid the tears and benedictions of all the people.

Mr. President, only four days ago the Senate adopted Resolutions of respect to the memory of an ex-President of the United States—a venerable man, who, in the fulness of years, has passed away from the scenes and responsibilities of earth; and now we pause to pay a similar tribute of love and regard for one greater than he—one nearer and dearer to all our hearts, the recognized champion of the oppressed, the friend of the friendless the wide world over.

Well might we be distrustful for the future, as, one by one, the men who have upheld our country's honor and fame, faint or fall; were we not assured that others, brave and true, will come forth to fill the places made vacant by their departure; and that to-day, upon a thousand altars, from the Atlantic to the Pacific, they are ready to pledge anew their lives, their fortunes and their sacred honor, that they will transmit to their children the heritage we have received from our fathers—the priceless blessing of a Republican Government.

Hon. GEORGE B. LORING, President of the Senate, having called Mr. BAILEY to the Chair, made the following address:—

Mr. PRESIDENT: The sad and startling event which has suddenly arrested the attention and stricken the heart of this Commonwealth and the country, falls with peculiar and touching force upon us who are assembled here. For nearly a generation of men the name of CHARLES SUMNER has been held dear and sacred in these halls. His humane and lofty sentiments have inspired the legislative action of Massachusetts to high and honorable purpose in the great public trials of our day; at his feet have sat those who have pointed the way to an immortal service, and whose short and brilliant career has taught the world what a free Commonwealth can do on the field of battle, and in the executive council, to purify and elevate mankind; and his name has been a watchword for those who believe in humanity, and integrity, and justice, and equality, as the foundation of an imperishable Republic.

Around CHARLES SUMNER as Senator and citizen, as associate and friend, have circled, for a quarter of a century, the best aspiration, the highest culture, the loftiest purpose, and the most earnest hopes of our people, high and low, rich and poor. To him it was given in the same hour to warm the thought of the scholar, and to cheer the heart of the down-trodden and the oppressed. As he walked along the path of life, he led with one hand the wise and the thoughtful to a lofty sphere of duty, and with the other hand the poor and the lowly to the great opportunity and the sweet consolation which attends untrammelled manhood. Not always in accord with popular demand, he was always found proudly in the fore-front of popular honor. Not always an ingenious legislator, he furnished the broad, general principles upon which the more expert might build with entire safety and for the highest welfare of the country. To his mind the animating sentiment of a Republic is virtue; and so he demanded for the people complete social and civil equality, and of the government a patriotic and honest administration of public affairs. Exposed at all times by his sturdy and uncompromising faith to the severest criticism, he set his standard of public service high, and made his demands upon his associates imperative. No man can now recall a word of toleration for a low and equivocal design which ever fell from his lips; and many a man can remember the kind encouragement which he warmly bestowed upon humane and manly purpose.

It is usual, Mr. President, to attribute the result of a brilliant and successful voyage through life to the favoring gales of fortune. Of many of us this may be true; but not so of him whose high and commanding career we are suddenly called upon to contemplate in all its grandeur, and whose untimely death we now deplore. To no man, in any age, has the law of cause and consequence been more thoroughly and consistently applied than to Mr. SUMNER; from no man in public life have we been able to promise mankind a larger and more benignant service than from him whose characteristics, from youth upward, were peculiarly adapted to the times in which he lived. A constant, patient and devoted student, he stored his mind with the broadest principles of humane and Christian statesmanship as the foundation of his service in the cause of freedom; he became familiar with the most righteous doctrines of international law, as a guide for the Republic in its relations with foreign powers; he established a fraternal sympathy between himself and large-hearted statesmen and philanthropists everywhere; he joined himself with the fraternity of scholars throughout the world; he brought to his side, in all his trials, the thoughtful of his own land, and the aspiring of States less favored; and he elevated the political controversies

in which he was engaged up to a standard attractive to
the cultivated and sincere. Not by accident, nor by
good fortune alone, did he accomplish this. It was not
accident which, in his youth, opened the best homes in
Boston to him, in order that affectionate parents might
set his example before their children; it was not accident
which gathered around his early manhood a circle of literature and refinement, where the last bright volume and
the rising author found a welcome into the best companionship of letters; it was not an accident which secured
for him the esteem of the best jurists of America, and
the admiration of the great lawyers who throng Westminster Hall; it was not accident which led him to
advocate the doctrine of peace as the only foundation of
true national grandeur, and to proclaim the doctrine of
freedom as the only sure foundation of the American
Republic; it was not accident which elevated him to the
championship of human equality, and brought him to martyrdom in the holy cause. No. The high purpose, the
devotion to the best mental culture, the eager demand for
the companionship of the wisest and the best, the resolute determination to get wisdom as the "principal thing,"
"more precious than rubies," the early, constant and lasting intimacy with high-toned speculation, the defiance of
social position before the imperative call of conscience,
the unyielding grasp upon a grand and fundamental idea,
the dedication of himself to the great principles, the lofty
scorn of party dictation which marked his course, combined to build for him an imposing monument of civil
labors, whose symmetry and fine proportion no mere
chance could create and which no accident can destroy.
He is known, and will be known, in American history, as
THE SENATOR; no more, no less. One grand, imposing,
perfected structure is his, complete in all its parts, dedicated to one service—a type of what can be accomplished
by the American statesman whose honesty and devotion

secure the confidence of the people, and whose heroism
and courage command their admiration and lay hold upon
a controlling and commanding force, before which all
political machinery is powerless and contemptible. Let
him stand forever in our annals as THE SENATOR—the
product of those institutions which are founded on popular intelligence and freedom, and rely for their defence
and development upon an educated and Heaven-directed
conscience.

And now that he is gone, the best sentiments of our
· hearts struggle for expression. Fortunate as he was, not
so much in the accidents of public life as in that constant
preparation which made him the central figure of every
momentous event in a most critical period in our history,
he was also fortunate in the respect and admiration which
his career secured from all classes and orders of men.
For him the poet sang, the historian wrought, the scholar
labored, the orator warmed, the suffering prayed, the
emancipated poured forth their blessings. When we
remember his characteristics and call up the events of
his life, to no man of our day and generation so truly
applies that familiar and delightful tribute, drawn from
the ancient tongue he loved so well :—

> "Justum et tenacem propositi virum,
> Non civium ardor prava jubentium,
> Non vultus instantis tyranni
> Mente quatit solida."

And as we contemplate his closing hours, to no man
belongs more sublimely those diviner words : —

> "Mark the perfect man and behold the upright ; for the end of
> that man is peace."

Hon. FRANCIS B. HAYES, of the Second Suffolk District, said:—

MR. PRESIDENT: At this time, when death has struck down with awful suddenness the senior representative of this Commonwealth in the councils of the Nation, we cannot refrain from the public expression of sorrow, nor fail to manifest our respect for the memory of the departed. It is the reward of the patriot to be remembered gratefully by his countrymen after he has passed from earth; and we but pay a just debt in recognizing, with the warmest expression of our hearts, the great services which the illustrious statesman, whose death we deplore, has rendered to the State and to all mankind. We do not allow our political opinions nor our personal preferences, in the consideration of subjects upon which men may honestly entertain different views, to prevent us from doing full justice to him who lies now in the cold embrace of the invincible conqueror of mortality. We all hasten to honor him whose useful and noble life has added lustre to the honor of our State and Nation.

The character of CHARLES SUMNER was typical of his New England birthplace. His mind was as capacious as the ocean which beats upon our coast. In his principles he was as immovable as our lofty hills. Though he might not have been so demonstrative as many in the expressions of cordiality, yet his large heart embraced in its affections all mankind, and throbbed with the warmest sympathy for the weak and friendless. The earliest efforts of his manhood were directed to the amelioration of the wretched prisoner in his cell, and in his maturer years he knew no rest until the oppressed were freed from bondage. Justice having been done to the slave, he was then equally anxious that justice should be done to the master. The down-trodden could always look up to him in hope and confidence to alleviate their misery and

to raise them from degradation. He was emphatically
the friend of the friendless.

Mr. SUMNER was a thoroughly honest man. Even
calumny, so ready to destroy the character of good men,
dared not breathe a suspicion against the integrity and
purity of life of our deceased friend. He could not be
approached by any unworthy inducements. His opinions
were always frankly and boldly expressed. He cared not
if he differed from those of high social or official position
if he believed his cause was right. He was no time-
server. While not regardless of the good opinion of
men, he looked first for the approval of Heaven. However his associates in public life might differ with him,
however much some of his friends might regret the
course he thought proper to adopt at times upon matters
of great public interest, yet all will readily accord to him
their respect for his manliness and unflinching courage
in expressing his opinions, which were founded upon his
honest convictions.

Mr. President, I did not rise to pronounce a eulogy
upon CHARLES SUMNER. My feeble words can add nothing to his glorious fame. I simply desire to express my
appreciation of the great loss which has happened to all
in the death of the ripe scholar, the distinguished statesman, the true patriot and honest man. He was a resi-
dent of the district which I have the honor to represent
in this body. But no local boundaries limited his usefulness. He belonged not merely to Massachusetts, but to
the Nation and the whole world, which have been bene-
fited by his life, devoted to the sacred cause of truth and
to the relief of suffering humanity.

It will be, I doubt not, Mr. President, a melancholy
pleasure for us all to unite in manifesting in the most
appropriate manner our respect for the memory of the
long tried, faithful and honored servant of this Commonwealth, now at rest from his labors.

Hon. Thomas N. Stone, of the Cape District, then rose and said :—

Mr. President : Amid the wreaths so rare in their beauty that are laid upon the coffin of our deceased Senator, permit me to place a simple wild-flower as a token of my humble love. For truly has the great iconoclast entered into the house of my idols and stricken from his pedestal one before whom my soul had long bowed with reverence akin to devotion. Ever since I read his "True Grandeur of Nations" CHARLES SUMNER has been to me a model statesman, towering high above his fellows. And amid all the political changes of our country, amid all the clouds and sunshine that have been thrown upon his pathway, my soul has been true to its first love. I was proud to be in the minority last year, as I was glad to be in the majority this year, on that vote which tore the hateful cypress from his brow, just in time for death to place his laurel there. Mr. President, there will be noble praises sung over CHARLES SUMNER's grave, and grand orations pronounced on his life and death. But nowhere in the Old Bay State will CHARLES SUMNER have more sincere mourners than among the sand-hills of my native shore, where old Atlantic, beneath the rude winds of March, is thundering a requiem alone worthy the fame of Massachusetts' noblest son. To us, amid all the suspicion and doubt which have fallen in lighter or darker cloud upon other statesmen, CHARLES SUMNER has ever stood forth sublime in his purpose and grand in his integrity,—

"As some tall cliff that lifts its awful form,
Swells from the vale, and midway leaves the storm,
Though round its breast the rolling clouds are spread,
Eternal sunshine settles on its head."

An eagle-eyed statesman, he saw the foe before he was reached by our shorter vision, and he met that foe when his great heart. which death has now stilled, was the only drum to beat the charge, and his own grand inspiration his only henchman in the field. He has died, leaving no superior behind in his chosen field, and few—for our country all too few—who, in grandness of aim and integrity to right, are worthy to be called his peers. But CHARLES SUMNER has left to posterity a character and a fame after which, it is to be hoped, future statesmen will model their own.

Drape the banner my State,
    For thy chieftain lies low ;
In the field of his conquest
    He has met his last foe.

Hang his shield on thy wall—
    It was dented for thee ;
His war-cry no longer
    Waketh mountain and lea.

The March winds are moaning
    O'er thy forest and plain,
As back to his mother
    Comes thy child once again.

Now his life's work is done,
    Let him sleep on thy breast ;
For of all our broad States
    He has loved thee the best.

The following remarks were then made by Hon. E. H. LATHROP, of the First Hampden District :—

Mr. PRESIDENT : While I fully accord with the sentiment of the Resolutions, and desire for myself to add thus publicly my fealty to, and respect for, the memory of the Senator who has departed, it is to me, sir, a matter of comfort and congratulation that when a Commonwealth sits in the shadow of a great calamity the shackles of party and the prejudice of faction fade away and fall. As has been well said by the Senator who preceded me, I have no eulogy to pronounce upon the character of CHARLES SUMNER; the path of the history of State and Nation for the last twenty-five years is illustrated with the monumental record of his life.

It is peculiarly appropriate, as it is true, while the spirit of the Commonwealth and of the Nation stands in bowed bereavement at the door of his open tomb, that there should exist within the hearts of the people the elements of a great content,—content in this, that the rare symmetry of this man's life is so roundly and nobly perfected in his death.

It remained for him, in the later days of his life, to illustrate to the people of this Commonwealth how possible it is for one large-brained, great-hearted, clear-visioned man to be nearer right than the whole Commonwealth of Massachusetts; and how happily is it true that, after the soreness and the sorrow, and just as his hand was lifted to knock at the gates of the Everlasting City; just before the call was sounded which summoned him to solve the great sad problem of the immortality, there came to him, by tender ways and honored paths, the renewed loyalty, fealty and faith of his Commonwealth.

Now, sir, to the tender tributes that have been offered to his memory, not only in the hearts of this people but by Senators in this chamber, I can add nothing more tender than has been sung by the sweet-voiced laureate of England, of one whom England loved and honored :—

> " We know him now ; all narrow jealousies
> Are silent ; and we see him as he moved,
> How modest, kindly, all-accomplished, wise ;
> With what sublime repression of himself,
> And in what limits and how tenderly—
> Not swaying to this faction or to that,
> Not making his high place the lawless perch

5

Of winged ambition, or a vantage ground
For pleasure. But through all this tract of years
Wearing the white flower of a blameless life,
Before a thousand peering littlenesses,
In that fierce light that beats upon a [public man]
And blackens every blot; for where is he
Who dares foreshadow for an only son
A lovelier life, a more unstained than his?"

Hon. NATHANIEL P. BANKS, of the Second Middlesex District, then addressed the Senate in the following words,—after which the Resolutions were unanimously adopted, amid profound silence, by a rising vote.

The death of Mr. SUMNER has fallen upon us with such startling effect, Mr. President; it has been "so unadvised, so sudden, so like the lightning, which is here and gone ere one can say, 'it lightens,'" that it is quite impossible for us to present even the general appreciation of the character of the great man whose loss the State we represent is especially called to mourn. The members of the Senate have been engaged in a more practical and important duty than that of presenting their opinions as to the services of the illustrious Senator, in making arrangements for the last final honors that are to be paid him by the State and the people of this Commonwealth. Yet, nevertheless, sir, it is due to his memory, and still more to the State and ourselves, to suggest some views of his services and character, however imperfectly they may be presented.

Mr. SUMNER had an established reputation before he was charged with the partial representation of the people of Massachusetts in the Senate of the United States. In his own honored university at Cambridge he was a marked man. He was the flower of its literary societies, and the recipient of high classical honors; and had been offered an appointment to the law professorship as the successor of Judge Story. His eloquent voice had recalled the virtues and the genius of some of the most brilliant men of the time—scholars, artists, philanthropists and jurists. His name was celebrated in the capitals of Europe. He was, therefore, not unknown when he came to the service of the Commonwealth. It is as the Representative of the Commonwealth in the Senate of the United States, however, that his character will be judged and his fame will rest.

The office of Senator of the United States was, in point of fact, the only public office he ever held. It is true he had held a commission at an early period of his life as one of the ministerial officers of the Government of the United States, but it was an uncongenial position, unsuited to his capacity, not at all in accordance with his principles; and when an important change had been made in the legislation of the country, it became morally impossible for him to discharge its duties. So, sir, the office of Senator of the United States was, in truth, the only public office he ever held. How well, sir, he filled that high station, we all know. None of us can well state in such terms as here occur to us the full measure of his success. But we can all comprehend and appreciate the great events of his life, which in themselves convey to the world a proper estimate of his capacity and character. His election occurred in April, 1851. A few months earlier the Congress of the United States had passed what was known as the compromise measures, designed to settle all questions of difficulty between the North and South.

Mr. SUMNER was elected and entered upon his term of service as an opponent of these acts. He stood, therefore, among those with whom he was officially associated, as a representative of a distinct principle, in opposition to the policy which the Government had adopted. The Administration party, with the honored and distinguished ex-President of the United States, Mr. Fillmore, at its head, whose memory was appropriately noticed the other day; whose mortal remains but yesterday, sir, were waiting, in common with those of our own beloved Senator, the last sad honors of their respective States, before the tomb should shut them from our sight forever,—Mr. Fillmore and the great men associated with him, the two houses of Congress, and a large majority of the people, had determined that a policy of concession was necessary and just. It was assumed to be the voice of the people. It would lead, as they supposed, to peace, and avoid an impending fratricidal war. Against that policy Mr. SUMNER appealed as the representative of a different spirit. He conceded nothing. He demanded everything essential to the personal and public liberty guaranteed by the Declaration of Independence.

Undoubtedly the great majority of the people were against him, regarding him as a disturber of the public peace. But the result shows upon whom the gift of prophecy had descended. The parties for whom these concessions had been made were determined to accept nothing that did not recognize slavery as the law of the land, and this extreme demand being rejected, they seemed ready, and, indeed, determined, to destroy the Government itself. And thus, sir, when, at last, the long threatened assault on the part of the Southern States was made, the whole country had to recognize the fact that the illustrious Senator of Massachusetts had stated the only correct principle of action for the General Government in its dealings with the slave-power. And it was then conceded on all sides that compromise as a basis of settlement was impossible. It is upon this historical fact that his reputation must forever stand. It proclaims him the foremost man of his time. For, though he had many able, patriotic, and eloquent coadjutors in defence of the principles of freedom, which ought to have been accepted as the landmark of the Nation, it is well known that from the earnestness of his nature, the intensity of his feelings on this question, he pronounced such eloquent invocations in behalf of liberty, such appeals to the sense of national justice, such stinging rebukes and scathing denunciations of his opponents, that they selected and marked him, the young giant of Massachusetts, as the man who must be overthrown if their cause was not to be destroyed. The deceased Senator in this conflict stood almost alone. Older Senators, who had been taught by experience how far in opposition to the predominant policy they could safely go, had followed a more prudent course. They had even counselled the Massachusetts Senator that his sharp methods of controversy were impolitic and perhaps unsafe. But he did not desist. He returned denunciation for denunciation and scorn for scorn. Like Milton's angel, faithful among the faithless, —

> " From amidst them forth he passed
> Long way thro' hostile scorn, which he sustained
> Superior; nor of violence feared aught;
> And with retorted scorn his back he turned
> On those proud towers to swift destruction doomed."

Thus, Mr. SUMNER, in the Senate of the United States, endured for ten long years the hostility of those that opposed the principles of which he was the representative, and thus he turned his back upon them "with retorted scorn" till those great States suffered the swift destruction to which they had been doomed. In this manner, sir, he became the representative of his country, from his fidelity to its principles. He was entitled to the consideration and marked respect of the whole people, whether they had been enemies or his friends. As an orator, he had in his time few equals, certainly no superior. It is unnecessary for us to speak of him in comparison with ancient orators. We know little about

them. We know of them only by tradition, and we
know enough of tradition to doubt much, if not all,
that is said in praise of them. But the early orators
of our own country we know perfectly well, and however much we esteem them and approve their efforts, we
must remember that the same orations which were then
delivered with studied phrase, modulated voice and pre-
arranged action, would not suit the people of our day.
It is doubtful if the orations which thirty or forty years
since so entranced the people of the United States would
be now appreciated as they were then.

The world is too busy to listen to artistic and studied
harangues. We want to come directly to the points at
issue, and understand the reasons for and against them;
and, measured in this way, Mr. SUMNER had no superior.
He was not only an orator, an instructive speaker upon
all great subjects which he was called upon to discuss,
but he was a keen and able debater, which demands
very different, if not higher powers. And, although
debate involved those sharp thrusts and retorts which
were offensive to him, yet, when necessary, he had as
sharp and bitter a tongue as any man he encountered.
I myself once heard a few words uttered by him
in the Senate of the United States, in the midst of
the personal assaults that were made upon him, that
seemed to impregnate the very atmosphere of the hall
in which he stood. Such was his character, such his
power of language in debate. It has been said, here and
elsewhere, that he was cold and distant. But this was
not the character of his heart or nature. The man who
in the service of the Government has to consider a
hundred different subjects in a day, must dismiss them
promptly, decidedly, but with kindness.

It is quite competent for a man to say yes and no to
everybody, and give the impression to the country, far
and wide, that he is a man of feeling. But he is not a

true man. The true man is he who considers everything presented to him, and speaks honestly and truthfully upon each question. And the deceased Senator never dealt otherwise with man or woman. Thus, when he was thought to be lofty and cold, it was because he was engaged upon those practical matters of business where it was impossible for him to delay or waste his time. But at the foundation of his being, in the depth of his soul, all his warm and strong personal friends say there was a never-failing well of generous and heart-felt sympathies. We can well believe that it was this generous and sympathetic nature which led him to support the great cause to which he dedicated his life.

My honored colleague of the city of Cambridge, my associate upon the committee, informs me, when, a few days ago, the Resolutions of the State of Massachusetts, rescinding the Resolution of condemnation that had been passed against him, were presented to him, he received them with equanimity; that he spoke a few words to one or two gentlemen connected with the Government whom he knew, and then, overcome with emotion, wept as a child. That, sir, was the character of the Senator, when stripped of the husk, the rhinoceros hide, that every public man must sometimes put on to protect him from the assaults of friends as well as enemies.

There is another consideration, more important in estimating the character of the Senator than those which have been suggested. He was a point of union among the people; not a point of union for partisan success, but for necessary and novel combinations and the success of great principles. It was in this way he came to be a Senator of the United States. He did not seek the office. When he was chosen he deemed it proper to recognize his election by notifying the Legislature of his acceptance, and he then declared that while he accepted the office to which he had been elected, and

returned his grateful thanks for the honor conferred
upon him, he had not lifted his hand to obtain it. The
young men of the Commonwealth met this young giant,
as Frederika Bremer called him, soon after his return
from Europe, where he had been honored by the friendship of its scholars and statesmen, and observing his
interest in the philanthropic questions of the day, following in his footsteps as he passed through the streets
— a man of perfectly symmetrical form and vigorous
and manly beauty — and feeling that there was for him
a destiny in connection with the future of his country,
made him their representative.

There were plenty of men in the same organization
in which he moved and with which he acted, that would
have been capable of serving the State in that regard,
but they had not the power of union ; they had not
those qualities that drew men to him. Mr. SUMNER
became a Senator of the United States, after a desper-
ate struggle here in the State of Massachusetts, which
occupied the two houses to the exclusion of almost all
other business for nearly four months, and which tested
the sincerity and integrity of men more than any other
question ever presented to the Legislature. Two or
three hundred men stood up for him or against him,
day and night, until he was triumphantly elected. It
must have been believed that there was something in
his character to support or something in his principles
to oppose, that was important to themselves or to the
country. Then came another opportunity when he could
unite men of different parties for the success of great
principles.

After some years' service, having spoken for the people
of Massachusetts strongly and clearly, he was made the
subject of a brutal and cowardly assault as he sat,
pinioned, as it were, at his desk, and unable to meet
either of the assailants who surrounded him. Men some-

times are able to concentrate masses of men by mere accident as well as by force of intellect. No sooner was this assault upon the Senator of Massachusetts known, than the people of every loyal State, with one voice, avowed their determination to defend his position and his principles. The great revolution, began in 1856, and culminating finally in the war, and the incorporation for the first time of the principles of the Declaration of Independence into the text and body of the Constitution of the Republic, is due to the union formed by the people of the loyal States over his prostrate body in the Senate Chamber. And now, sir, that he is taken away, we feel that in the fulness of his time he had come to another point of union when he, if his life had been spared, would have led us to other and necessary changes in the policy and objects of the Government. This, sir, is what we lose.

It is this, sir, that makes us pause and ask, not of man but of God, "What is your will and what is our duty?" The great man of whom we spoke the other day—I am not ashamed nor afraid to speak of Mr. Fillmore as a patriotic man—had finished his career. Other illustrious statesmen have passed away. They had fulfilled their mission; there was no further duty for them, and God, in his providence, took them to himself. But this man whom we mourn, who lies in the capitol at Washington, and over whom, perhaps at this moment, is pronounced the benediction of the people—this man had just commenced life. He had dismissed many of the personal considerations which had controlled him, and was ready for new fields of service, as essential to the prosperity of the black man, to whom he had dedicated his earlier life, as for that of his own class.

The people of the country would have turned to him, not perhaps as a standard-bearer—there are always standard-bearers enough—but as one who could have given

6

counsel which the people of the North, South, East and
West would have gladly followed. Thus separated from
all personal controversies and personal interests, the
country would have accepted his judgment and followed
his example, knowing well that when he stood alone,
with scarcely a man to back him, and with a whole
country against him, he had judged justly and advised
them wisely. It is for this, sir, that we should regret
his loss. Where is the man to supply his place? Undoubtedly it will hereafter be supplied. Men have
been thus supplied heretofore and will be again. If he
were with us there would be multitudes who would
accept his counsels, assured of safety for the future.
But our loss is his gain. It is not for the dead, but
the living, that we mourn. He is at this hour, yes,
this hour, the recipient of a purer liberty than any that
entered into his conception, or that has ever been
enjoyed by man.

> " There is yet a liberty, unsung
> By poets and by Senators unpraised,
> Which monarchs cannot grant, nor all the powers
> Of Earth and Hell confederate take away ;
> A liberty which persecution, fraud,
> Oppression, prisons, have no power to bind ;
> Which whoso tastes can be enslaved no more.
> 'Tis liberty of heart, derived from Heaven,
> Bought with His blood, who gave it to mankind,
> And sealed with the same token. It is held
> By charter, and that charter sanctioned sure
> By the unimpeachable and awful oath
> And promise of a God. His other gifts
> All bear the royal stamp that speaks them his,
> And are august ; but this transcends them all."

And this is now the ineffable joy and the just reward
of the illustrious dead Senator of Massachusetts.

PROCEEDINGS IN THE HOUSE OF REPRESENTATIVES.

HOUSE OF REPRESENTATIVES, March 13, 1874.

THE Resolutions from the Joint Special Committee on the Message of the Governor were reported by Mr. WILLARD P. PHILLIPS of Salem, and were read by the Speaker.

Mr. PHILLIPS then addressed the House as follows:—

Mr. SPEAKER: In rising to move the adoption of the Resolutions which have just been read from the chair, I shall utter but few words.

It is true that CHARLES SUMNER no longer lives. The great Senator we have loved so well has passed from earth. His life is ended; his record is made up. It remains for us, the Legislature of the Commonwealth he has served so long and honored so much, to take such action as the sad occasion requires.

For twenty-three years he has been our Senator. Entering the Senate when comparatively unknown to the country, he has there earned a name which is eminent throughout the civilized world. He stood there but yesterday, recognized everywhere as the great champion of freedom, the defender of justice, the advocate of equal rights. To-day there is a vacant place which can be filled by no living man.

Chosen to his high office as an opponent of the then dominant slave power, he applied himself untiringly to the great duty he had undertaken—regardless alike of labor and of personal danger; and while so performing

44 CHARLES SUMNER.

his duties in the Senate chamber, he suffered those
injuries from which he never recovered. But he lived
to see the slave power powerless, slavery itself destroyed,
and four millions of slaves enfranchised. All this he
labored for and did much to accomplish.

But, sir, it is not only in the advocacy of great truths
and of just causes that he has achieved fame. His pure
and honest life, unsullied by any wrong act, was worthy
of the man, an honor to the State and Country. In the
midst of political contests, with corruption charged upon
almost every public man, he was never charged with or
suspected of any wrong-doing.

The people of the Commonwealth have loved and honored Mr. SUMNER from his first entry into public life.
Never, when his election has been in controversy, have
they failed so to vote as to make his return absolutely
certain; but at the extra session of the Legislature held
in November, 1872, a Resolution was adopted, perhaps
hastily, which he considered a censure and a rebuke. To
him it seemed undeserved. It affected his health and
caused him many hours of suffering and pain. The next
Legislature, already elected when the Resolution was
adopted, refused to rescind it, and it remained unrepealed
for more than a year. But when the people of the Commonwealth could act, they elected the present Legislature,
which has, without delay, annulled the resolution of
censure, and sent to our Senators and Representatives in
Washington copies of the rescinding Resolution, which
had been read in both branches of Congress — in the
Senate, most singularly, at the very last session of that
body held before our Senator's death, and in his presence.

Surely, sir, we may felicitate ourselves that we have
done him justice, and that now no condemnation of him
stands unrescinded upon the records of this Commonwealth.

Sir, the great Senator, the honest man, the friend

of the oppressed, the illustrious citizen, honored and respected everywhere, has gone. In his dying hours he was true to the cause to which he had devoted his life, and urged almost with his last breath that his civil rights bill should be taken care of. May we do what we can to aid in the accomplishment of this, his last wish, and may it be our endeavor to emulate his example of devotion to every duty, and thus to show that we have not forgotten his teaching.

Mr. Speaker, I move that the Resolutions be adopted.

Mr. CHARLES R. CODMAN of Boston next spoke as follows:—

Mr. SPEAKER: He has read history to little purpose and with little thought, who has failed to perceive a divine law in human affairs. No great cause has ever triumphed, no great reform has ever been accomplished, no gigantic wrong has ever been redressed, without the personal agency of a great leader. To such men their fellow-men have always turned in seasons of peril, of doubt and of difficulty; and when in the fulness of time the hour has come for one of the great moral revolutions of the world, the hour has brought with it the man for the crisis. We read in the picturesque pages of our own historian, of the heroic struggles of the Dutch republicans, of their reverses, their sufferings and their final triumph; and the grand figure of William the Silent stands forth in bold relief as their leader, their guardian and their guide. We are told "that as long as he lived he was the guiding star of a whole brave nation, and when he died the little children cried in the streets." The name of Wilberforce is inseparably linked with that grandest act in English history, the emancipation of the slaves in the British colonies. This great and earnest man seems to have been providentially raised to awaken and inform the people, and without him, humanly speaking, the great act of justice would never have been performed. So, too, in our own revolutionary days, as we read the history of that time, it almost seems as if our independence could not have been achieved if we had had no Washington. And in the suppression of the great rebellion we are not too near those days of conflict and trial to fail to recognize that, in that crisis of our destinies, the wiser Will that governs human affairs gave us a heaven-born leader of men. In the providence of God there are no accidents, and it was something more potent than the chances of a political convention that gave us Abraham Lincoln for our President.

He whom we mourn to-day was one of these providential men. His was the allotted mission to rouse the conscience of the American people, and in season and out of season that resolute and unfaltering voice was heard, not so much pleading as demanding, ever urging, ever pointing the way. No rest for SUMNER if a single step was gained. Others would fain pause, if only to take breath and note what had been done, but with restless energy he was always crying " Excelsior," counting nothing as done while anything remained to do, struggling, urging, exhorting, remonstrating, reproving, denouncing, never satisfied, never believing the work at an end, in the vanguard always, foremost for the restriction of slavery, foremost for emancipation, foremost for reconciliation.

And now, Mr. Speaker, he is gone, and his great task is left well-nigh finished. As we cast our tributes upon his grave, we will not say that his end is untimely. He has done a great and noble work, and he falls at last in the full possession of his great mental powers, with his eye not dim nor his natural force abated, as the good soldier falls at his post with all his armor on.

Mr. Speaker, I do not forget that it is my privilege to speak here to-day as one of the representatives of the city and of the ward in which he lived for so many years. Born almost under the shadow of this State House, bred in our public schools, he was always in heart and soul, as well as by birth, a Bostonian. With devoted friends throughout the whole civilized world who revered and admired him—for in all countries the lovers of art, of literature, of science and of liberty were his friends—it is here in Massachusetts, and chiefly in the neighborhood of Boston, that his death will be felt as a personal loss. We in Boston love to think of him as one of our boys, going to the Latin school and taking the Franklin medal, and giving an early promise of future greatness. We delight to remember that his home for many years, on the north side of Beacon Hill, was in the street next to that which contains the little colony of colored people. The great champion and advocate of their race was well placed in their neighborhood. Many a fugitive slave has found refuge and concealment in those lanes and alleys, and some are living there to-day; and the devotion of all of them to CHARLES SUMNER is equalled only by his loyalty to them. Deep is their grief at his loss, and all their brethren are mourners with them; for nothing has ever shaken their faithful attachment. No matter if the Senator changed his party associations; they well understood that he was always faithful to them. If they could not vote with him, they were always ready to vote for him. Some of them may have been ignorant, uneducated, simple, but their hearts always told them that their friend was true, and it was simply impossible to make them believe otherwise.

But I should do feeble justice to a fragrant memory if I do not call to mind the essential purity of the personal character of CHARLES SUMNER. Lofty as were his aims as a public man, stainless as was his integrity as a statesman, his private and daily life was absolutely unspotted and blameless. The driven snow is not whiter than his reputation, and slander itself can find nothing to assail in any act of his. The frailties of many a great statesman, of many an honest public man, have marred his fame and diminished his usefulness, but no blot will stain the historic page that records the services and virtues of our great Senator.

Mr. GEORGE J. SANGER of Danvers, then addressed the Chair and said:—

Mr. SPEAKER: When the great and good die it is well to pause, and looking at what they have been, calling up their virtues, their achievements, their character, fix in our hearts the memory of these, and thus put ourselves to fresh obligation for their existence. And to-day it is well to call before us the great and noble life of CHARLES SUMNER—our fellow-citizen, reared amid the influences of our institutions, surrounded in youth and early manhood with the moral atmosphere of our Commonwealth—cultured in our schools and university; ours by official position, ours because he gave honor to the position of trust we had committed to his keeping. But he was not only a citizen of Massachusetts; he was a citizen of our whole country. His was a wider field than a city or State. He loved the unit only as a part of the whole and for the good of the whole. And the love of his country was so true and wise, that it sought no good even for his country that came through wrong and injustice to any. His was a charity—in the true apostolic sense of the word—that never failed; in which hope found its fruition and faith became sight. But he has gone from us; for us no more to toil, for us no more to stand as the impersonation of justice, as the concentration of rectitude. We can give his dust our tears, and with gentle hand commit it to the kindred earth. We can give him, as a State, our mournful farewell, and with all the lovers of good men, pray that his mantle may fall on those who shall succeed him.

Great as a scholar, his admiration for the great never cooled his love for the lowly. Great as a statesman, his was the wisdom that saw that only "righteousness exalteth a nation." He was a man of "open vision." The past he made tributary to his judgment, and with reverence for what age had to teach, he combined the insight to see the demand of the hour and the courage to go forward. He knew, what the world has been slow to learn, that in righteousness there is no failure. His day was a day of great responsibility. A wrong, colossal in proportions and foul in every attribute, held control of the Government. Men had compromised; but only evil thrives under such treatment. To him there came the clear sight that is the reward of unbending rectitude, and his voice gave no uncertain sound. Neither proffered honor nor intimidation could bind him; he had found the strait and narrow way, and to him it was life. He had faith; not the faith of a dogma but of a principle; it might cost life, fortune, position to the individual, but the end would be a full compensation. It was this that constituted his greatness. The past witnessed its worth, and he knew the future would testify of its success. But why should I spend time in the analysis of his character; and surely I need say no word to touch your feelings. We say of the one we mourn, that he is dead. We speak of our loss. But nothing that is good ever dies, for it is everlasting. What he accomplished is secure. His pure life, his unbending rectitude, his complete fidelity—they are our possession. They belong to the world and can never pass away. They abide for us. They will live to teach the future. In the crisis-hour of the future, when men shall seek some light to guide, they will turn to this memory, and in it find counsel and support. What he has done, we will teach to our children, and our children's

7

children shall live anew in the benefaction of this life.
As the great river of our country has built up through
the ages on either bank the broad acres on which city and
village stand secure, so the great and good who leave us
make possible the future. Then, in the assured heritage
of his integrity, let us abide. In the light of his just
and perfect life, let us live.

Mr. JOSHUA B. SMITH of Cambridge, then addressed the Speaker
and was recognized.

[Mr. Smith's close relations with Mr. SUMNER for many years, his
recent return from Washington where he had been as the bearer of
the "Rescinding Resolutions," and where but a few hours before he
had felt the grasp of his friend's hand; the sacred memories and
personal griefs, and the quickened sense of the loss of a great and
true friend, made too large a demand upon his control of voice to
enable him to utter a word, and he presently resumed his seat.
The hushed stillness of the House was profoundly impressive,
making the "silence golden," and this was maintained for several
minutes.*]

Mr. CHARLES HALE of Boston then rose and said:—

Mr. SPEAKER: Our friend from Cambridge has made
the most eloquent speech that is possible. It is with
reluctance that I intrude upon the silence.

Mr. HALE continued:—

It is peculiarly fitting that in this hall expression
should be given to the grief which, at this moment,
oppresses the public mind everywhere. Everywhere it
is remembered that Mr. SUMNER was, at the time of
his decease, the "father" of the Senate of the United
States; the oldest Senator by consecutive service, the

* See page 57.

most conspicuous member of that illustrious body, and that he served as Senator from Massachusetts for a longer period than any of his predecessors. The eulogists of public men, dying in posts of high station or in retirement after having held such posts, have generally been called to recount the many offices they have held; to point out how they have risen—sometimes how rapidly they have risen—from one round of the political ladder to another; how, having been found faithful in a few things they have been put over many things, and have held town, county and State offices, and then one and other position in the national councils. So, too, we have been asked to admire the honorable service of our statesmen in diverse positions of public trust; in executive office or administrative positions of the State or Nation; in service abroad or at home relating to the foreign relations of the country; sometimes, also, in military service, diversifying their labors in civil life. Mr. SUMNER's public life, not less illustrious, has none of these characteristics of variety. He entered the public service as a Senator in the Congress of the United States from the State of Massachusetts; and in that place, without interruption of that service, he has died. From an early age he held a State commission as justice of the peace; and he was a member of the Convention in 1853 for the revision of the State Constitution. With no other exceptions, I think, than these, he never held office by popular election, and he never held office by executive appointment. No mandate of commission summoned him into public life less distinguished than that of the Commonwealth of Massachusetts, expressed by the voice of her Senate and House of Representatives in General Court assembled; from the beginning to the end, no field of public service engaged his mighty powers less broad or less elevated than that of the Senate of the whole Union.

This hall was the scene of that extraordinary summons

to exalted public position of one who had never placed himself among aspirants for office. Of the circumstances attending that summons nothing more need be said than that, to whatever criticism they may be obnoxious, no criticism can attach to Mr. SUMNER's part in them; or, rather, it is to be said that he had no part in them whatever. Indeed, some of his supporters were disposed to make it a matter of complaint that during the memorable contest which introduced him to public life, not a word, a syllable, or even whisper, could be elicited from their candidate to aid in his election. Whatever combinations may have been made, he had no hand in them; from all such things he held himself wholly aloof. He sometimes made addresses at public meetings and conventions, but he took no part in any legislative caucus—if any there were—in which his name was brought forward as a candidate for office; and after that first extraordinary election in 1851, so honorable to him, on each recurrence of the expiration of his six years' term, never was there occasion for a caucus; his reëlection to the Senate in each case, generally almost unanimous, always without arrangement or management by anybody, certainly without a word from himself, occurred as regularly as the return of the seasons in their due order. Mr. SUMNER had no occasion to lift a finger to help it; he might with as much reason have beckoned the sun to rise.

In viewing the public life of Mr. SUMNER as Senator, it will perhaps be said that his character did not particularly fit him to lead in a parliamentary assembly; or, in other words, that he was an orator rather than a debater. Such a criticism would reflect no discredit on the talents and attainments of Mr. SUMNER, even if it had more solid foundation than can justly be claimed for it. The Senate of the United States, as he rightly considered, is not precisely to be regarded as a mere assembly for the taking of votes and the passing of laws. Whether from the cir-

cumstance that thither are sent the greatest men of the
Nation, or that in the lower house, by reason of its numbers, or of the immense accumulation of business there,
or from some other cause, debate is rather stifled than
allowed, the Senate has become to a much greater degree
than the lower chamber in our National Government what
the House of Commons is under the British Constitution:
the great forum of the nation for the general discussion
of public affairs in all their bearings. But apart from
this, I should not be disposed to admit the force of the
criticism. The four great qualities of a model debater
have been thus defined: A genial temper in debate;
courtesy and dignity of deportment; profound knowledge of his subject; a thorough preparation. Which of
these did not Mr. SUMNER possess? or, rather, which of
them did he not possess in the most eminent degree?
The fact is, Mr. SUMNER knew parliamentary law as he
knew all other law, from a profound study going back to
first principles; and he had ever in mind the rules based
on the fundamental principle, that its purpose is to aid in
giving faithful expression to the true opinion and will of
the assembly; and that in coming to that expression it is
not so much the right of every member to be heard, as it
is the duty of the assembly to collect every contribution
to the common stock of knowledge or information which
any member may be able to furnish, to aid the assembly
in coming to the best result. For parliamentary law,
considered as a series of artificial rules capable of use in
cunning hands to pervert it from this, its true purpose,
he had no taste. Sir, Mr. SUMNER was an accomplished
debater; a debater of the school which thinks of the
soundness of its cause, the strength of reason and the
force of argument; not one who seeks to gain personal
adherents for the measure he advocates, irrespective of
its intrinsic merits, eager to carry it by some parliamentary artifice, by which an assembly may ingeniously

be forced, almost against its will, to accept worse for
better.

In the national loss, there is a mitigation in the value
of the lesson that may be learned from it. As we gather
round the grave of our illustrious Senator, may we all
remember, especially may the young men now coming
forward observe, that this great man, whom the whole
world mourns, attained and held his high place, although
he never packed a caucus, pulled a wire, or rolled a log;
that he never sought office for favorites or personal adherents; was never concerned in any use of money for
elections; and let us resolve, each for himself, so far as
in him lies, that as the assault on Mr. SUMNER in 1856
was the signal for a great national movement which
removed from the Nation the ban of slavery, so may we
hope that his death in 1874 may prove the signal for a
great national movement that shall give to the country a
pure political atmosphere such as he would have loved
to breathe.

Mr. JOHN E. FITZGERALD of Boston then spoke as follows :—

Mr. SPEAKER : We read in the history of the ancient
Republic of Greece, that when the Spartan General
Brasidas died in battle, the leading Spartans came to
condole with his mother. Having asked those who visited
her, if her son died as became a Spartan, they said, "He
has left no man in Sparta like him." She answered,
"Not so, my friends, Brasidas was an honorable man, but
Sparta has many nobler and greater than he." And
to-day, sir, the Commonwealth of Massachusetts mourns
the loss of her greatest son, and from one end of the
Republic to the other, the universal verdict comes to her,
"He has left no man in the Republic like him." Would
that Massachusetts could say, as did the Spartan mother
of old, "SUMNER was a great man but we have many

nobler and greater than he." Twenty-three years ago Massachusetts clothed him with the official robe of Senator; to-day that official mantle is laid at the feet of Massachusetts, pure and unsullied, without spot or blemish. What means, sir, this universal grief of the Nation for the death of one man? Ah! sir, it is a tribute of respect, not so much to the eloquence, scholarly attainments and statesmanship of CHARLES SUMNER, as to his honesty and patriotism, equalling those of the better days of the ancient Republics. In high-toned patriotism, spotless purity of character, and unswerving fidelity to duty, he had no superior in the Senate of the Nation. Threats could not deter him, nor (what is often more dangerous) the soft blandishments of friends mislead him from the path of rectitude. Hence, sir, the nation mourns his loss at a time when the example of his noble qualities is most needed; at a time when statesmanship like his is becoming more rare and less influential; and the qualities that make up the wire-puller and trickster, more frequent and powerful in the politics of our Republic. And standing by his bier to-day, how best can we show our appreciation of the great virtues that have made SUMNER'S name famous forever more! Unhappily we cannot say "Massachusetts has many nobler and greater than he," but we can select a son of Massachusetts possessed in some degree of the virtues which characterized him, of his honesty and independence at least. Doing this we honor ourselves and pay the highest tribute of respect to the life and services of CHARLES SUMNER.

Mr. ALBERT PALMER of Boston closed the addresses of the day in the following words:—

Mr. SPEAKER: No power of thought or speech can measure or express the grief and mourning of this hour. No living tongue can now fully portray the nation's loss,

or speak the fit consoling word.   The lips that once could
best do such service are now silent and sealed in death.

Mr. Speaker, not only has America lost her greatest
and best statesman, but the world has lost its ablest and
most devoted friend.   It was said of Webster, when he
died, "The nation's heart beats heavily at the portals of
the tomb."   SUMNER is dead, and the whole world's heart
will beat heavily at the portals of his tomb.   The Resolutions fitly enumerate the great and wonderful accomplishments of the peerless Senator—his scholarship, so varied
and profound; his statesmanship, so wise, so impartial,
so just; his vast and unequalled knowledge of law, constitutional and international; his mighty power of speech
and argument, which made the world his audience-room
and nations willing listeners; his industry, so untiring
and unremitting, as if he needed to supplement merely
ordinary powers by extraordinary diligence.   But above
all these shining qualities and accomplishments of genius
and intellect, or rather permeating all, was that unsullied
virtue and perfect integrity which now in this sad hour
command universal assent and homage.   All men and
parties hasten to say he was an honest man.   His brilliant
and unrivalled intellectual powers compel universal admiration.   His moral integrity will inspire universal homage
and love.   His character was monumental; pure, white
and unstained, from pedestal to capstone.   In council
chambers and legislative halls of State and Nation he will
be missed and mourned, but not less in every humble
hamlet throughout the country.   The full and almost
broken heart of my friend, the member from Cambridge,
too full for utterance, pays the best and most eloquent
tribute to our loved and noble statesman.   Let not our
friend seek to hide the tears that close his utterance and
forbid him speech :

     " 'Tis manliness to be heart-broken here,
For the grave of earth's best nobleness is watered by the tear."

We love to recall the dying words of our great men. "Remember my civil rights bill," said the great Senator on his death-bed; and shall we not consider those words as an inheritance? As we cherish and defend the civil and equal right of all, we shall honor and cherish the memory of CHARLES SUMNER; and thus shall we best commend his great example to the world.

The question was then put upon the Resolutions, and they were unanimously adopted, by a rising vote.

At the earnest request of the Committee entrusted with the duty of preparing this volume for the press, Mr. J. B. SMITH of Cambridge has written out the remarks which he intended to have made in the House of Representatives, when he addressed the SPEAKER as described above, at page 50. They are as follows:—

Mr. SPEAKER: Thirty-five years have passed since Colonel Robert G. Shaw was a babe in his cradle. On an occasion that I well remember, CHARLES SUMNER was a guest at his father's table, and I was a servant standing behind his chair. The question of slavery, then the general topic of conversation, was under discussion. One of the guests gave expression to the most bitter feeling I ever heard, saying that "the Abolitionists, with their negro friends, ought to be hanged." But Mr. and Mrs. Shaw, the father and mother of the infant, spoke strongly in favor of justice and freedom. The gentleman who had been speaking so bitterly asked Mr. SUMNER what he thought of the negro question. Pointing to me he replied, "Would you have that man a slave?" And that expression, with other words then spoken, cost him his social position for years in Boston. Slavery had struck its roots wide and deep; but for me the star of

8

justice rose in that hour, and I saw it shining, for the
first time, through the dark clouds of prejudice that
surrounded me.

A few years after that I was with that child on Boston
Common. As we were sitting there, I noticed that he
looked intently at me, and presently he said, "Smith,
what makes your hands black?" "Why, my boy, God
made them so," I replied. "Well," said he, "if God
made them so, why do people find fault with it?"
"Because they are bad," I answered. He gazed at me
a few moments without speaking, and then said, "Smith,
some day I'll fight for you."

When he was only twenty-five years of age this child
was made Colonel of the Fifty-Fourth Massachusetts Volunteers, the first regiment of colored soldiers recruited
in this State; and then, as Colonel Shaw, led the colored
troops at Fort Wagner, and there gave his life for his
country and for that justice and freedom that had been a
part of his early training.

Thirty-two years after the noble expressions referred to,
of Mr. SUMNER, I was a guest at his table in Washington. While we were seated there, a party of Southern-
ers, from Georgia, called upon Mr. SUMNER to secure
his influence in what he considered would be unjust legislation. The great Senator turned again, pointing to me,
and said: "There is my friend; my equal at home and
your equal anywhere; and when you are ready to make
eternal justice law, then call upon me and I will help
you, and not before."

Mr. Speaker, I have lived out two generations, and
have tasted the bitter fruit of the seed planted by our
fathers eighty years ago. I have had the doors of the
Church and of the State House shut in my face; but I
have lived to enjoy the blessings of liberty, and to-day I
stand the peer of every man in this House, and this, as
I believe, through the life and labor of CHARLES SUMNER.

What a change has taken place within the forty years of my remembrance! I wish I could picture it. In those days I was a servant in a family travelling through the South. They stopped in Washington, and I there saw, for the first time, men, women and children sold on the auction-block as cattle are sold. No regard was paid to age, sex or relationship. Husband and wife, mother and child, were parted to meet no more. At that time, if a black man's child, or dying wife, cried for water after ten o'clock at night, he dared not go into the streets to get it, for fear of arrest and the watch-house. And if the master did not pay the fine the next morning, thirty-nine lashes on the bare back was the black man's penalty. In those days I would have given a kingdom to have been a dog, with a collar on my neck with the owner's name upon it, for that would have protected me.

The family to which I have referred was invited into the country to dine, and I stood to wait upon them. After dinner I heard the sound of the lash, and a voice crying, "O God, have mercy!" I stepped out into the garden, and, looking about me, saw a poor girl with the blood running down her neck, with her eyes fixed on the shining clouds towards the setting sun, and saying, "O Jesus, I will soon be with thee, and then my soul will shine as those clouds, and I will be thy child." It was the first prayer I had ever heard, and there I swore eternal hatred to slavery.

Forty years after that I went again to Washington. Slavery had disappeared. The whipping-post and auction-block were gone. The star that I saw rise was now at its meridian. It shone full in my face. I was in a new world. I was as free as air. I went as any gentleman might go. I walked to the cars, I went to Arlington, and heard no word of insult. I had every attention paid to me as a gentleman, and should not have known that I was a black man if I had not looked in the mirror.

Now, Mr. Speaker, CHARLES SUMNER did it. Five-and-twenty years ago the Anti-Slavery sentiment of New England fixed upon SUMNER as the man to go to Washington to strike the first blow. You speak of Sherman's march from Atlanta to the sea as a great victory. But that was nothing compared to the success of SUMNER. Sherman had the Nation at his back. SUMNER had simple justice. Sherman had a hundred thousand men. SUMNER fought single-handed and alone. Sherman had the wealth of the Nation laid at his feet, and SUMNER had only the prayers of the poor.

Mr. Speaker, I stand here amazed. One week ago this day I placed in the hands of our great Senator the Rescinding Resolutions of this Legislature. As he read them he turned his head and wept as I never saw man weep before. He then said, "I knew Massachusetts would do me justice."

As I stood here I could not but think of that passage of Scripture which says, "Jesus wept." Not for himself, but for a poor, unbelieving world. SUMNER wept; not for himself, but for the State he loved and served so well.

Sir, I do not forget in this hour that, little more than one year ago, the Legislature censured him. To-day this House stands ready to lay the wealth of the State at his feet to honor his great name.

And now, sir, that great life has ended here. That star has set. And while it rests on the banks of eternity, awaiting its assignment amid the bright and shining lights in the canopy of heaven, its rays still lingering on the clouds and the mountain-tops, O God, I pray thee, give us one to take hold where he let go—one who can lighten us through this dark and unkind world, until thy glory shall shine on a regenerated land. Then justice, honesty and peace shall rule the Nation.

COMMONWEALTH OF MASSACHUSETTS.

——— ——

In SENATE, March 13, 1874.

ORDERED, That a committee of three on the part of the Senate, and five on the part of the House, be appointed to meet the Congressional Committee having in charge the remains of SENATOR SUMNER, at the boundary line of the Commonwealth.

And Messrs. HAYES, JACOBS and WARDWELL, were appointed the committee on the part of the Senate.

Sent down for concurrence.

S. N. GIFFORD, *Clerk.*

HOUSE OF REPRESENTATIVES, March 13, 1874.

Concurred: And Messrs. CODMAN of Boston, ADAMS of Quincy, NOBLE of Westfield, BLUNT of Haverhill, and CUMMINGS of Woburn, are joined.

GEO. A. MARDEN, *Clerk.*

COMMONWEALTH OF MASSACHUSETTS.

In SENATE, March 13, 1874.

ORDERED, That a committee of three on the part of the Senate, and five on the part of the House, be appointed to make all necessary arrangements for the reception of the body of SENATOR SUMNER and for the funeral obsequies in this Commonwealth, which shall be held in King's Chapel on Monday, the 16th inst., at 3 o'clock, P. M.

And that the committee be authorized to provide appropriate drapery for the Chapel on the occasion; and also to extend an invitation to the City Government of Boston to be present.

And Messrs. STICKNEY, BACON and MERRILL, were appointed the committee on the part of the Senate.

Sent down for concurrence.

S. N. GIFFORD, *Clerk.*

HOUSE OF REPRESENTATIVES, March 13, 1874.

Concurred: And Messrs. PERKINS of Boston, BUFFUM of Lynn, SLADE of Somerset, CROCKER of Boston, and ESTABROOK of Worcester, are joined.

GEO. A. MARDEN, *Clerk.*

COMMONWEALTH OF MASSACHUSETTS.

IN SENATE, March 13, 1874.

ORDERED, That a Committee of two on the part of the Senate, and three on the part of the House, be appointed to take suitable measures to provide for the delivery of an Oration before the Executive and Legislative branches of this Commonwealth, upon the life, character and public services of CHARLES SUMNER, by such person, and at such time and place, as may seem to them appropriate.

Sent down for concurrence.

S. N. GIFFORD, *Clerk.*

HOUSE OF REPRESENTATIVES, March 13, 1874.

Concurred: And Messrs. SMITH of Cambridge, PHILLIPS of Salem, and PHILLIPS of Springfield, are appointed the Committee on the part of the House.

GEO. A. MARDEN, *Clerk.*

IN SENATE, March 17, 1874.

Messrs. MERRILL and VERRY are appointed on the part of the Senate.

S. N. GIFFORD, *Clerk.*

COMMONWEALTH OF MASSACHUSETTS.

By His Excellency WILLIAM B. WASHBURN, Governor:

A PROCLAMATION.

WHEREAS, Three o'clock of Monday afternoon, sixteenth instant, has been determined upon as the hour for the funeral of CHARLES SUMNER; and

WHEREAS, It is believed the people of the Commonwealth, without distinction of party, will desire to participate in this last tribute of respect and affection to the great Senator who served them so long and so well;

Therefore, I request the officials of cities and towns throughout the Commonwealth to make provision for solemnizing the hour named, by the tolling of bells, and such other services as they may deem appropriate to the occasion.

Given at the Executive Department, Boston, under the seal of the Commonwealth, this fourteenth day of March, A. D. one thousand eight hundred and seventy-four.

WILLIAM B. WASHBURN.

By His Excellency the Governor:

OLIVER WARNER, *Secretary.*

God save the Commonwealth of Massachusetts.

THE OBSEQUIES.

9

THE OBSEQUIES.

THE announcement in Washington that CHARLES SUMNER was dead, fell like a pall upon the Capitol.

In each Legislative Chamber there was the hush of death.

In the Senate, all eyes were turned upon the vacant chair.

The simple words of mourning, spoken by Senator ANTHONY when he announced the death of Mr. SUMNER, had a touching significance rarely equalled even in that chamber. But more eloquent than these words of tenderness was this vacant chair—a silent witness of the great Senator's departure. It was draped in black —a mute emblem of the national grief—and upon the desk before it were the fresh flowers which loving hands had placed there *in memoriam*.

The proceedings in both Houses on Thursday were brief, but the simple formalities of the passage of the Resolutions, and the appointment of the Committees to arrange for the funeral and to accompany the body to Massachusetts, were full of tenderness and solemnity.

On Friday morning the remains of Mr. SUMNER were placed in the Rotunda of the Capitol, where they lay in state until half-past twelve o'clock, the hour of the funeral services in the Senate Chamber.

At the close of these services the funeral procession moved to the station, and at three o'clock a special train started for New York, arriving at that city at midnight, where the Committee rested, and the honored remains were placed under guard.

On Saturday morning, the fourteenth of March, the special cars, draped in mourning, moved out of the station on their way to Boston.

The Joint Special Committee of the Legislature met the train at Springfield, where its Chairman (Hon. FRANCIS B. HAYES) addressed the delegation in the following words:

Mr. Chairman and Gentlemen of the Congressional Committee:

The Legislature of Massachusetts has charged us with the duty of waiting upon you and receiving the sacred remains of our beloved Senator. With the remains, permit us to conduct you and the members of the Massachusetts delegation in Congress, as honored guests of the State, to its capital, when it shall please you to continue your journey.

An appropriate reply to this greeting was made by Senator ANTHONY, in behalf of the delegation.

At every station a concourse of people received, with tolling bells, with craped and drooping flags, and with uncovered heads, the sacred dust of the man whom they loved and reverenced. Tenderly the great heart of Massachusetts beat, as she wept for her honored son. It seemed, at the moment, as if no tribute could express his high service; no loyalty or reverence his great fidelity. But the quickened sensibilities, the tenderest emotions, and even the tears of a great people were freely given.

At seven o'clock, on Saturday evening, the booming guns announced to Boston the arrival of the funeral train. For hours, awaiting patiently its approach, uncounted thousands, of every class, had thronged the avenues leading to the station.

The spontaneous impulse to do honor to the great soul that would no longer stand in the flesh, and move as aforetime with a presence so majestic in our streets, was as remarkable as it was significant.

The great meeting of the citizens of Boston, in Faneuil Hall, but a few hours before, had struck the key-note of the day. The student left his book, the clerk his desk, the artisan his tool, and the laborer his spade. The inspiration of the occasion, the touched and quickened sensibilities, intensified by the commingling of thousands of men with a common purpose, seemed to charge the city with an unusual emotion.

As the shades of evening fell upon the multitudes thronging the streets, few can forget the reverent hush which had settled upon them, or the expression in every face, of the solemn purpose that had drawn and held them waiting there.

The Legislative Committee having in charge the reception of the body of the Senator, was in attendance at the station. A procession was formed in silence, and moved to the State House, in the gloom of approaching night, through streets lined with people standing uncovered in honor of their dead.

In this great demonstration of respect, it seemed as if strong men bowed themselves. The doors were shut in the streets and the windows were darkened, because a great "man goeth to his long home, and the mourners go about the streets." A silver cord had indeed been loosed, and a golden bowl had been broken; the dust was to return to the earth as it was, as the spirit had returned to God who gave it. But the mourning of the people was not for him; it was for themselves and for their children.

A vast concourse of people were at the State House waiting the funeral procession. The coffin was borne slowly up into the Doric Hall and placed upon the catafalque.

Here the Governor of the State, the members of his Council and Staff, and the Legislative Committees, were in attendance to receive the Committee of the United States Senate, and the members of the Massachusetts Delegation in Congress by whom they were accompanied.

Colonel STORER then introduced Senator ANTHONY, Chairman of the Committee of Senators, who said:—

MAY IT PLEASE YOUR EXCELLENCY:

We are commanded by the Senate to render back to you your illustrious dead. Nearly a quarter of a century ago, you dedicated to the public service a man who was even then greatly distinguished. He remained in it, quickening its patriotism, informing its counsels and leading in its deliberations, until, having survived in continuous service all his original associates, he has closed his earthly career. With reverent hands, we bring to you his mortal part, that it may be committed to the soil of the renowned Commonwealth that gave him birth. Take it; it is yours. The part which we do not return to you is not wholly yours to receive, nor altogether ours to give. It belongs to the country, to freedom, to civilization, to humanity. We come to you with the emblems of mourning which faintly typify the sorrow that dwells in the breasts which they cover. So much we must concede to the infirmity of human nature. But in the view of reason and philosophy, is it not rather a matter of high exultation that a life so pure in its personal qualities, so lofty in its public aims, so fortunate in the fruition of noble effort, has closed safely, without a stain, before age had impaired its intellectual vigor, before time had dimmed the lustre of its genius !

MAY IT PLEASE YOUR EXCELLENCY : Our mission is completed. We commit to you the body of CHARLES SUMNER. His undying fame the Muse of History has already taken into her keeping.

Governor WASHBURN advancing towards the Senate Committee, replied :—

GENTLEMEN : It becomes my painful duty to receive from your hands all that remains of our great Senator. I wish to thank you, in the name of the State, for your labor of love, in thus transmitting to our keeping this precious dust. We receive it at your hands with the assurance that it shall be guarded most tenderly, and the spot to which it shall be borne for its final resting-place, being baptized by such precious blood, shall ever hereafter be looked upon as consecrated ground. In the meantime, I commit it to the careful keeping of the Committee of our Legislature, selected for this special purpose. Permit me now to welcome you to the hospitalities of our State, and to assure you that no efforts of ours shall be wanting to make your brief stay with us as agreeable as possible under the circumstances which have brought you hither.

Thanking you again for your marked sympathy in this hour of sore trial, I bid you all a hearty welcome, with the assurance that your tender regards on this occasion shall never be forgotten.

Doric Hall, with the sacred emblems of battle enshrined in its alcoves, was draped in mourning in honor of the illustrious dead.　The affecting historical associations which cluster about this beautiful hall made it the spot of all others in the Commonwealth, where, for a brief day, the worn and weary body of the dead Senator should rest.　Here, under the Dome of the Capitol, he was laid, canopied with flowers, and guarded with tender vigilance by a company of that race to whose protection he had consecrated his life.*

Sunday morning dawned.　The draperies of black and white, festooned from the cornices and arching door-ways, made of the silent corridors a mausoleum.　The catafalque was covered with flowers.　Over the coffin, depending from the ceiling, was a wreath of smilax, from which radiated a drooping vine, encircling the columns to their base.　From this wreath was suspended a crown of flowers, and from this, as if in flight, a white dove, and from its beak an olive-branch; while rare flowers, in masses of color, in every graceful form of cross and wreath and trailing vine, gave fragrance and beauty to the silent hall.

The public demonstration during the day in the streets leading to the State House was such as had never before been witnessed on any similar occasion in Boston.　Multitudes of people, who could not be numbered, crowded the avenues of Beacon Hill, and from early morning until dusk of evening, the tireless stream of humanity passed through the open doors where the great Senator lay in state.

Silently, decorously, sadly, the vast multitude availed themselves of this privilege.　The old and the young, the

---

* "Shaw Guards," Company A, 2d Battalion Infantry, Mass. V. M.

rich and the poor, the white and the colored, of every occupation and every class, from the city and from the country, those in high station and those in humble life, little children and gray-haired dames, all moved with one impulse to pay a last tribute to CHARLES SUMNER.

And who shall interpret the emotions of those who were privileged to stand there ! The history of a generation of the national life, its days of darkness and of woe, its throes of agony and its majestic triumphs, all this was epitomized as men looked on the silent dust of the man who for a quarter of a century had stood in the advance in the great struggle for freedom.

The silence was eloquent, and in that silence these sacred memories and the vision of his spotless career were renewed.

Monday, the sixteenth of March, was the funeral day. As its hours passed, the vast crowds which assembled before the State House and streamed through its open corridors, repeated the scenes of the day before. From every part of New England tens of thousands had come to join the funeral. All business was suspended. On the main avenues the stores were draped in mourning. Flowers and vines wreathing the portraits of the Senator, flags festooned and craped, with other memorial emblems, were seen everywhere. The city was filled with moving throngs, whose faces expressed the universal sorrow. There was a silent going about the streets, an unaccustomed hush in the marts of trade, which was in keeping with the solemn purpose of the day.

The tender interest that held the great multitudes for hours in the streets surrounding the Capitol, the gentle-

10

ness upon every face, the emotion in every heart, the
kindliness and courtesy apparent even in the densest
crowds, was a tribute in itself both affecting and significant.

The Senators and Representatives met in their respective Halls, and, at two o'clock, both branches assembled
in the lower corridors of the East Wing, while the
Executive Departments and distinguished delegations
gathered in the West corridors of the Capitol.

At half-past two o'clock the coffin was borne from
the State House, the solemn notes of the Dead March
awakening a response in ten thousand hearts. The procession was formed and moved with no audible sound,
save the measured tramp of feet and the mournful
strains of the band, amid thousands of uncovered spectators, who filled the sidewalks, and the doors and
windows of every house, through Beacon Street to King's
Chapel, where the services were held.

This venerable church, with its interesting historical
associations, was the family place of worship of Mr.
SUMNER. The beautiful interior, its quaint and massive
architecture, its richly painted windows, its mural tablets and monuments, were enriched by every delicate
device of flower, fern and trailing vine, to add bright-
ness and beauty to the solemnities.

The stained windows were crowned and festooned
with smilax, which drooped like a delicate veil over
the tablets of the commandments. The reading-desk,
pulpit and galleries were appropriately draped in black
and white, with threads of smilax in festoons, with
pinks and rosebuds intertwined.

The pew formerly occupied by Mr. SUMNER, was marked by a profusion of flowers. A loving and sympathetic taste had employed itself in the final arrangement of the beautiful offerings which had been placed within the chancel in affectionate remembrance.

For a brief hour of prayer, and choral song, and dirge, and benediction, King's Chapel was thus made ready to receive the mortal part of the Senator on its way to burial.

Profound silence reigned within the church; even in the streets surrounding it the din and hum of traffic were hushed. The distant strains of the funeral dirge were heard softly rising upon the air, and then, in clearer notes, the measured cadences of the Dead March resounded, as the cortège approached the open doors, deepening the solemn impressions of the hour.

At fifteen minutes before three o'clock the procession entered the church. His Excellency the Governor, and Staff, the members of the Executive Council, Heads of Departments and Senate, members of the Society of the Cincinnati and Board of Trade, were assigned seats on the left of the broad aisle. The pews on the left side aisle were occupied by the members of the House of Representatives. The pews at the head, on the right of the broad aisle, were allotted to intimate personal friends of the deceased Senator, the Vice-President of the United States, the Massachusetts delegation in Congress, the Congressional Committee, and the Chaplain and Sergeant-at-Arms of the United States Senate. Behind them were seated the Judges of the Supreme Court, Judges of the United States Courts, and Officers of the Army and Navy, Corporation and Overseers of Harvard College, members of the Class of 1830, the Reverend Clergy, Massachusetts Historical Society, and members of the New York Chamber of Commerce. The pall-bearers were seated at the head of the right side aisle, and below them the members of the City Government. Places were also assigned to the Trustees of the Public Library and Art Museum, and the Cambridge City Government.

It was with stately simplicity that the Commonwealth moved to the burial of her lamented son.

THE BURIAL SERVICE.

The Burial Service was according to the King's Chapel Liturgy, with special additions.

Rev. HENRY W. FOOTE officiated. He met the coffin at the door of the church and read the sentences :—

"I am the Resurrection and the Life, saith the Lord; he who believeth in me, though he were dead yet shall he live; and whosoever liveth and believeth in me shall never die.

"I know that my Redeemer liveth, and that he shall stand at the latter day upon the earth. And though after my skin worms destroy this body, yet in my flesh shall I see God.

"We brought nothing into this world and it is certain that we can carry nothing out. The Lord gave, and the Lord hath taken away; blessed be the name of the Lord."

An organ prelude followed; then Neumarck's Choral:

"To thee, O Lord, I yield my spirit,
  Who break'st in love this mortal chain;
My life I but from thee inherit,
  And death becomes my chiefest gain:
In thee I live, in thee I die
Content, for thou art ever nigh."

Then followed the Burial Psalms, the choir singing the responses :—

Lord, let me know my end and the number of my days; that I may know how frail I am.

Behold, thou hast made my days as it were a span long, and mine age is even as nothing in respect to thee; and verily every man living is altogether vanity.

For man walketh in a vain shadow, and disquieteth himself in vain; he heapeth up riches and cannot tell who shall gather them.

And now, Lord, what is my hope? Truly my hope is even in thee.

I became dumb and opened not my mouth; for it was thy doing.

But take thy plague away from me; for I am consumed by the blow of thy heavy hand.

When thou with rebukes dost chasten man for sin, thou makest his beauty to consume away, like as it were a moth fretting a garment; surely every man is vanity.

Hear my prayer, O Lord, and with thine ears consider my calling; hold not thy peace at my tears.

For I am a stranger with thee, and a sojourner, as all my fathers were.

Oh spare me a little, that I may recover my strength, before I go hence, and be no more seen.

Lord, thou hast been our refuge from one generation to another.

Before the mountains were brought forth, or ever thou hadst formed the earth and the world, even from everlasting to everlasting, thou art God.

Thou turnest man to destruction; and sayest, Return, ye children of men.

For a thousand years in thy sight are but as yesterday, when it is past, or a watch in the night.

Thou carriest them away as with a flood; they are even as a sleep; and fade away suddenly like the grass.

In the morning it is green, and groweth up; but in the evening it is cut down, dried up, and withered.

The days of our age are threescore years and ten; and though men be so strong that they come to fourscore years, yet is their strength then but labor and sorrow; so soon passeth it away, and we are gone.

So teach us to number our days that we may apply our hearts unto wisdom. Amen.

Then followed these Selections from Scripture : —

The burden of the valley of vision. What aileth thee now, that thou art wholly gone up to the housetops? Thou that art full of stirs, a tumultuous city.

Help, Lord! for the faithful fail from among the children of men.

All ye that are about him, bemoan him; all ye that know his name, say, how is the strong staff broken, and the beautiful rod!

To the counsellors of peace is joy. But His word was in mine heart as a burning fire shut up in my bones, and I was weary with forbearing, and I would not stay. For I heard the defaming of many, fear on every side. Report, say they, and we will report it. All my familiars watch for my halting, saying, Peradventure he will be enticed, and we shall prevail against him, and we shall take our revenge on him. . . . But, O Lord of hosts, that triest the righteous, . . . unto thee have I opened my cause.

Righteousness exalteth a nation; but sin is a reproach to any people.

Speak unto the children of Israel . . . and proclaim liberty throughout all the land unto all the inhabitants thereof. Is not this the fast that I have chosen? to loose the bands of wickedness, to undo the heavy burdens and to let the oppressed go free, and that ye break every yoke? As free, and not using your liberty for a cloak of maliciousness, but as the servants of God.

The people that sat in darkness have seen a great light; they that dwell in the land of the shadow of death, upon them hath the light shined.

When I went out to the gate through the city the young men saw me, and hid themselves, and the aged arose and stood up. The princes refrained talking, and laid their hands on their mouth. Because I delivered the poor that cried, and the fatherless, and him that had none to help him, the blessing of him that was ready to perish came upon me. I put on righteousness and it clothed me. I was a father to the poor; and the cause which I knew not I searched out. My glory was fresh in me; and my bow was renewed in my hand. Unto me men gave ear, and waited, and kept silence at my counsel.

Judge me, O Lord, for I have walked in mine integrity. I have not sat with vain persons, neither will I go in with dissemblers. I have hated the congregation of evil doers; and will not sit with the wicked. I will wash mine hands in innocency. Gather not my soul with sinners, nor my life with bloody men: in whose hands is mischief, and their right hand is full of bribes. But as for me, I will walk in mine integrity; redeem me and be merciful unto me.

Who shall ascend into the hill of the Lord, or who shall stand in his holy place? He that hath clean hands and a pure heart: who hath not lifted up his soul unto vanity nor sworn deceitfully. He shall receive the blessing from the Lord, and righteousness from the God of his salvation.

And now, behold, I am gray-headed . . . and I have walked before you from my childhood unto this day. Behold, here I am; witness against me before the Lord, and before his anointed: whose ox have I taken? or whose ass have I taken? or whom have I defrauded? or whom have I oppressed? or of whose hand have I received any bribe to blind mine eyes therewith?

But the souls of the righteous are in the hand of God, and there shall no torment touch them. There the wicked cease from troubling and the weary are at rest.

For the memorial of virtue is immortal; because it is known with God and with men. When it is present men take example at it, and when it is gone they desire it; it weareth a crown and triumpheth forever, having gotten the victory, striving for undefiled rewards.

Their bodies are buried in peace; but their name liveth forevermore.

He judged the cause of the poor and needy; then it was well with him. Was not this to know me? saith the Lord.

What shall one then answer the messengers of the nation? That the Lord hath founded Zion, and the poor of his people shall trust in it.

He that had received five talents came and brought other five talents, saying, Lord, thou deliverest unto me five talents; behold, I have gained beside them five talents more. His lord said unto him, Well done, thou good and faithful servant; thou hast been faithful over a few things, I will make thee ruler over many things; enter thou into the joy of thy lord.

Finally, brethren, whatsoever things are true, whatsoever things are honest, whatsoever things are just, whatsoever things are pure, whatsoever things are lovely, whatsoever things are of good report; if there be any virtue, and if there be any praise, think on these things.

Now is Christ risen from the dead, and become the first fruits of those who slept. For since by man came death, by man came also the resurrection of the dead.

For as in Adam all die, even so in Christ shall all be made alive.

There is one glory of the sun, and another glory of the moon, and another glory of the stars; for one star differeth from another star in glory. So also is the resurrection of the dead. It is sown in corruption, it is raised in incorruption; it is sown in dishonor, it is raised in glory; it is sown in weakness, it is raised in power; it is sown a natural body, it is raised a spiritual body.

Now, this I say, brethren, that flesh and blood cannot inherit the kingdom of God; neither doth corruption inherit incorruption. For this corruptible must put on incorruption, and this mortal must put on immortality. So when this corruptible shall have put on incorruption, and this mortal shall have put on immortality, then shall be brought to pass the saying that is written, Death is swallowed up in victory. O death, where is thy sting? O grave, where is thy victory? The sting of death is sin, and the strength of sin is the law; but thanks be to God, who giveth us the victory through our Lord Jesus Christ.

The following Anthem was then sung : —

" Happy and blessed are they who have endured! For though the body dies, the soul shall live forever."

At the close of the Anthem the Burial Service proceeded :—

Man that is born of a woman hath but a short time to live, and is full of misery. He cometh up, and is cut down like a flower ; he fleeth as it were a shadow, and never continueth in one stay.

In the midst of life we are in death ; of whom may we seek for succor, but of thee, O Lord, who for our sins art justly displeased?

Yet, O Lord God most holy, O Lord most mighty, O holy and most merciful Father, deliver us not unto the bitter pains of eternal death !

Thou knowest, Lord, the secrets of our hearts ; shut not thy merciful ears to our prayers ; but spare us, Lord most holy, O God most mighty, O holy and merciful Father, thou most worthy Judge Eternal, suffer us not at our last hour, for any pains of death, to fall from thee.

Forasmuch as it hath pleased Almighty God to take unto himself the soul of our brother, here departed, we therefore commit his body to the ground ; earth to earth, ashes to ashes, dust to dust ; in sure and certain hope of the resurrection to eternal life, through our Lord Jesus Christ, when the earth and the sea shall give up their dead, and the corruptible bodies of those who sleep in Jesus shall be changed and made like unto his glorious body, according to the mighty working whereby he is able to subdue all things to himself.

Then the following Choral by Gastorius was sung :—

> " Leave God to order all thy ways,
>   And hope in him, whate'er betide ;
>   Thou'lt find him in the evil days
>   Thy all-sufficient strength and guide.
> Who trusts in God's unchanging love
> Builds on the rock that nought can move

11

"He knows when joyful hours are best,
   He sends them as he sees it meet;
   When thou hast borne the fiery test,
   And art made free from all deceit,
He comes to thee all unaware,
And makes thee own his loving care.

"Sing, pray, and swerve not from his ways,
   But do thine own part faithfully,
   Trust his rich promises of grace,
   So shall they be fulfilled in thee;
God never yet forsook at need
The soul that trusted him indeed."

Then followed the Collect and the special Prayer :—

Almighty God, with whom do live the spirits of those who
depart hence in the Lord; and with whom the souls of the
faithful, after they are delivered from the burthen of the flesh,
are in joy and felicity, we give thee hearty thanks for the good
examples of all those thy servants who, having finished their
course in faith, do now rest from their labors. And we beseech
thee that we, with all those who are departed in the true faith
of thy holy name, may have our perfect consummation and bliss
in thy heavenly and everlasting glory, through Jesus Christ our
Lord. Amen.

O Almighty and ever-living God, we fly to thee as our eternal
refuge ; we rest ourselves upon thee, the Rock of Ages.
Blessed be thy holy name for the assurance of eternal life which
thou hast given us by thy beloved Son ; blessed be thy holy
name for the faith which we cherish that this corruptible shall
put on incorruption, and this mortal, immortality.

Let this immortal hope and the comforts of thy gracious
Spirit sustain in this their bereavement the kindred and friends
of our departed brother, those who are near and those who are
far away. May the sorrow of the land bear up their hearts
with precious consolations, and the land's sorrow be full of
consecration for this great people.

Bless our beloved country, and make its rulers to rule over us for good. Teach its senators wisdom, and give to all its people a spirit of purer patriotism, inspired by thy faith and fear. May we trust not in any arm of flesh, but in the living God. Raise up wise and faithful men to guide us in the place of thy servant whom thou hast called to thy nearer service from the single-hearted and loyal discharge of his great office; and, O God, teach us in our great loss the full lessons of his eminent and faithful life, that our gratitude may be attested by our dedication of ourselves to thy truth and thy law.

In this community, whose son he was, we thank thee for every great gift in him, of example in constancy and courage for the right, and scorn of all that was mean and low, and incorruptible integrity,—for his pleading the cause of the down-trodden and his hearing the sighing of the sorrowful, his zeal for justice and truth, for every wise word and brave and honest deed. And chiefly do we thank thee for the lofty purpose which inspired his service of his country, to give to her the best he had to give. Sanctify these great memories to us, and make them fruitful in high thinking, and faithful living, to the people of this land.

Visit this mourning Commonwealth, whose heart is melted in a common sorrow, with thy Spirit of grace, to renew in us the best example of loyalty to truth and duty and thee. Purge us from all self-seeking counsels. Teach us to honor only that which is worthy of honor, and to trust only them who put their trust in thee.

Be thou, O God, our refuge and our consolation and our sure trust. The more we are brought to perceive that things seen are temporal, so much the more may we find that the things which are unseen are eternal; that thou art faithful, and that Christ is worthy, and that heaven and not earth is our home. May we embrace thy promises and be thankful; may we know that thou art God, and be still. And grant, we beseech thee, O Holy Father and Eternal Judge, that we may all live mindful of our duty and our trust, and waiting on thy will; that, when we have served thee in our generations, we may be gathered unto our fathers, having the testimony of a good conscience, and in the hope that neither death nor life, nor things present, nor things to come, will be able to separate us from the love of God, which is in Christ Jesus our Lord. Amen.

The following hymn by Montgomery was then sung by the congregation,—

> " Servant of God, well done!
>   Rest from thy loved employ ;
> The battle fought, the victory won,
>   Enter thy Master's joy.
>
> " The voice at midnight came,
>   He started up to hear ;
> A mortal arrow pierced his frame,—
>   He fell, but felt no fear.
>
> " Tranquil amidst alarms,
>   It found him on the field,
> A veteran, slumbering on his arms,
>   Beneath his red-cross shield.
>
> " The pains of death are past ;
>   Labor and sorrow cease ;
> And, life's long warfare closed at last,
>   His soul is found in peace."

The Benediction followed :—

" The grace of our Lord Jesus Christ, and the love of God, and the fellowship of the Holy Ghost, be with us all ever more." Amen.

And the service was concluded with Mendelssohn's "Funeral March" and Pergolesi's "Stabat Mater."

As the organ notes softly interpreted the great theme, the coffin was borne to the hearse, and the imposing procession moved on its way.

During the funeral service a number of organizations of colored men took positions on Beacon Street, in open order, standing uncovered, as the cortege moved through the long and silent lines.

THE PROCESSION.

The Procession was formed as follows:

MOUNTED STATE POLICE.

BAND.

SERGEANT-AT-ARMS.

LEGISLATIVE COMMITTEE OF ARRANGEMENTS.

THE OFFICIATING CLERGYMAN.

THE PALL-BEARERS.

MOUNTED ESCORT.   **THE HEARSE.**   MOUNTED ESCORT.

M O U R N E R S.

THE VICE-PRESIDENT.

MASSACHUSETTS CONGRESSIONAL DELEGATION.

COMMITTEE OF CONGRESS.

CHAPLAIN AND SERGEANT-AT-ARMS OF THE UNITED STATES SENATE.

HIS EXCELLENCY THE GOVERNOR AND STAFF.

HIS HONOR THE LIEUTENANT-GOVERNOR, AND THE COUNCIL.

HEADS OF DEPARTMENTS.

PRESIDENT OF THE SENATE, SENATORS AND OFFICERS.

SPEAKER OF THE HOUSE OF REPRESENTATIVES, REPRESENTATIVES AND
OFFICERS.

THE MAYOR OF BOSTON, AND THE CITY COUNCIL.

SHERIFF OF SUFFOLK COUNTY.

THE CHIEF JUSTICE AND THE ASSOCIATE JUSTICES OF THE SUPREME
JUDICIAL COURT.

JUDGES OF THE UNITED STATES COURTS.

OFFICERS OF THE ARMY AND NAVY.

PRESIDENT AND FELLOWS OF HARVARD COLLEGE.

OVERSEERS OF HARVARD COLLEGE.

CLASS OF 1830.

THE REVEREND CLERGY.

OFFICERS OF THE MASSACHUSETTS HISTORICAL SOCIETY.

STANDING COMMITTEE OF THE MASSACHUSETTS SOCIETY OF THE
CINCINNATI.

GOVERNMENT OF THE BOSTON BOARD OF TRADE.

DELEGATION FROM THE NEW YORK CHAMBER OF COMMERCE.

TRUSTEES OF THE BOSTON PUBLIC LIBRARY.

TRUSTEES OF THE ART MUSEUM.

REPRESENTATIVES OF THE CAMBRIDGE CITY GOVERNMENT.

ORGANIZATIONS OF COLORED CITIZENS.

COLORED CITIZENS TO THE NUMBER OF TWO THOUSAND,

(Including Fraternal and Hancock Associations of Boston, and Post 134, of the "Grand Army of the Republic.")

DELEGATIONS OF CITIZENS FROM DEDHAM, PROVIDENCE AND WORCESTER.

All the way from King's Chapel to Mount Auburn, a distance of at least five miles, the streets were lined with expectant but hushed and reverent crowds. This imposing demonstration has had but one parallel in our history, and that was the day set apart by proclamation for the contemplation of the virtues and sorrow for the death of ABRAHAM LINCOLN. Then "fears were in the way, and the keepers of the house trembled," and strong men wept;—it was the supreme hour of the nation. But this was the mourning of a State for her Senator, who, after matchless fidelity, had fallen at his post; and the startled community were uniting in a great sympathy and a tender yearning to do him honor.

It was nearly six o'clock when the long procession passed under the massive gateway of Mount Auburn, and began its winding march through Central and Walnut Avenues and Arethusa Path, to the grave. The coffin was covered with beautiful flowers, which were buried with it. The officiating clergyman, the pall-bearers, and other gentlemen at the head of the procession, took position about the grave, Mr. SUMNER's nearest friends and the Massachusetts Delegation in Congress standing at its foot and a little at the left, with the Committee of the Legislature by their side at the right. At its head, and just behind the minister, were the few surviving members of Mr. SUMNER's class in Harvard College; while on the rising slope above and north of the grave, stood the Congressional Committee, the members of the Legislature, and invited guests. Behind, clustering on every hillock, and climbing to the very summit of the hill where the Tower stands, was the vast crowd of spectators, numbering many thousands, who waited in silence the last rites of sepulture.

THE BURIAL.

As the body was deposited at the side of the grave a chorus of male voices, selected from the Apollo Club, sang the first eight lines of the Ode of Horace :—

> " Integer vitæ scelerisque purus
> Non eget Mauris jaculis neque arcu
> Nec venenatis gravida sagittis,
> Fusce, pharetra,
> Sive per Syrtes iter æstuosas
> Sive facturus per inhospitalem
> Caucasum vel quæ loca fabulosus
> Lambit Hydaspes."

While the solemn music was rising, two daughters of Dr. Samuel G. Howe, the only persons of their sex within the enclosure, stepped forward in behalf of Mrs. Hastings of San Francisco, the absent sister of Mr. SUMNER, and placed upon the coffin, already covered with flowers of rarest beauty, one a cross and the other a wreath.

Hardly had the sounds of the singers' voices died away upon the air, when the minister, speaking so that he could be heard by all around, said:—

"I heard a voice from heaven saying unto me, Write, From henceforth blessed are the dead who die in the Lord: even so saith the Spirit; for they rest from their labors and their works do follow them."

The Lord's Prayer was afterwards said by the minister and mourners, and while the remains were slowly lowered into their final resting-place, the choir sang Dr. Hedge's version of Luther's Choral:—

"EIN FESTE BURG IST UNSER GOTT."

"A mighty fortress is our God,
    A bulwark never failing;
Our helper he amid the flood
    Of mortal ills prevailing;
For still our ancient foe
Doth seek to work us woe,
His craft and power are great,
And, armed with cruel hate,
    On earth is not his equal.

"Did we in our strength confide,
    Our striving would be losing,—
Were not the right man on our side,
    The man of God's own choosing.
Dost ask who that may be?
Christ Jesus, it is he,
Lord Sabbaoth his name,
From age to age the same,
    And he must win the battle.

"The word above all earthly powers,—
    No thanks to them—abideth,
The spirit and the gifts are ours
    Through Him who with us sideth.

Let goods and kindred go,
This mortal life also;
The body they may kill,—
God's truth abideth still,
His kingdom is forever."

During this beautiful service, the chorus chanting in solemn monotones the responsive "Amens," the scene was deeply impressive.

The sky had taken on a subdued gray tinge, through which the light of the setting sun shone but faintly over the city of the dead. The air was silent, the vast assembly was hushed, and in the pauses of the service, from Boston—which lay plainly in sight towards the sea—and Cambridge, and Brookline, and all the neighboring towns, came slowly and faintly the vibrations of the tolling bells.

After a few moments the benediction was pronounced.

Thus with the mighty mourning of a sovereign State, the body was left with its kindred dust and to the vigils of the silent stars.

" Revive again thou summer rain
The broken turf upon his bed!
Breathe, summer wind, thy tenderest strain
Of low, sweet music overhead!"

12

COMMEMORATIVE OBSERVANCES.

COMMEMORATIVE OBSERVANCES.

TUESDAY, the ninth of June, having been appointed for the delivery of the Eulogy, on that day a procession was formed in Doric Hall, and marched from the State House to the Music Hall, in the following order:—

STATE POLICE.

BAND.

THE SERGEANT-AT-ARMS.

THE COMMITTEE OF ARRANGEMENTS.

THE GOVERNOR AND STAFF.

THE LIEUTENANT-GOVERNOR, AND THE COUNCIL.

HEADS OF DEPARTMENTS.

THE PRESIDENT OF THE SENATE, SENATORS, THEIR CHAPLAIN, AND CLERK.

THE SPEAKER OF THE HOUSE OF REPRESENTATIVES, REPRESENTATIVES, THEIR CHAPLAIN AND CLERK.

EX-GOVERNORS AND LIEUTENANT-GOVERNORS OF MASSACHUSETTS.

DISTINGUISHED GUESTS.

GOVERNORS OF OTHER STATES.

THE SHERIFF OF SUFFOLK COUNTY.

THE CHIEF JUSTICE AND ASSOCIATE JUSTICES OF THE SUPREME JUDICIAL COURT.

JUDGES OF UNITED STATES COURTS

MEMBERS OF CONGRESS.

THE COLLECTOR OF BOSTON.

INVITED GUESTS.

The Committee endeavored to make the services on the occasion worthy of the State, and a fitting tribute to the memory of her great Senator.

The Music Hall was decorated with care. The black and white hangings, the vines and flowers, the drooping laurel wreaths, and the organ veiled in a delicate drapery of smilax, gave grace and beauty to the spacious interior. A life-size portrait of Mr. SUMNER, of striking excellence, recalled to the great assemblage his commanding and attractive presence.

At one o'clock, the appointed hour, the service began with the Organ Voluntary, followed by a Chant by the Temple Quartette of the words :—

" Remember now thy Creator in the days of thy youth, while the evil days come not, nor the years draw nigh, when thou shalt say, I have no pleasure in them ;

" While the sun, or the light, or the moon, or the stars, be not darkened, nor the clouds return after the rain :

" In the day when the keepers of the house shall tremble, and the strong men shall bow themselves, and the grinders cease because they are few, and those that look out of the windows be darkened,

" And the doors shall be shut in the streets, when the sound of the grinding is low, and he shall rise up at the voice of the bird, and all the daughters of music shall be brought low ;

" Also when they shall be afraid of that which is high, and fears shall be in the way, and the almond tree shall flourish, and the grasshopper shall be a burden, and desire shall fail : because man goeth to his long home, and the mourners go about the streets :

" Or ever the silver cord be loosed, or the golden bowl be broken, or the pitcher be broken at the fountain, or the wheel broken at the cistern.

" Then shall the dust return to the earth as it was : and the spirit shall return unto God who gave it."

Prayer was then offered by Rev. JAMES FREEMAN CLARKE, in the following words :—

Who shall ascend into the hill of the Lord : and who shall stand in his holy place? He that hath clean hands and a pure heart, who hath not lifted up his soul unto vanity, nor sworn deceitfully.

O thou most righteous God, who lovest righteousness ! we, the people of this Commonwealth, assemble this day by our lawmakers and magistrates, to commemorate with glad and grateful words the life of a good man, who has finished the work given him to do.

From thee we begin, Infinite Friend, from whom cometh every good gift, recognizing as among thy best gifts to us the good and the wise, who in the time of our need have stood up as a fire, and whose words have burned as a lamp—sending its beams far into the night and storm.

Blessed be thy name that thou didst build this State on the foundation of just and wise men, Jesus Christ himself being its chief corner-stone : and that, from time to time, whenever new occasions have taught new duties, there have never been wanting, in thy good Providence, men of self-forgetting integrity, who have led us through every wilderness, and brought us in safety to the promised land.

And we thank thee to-day that, when our iniquities separated between us and God, and our hands were defiled with blood; when we enslaved our brother man and ground the faces of the poor; when the prophets prophesied falsely, and the people loved to have it so; that then thou didst raise up among us those who proclaimed liberty to the captives, and taught us to loose the bands of wickedness, and let the oppressed go free, and to break every yoke.

And, among these, we thank thee for our brother, who was called to stand so many years face to face with the advocates of tyranny and injustice. Thou didst make his face strong against their faces, and his forehead strong against their foreheads ; and he was not dismayed because of their looks, though they were a rebellious house.

He put on justice, and it clothed him. Righteousness was the girdle of his loins, and faithfulness the girdle of his reins.

Thou didst endow him richly with elevation of moral sentiment, combined with breadth of intellectual culture; and thou didst help him in the lingering conflict, through weary day and weary year, so that he did not heed the stinging bolts of scorn, or the words of fools who accounted his life madness, but fought the good fight to the end; approving himself in all things a true servant of God, in much patience, in afflictions, in distresses, in stripes, in tumults; by pureness, by knowledge, by long-suffering, by kindness, by love unfeigned, by the word of truth, by the armor of righteousness on the right hand and the left, by honor and dishonor, by evil report and good report; as a deceiver and yet true; as unknown and yet well-known; as dying, and behold! he lived; as chastened, and not killed; as poor, but making men rich; as sorrowful, and yet always rejoicing.

We thank thee that he was enabled to outlive all calumny, all censure, all evil report; and that when he died the great heart of the nation, from ocean to ocean, testified to his worth by a universal sorrow, and has thus shown that the memorial of virtue is immortal. We thank thee that his own dear State, which for a moment misunderstood him, once again uttered, while he could still hear her voice, her familiar blessing, and say, Well done, good and faithful servant!

And now, God save the Commonwealth of Massachusetts! May it be saved in the present and future, as it has been saved in the past! May it be saved from the cunning of selfish politicians, who care only for personal triumph, not for the good of the State; from those who make party success the highest good; from the corruptions of avarice and ambition! May not the labors be wasted of the wise and generous souls who have illustrated its noble history! May not their toils and sorrows be in vain! May not the blood shed on a hundred battle-fields for freedom and union be shed in vain!

But, seeing that we are compassed about with so great a cloud of witnesses, may we lay aside every weight; and be followers of them who through faith and patience have inherited the promises.

Miss CLARA LOUISE KELLOGG then rendered, from Handel's Oratorio of the Messiah, the Aria :—

"I know that my Redeemer liveth, and that He shall stand at the latter day upon the earth:

"And though worms destroy this body, yet in my flesh shall I see God."

"But now is Christ risen from the dead, and become the first fruits of them that slept."

The following poem, written for the occasion, by JOHN GREENLEAF WHITTIER, was then read by Prof. J. W. CHURCHILL :—

SUMNER.

"I AM not one who has disgraced beauty of sentiment by deformity of conduct, or the maxims of a freeman by the actions of a slave; but, by the grace of God, I have kept my life unsullied."—*Milton's Defence of the People of England.*

O MOTHER STATE!—the winds of March
　　Blew chill o'er Auburn's Field of God,
Where, slow, beneath a leaden-arch
　　Of sky, thy mourning children trod.

And now, with all thy woods in leaf,
　　Thy fields in flower, beside thy dead
Thou sittest, in thy robes of grief,
　　A Rachel yet uncomforted!

And once again the organ swells,
　　Once more the flag is half-way hung,
And yet again the mournful bells
　　In all thy steeple-towers are rung.

And I, obedient to thy will,
　　Have come a simple wreath to lay,
Superfluous, on a grave that still
　　Is sweet with all the flowers of May.

13

I take, with awe, the task assigned;
  It may be that my friend might miss,
In his new sphere of heart and mind,
  Some token from my hand in this.

By many a tender memory moved,
  Along the past my thought I send;
The record of the cause he loved
  Is the best record of its friend.

No trumpet sounded in his ear,
  He saw not Sinai's cloud and flame,
But never yet to Hebrew seer
  A clearer voice of duty came.

God said: "Break thou these yokes; undo
  These heavy burdens. I ordain
A work to last thy whole life through,
  A ministry of strife and pain.

"Forego thy dreams of lettered ease,
  Put thou the scholar's promise by,
The rights of man are more than these."
  He heard, and answered: "Here am I!"

He set his face against the blast,
  His feet against the flinty shard,
Till the hard service grew, at last,
  Its own exceeding great reward.

Lifted like Saul's above the crowd,
  Upon his kingly forehead fell
The first, sharp bolt of Slavery's cloud,
  Launched at the truth he urged so well.

Ah! never yet, at rack or stake,
  Was sorer loss made Freedom's gain,
Than his, who suffered for her sake
  The beak-torn Titan's lingering pain!

The fixed star of his faith, through all
   Loss, doubt, and peril, shone the same;
As, through a night of storm, some tall,
   Strong light-house lifts its steady flame.

Beyond the dust and smoke he saw
   The sheaves of freedom's large increase,
The holy fanes of equal law,
   The New Jerusalem of peace.

The weak might fear, the worldling mock,
   The faint and blind of heart regret;
All knew at last, th' eternal rock
   On which his forward feet were set.

The subtlest scheme of compromise
   Was folly to his purpose bold,
The strongest mesh of party lies
   Weak to the simplest truth he told.

One language held his heart and lip,
   Straight onward to his goal he trod,
And proved the highest statesmanship
   Obedience to the voice of God.

No wail was in his voice,—none heard
   When treason's storm-cloud blackest grew
The weakness of a doubtful word;
   His duty, and the end, he knew.

The first to smite, the first to spare;
   When once the hostile ensigns fell,
He stretched out hands of generous care
   To lift the foe he fought so well.

For there was nothing base or small
   Or craven in his soul's broad plan;
Forgiving all things personal,
   He hated only wrong to man.

The old traditions of his State,
    The memories of her great and good,
Took from his life a fresher date,
    And in himself embodied stood.

How felt the greed of gold and place,
    The venal crew that schemed and planned,
The fine scorn of that haughty face,
    The spurning of that bribeless hand!

If than Rome's tribunes statelier
    He wore his senatorial robe,
His lofty port was all for her,
    The one dear spot on all the globe.

If to the master's plea he gave
    The vast contempt his manhood felt,
He saw a brother in the slave,—
    With man as equal man he dealt.

Proud was he?   If his presence kept
    Its grandeur wheresoe'er he trod,
As if from Plutarch's gallery stepped
    The hero and the demi-god,

None failed, at least, to reach his ear,
    Nor want nor woe appealed in vain;
The homesick soldier knew his cheer,
    And blessed him from his ward of pain.

Safely his dearest friends may own
    The slight defects he never hid,
The surface-blemish in the stone
    Of the tall, stately pyramid.

Suffice it that he never brought
    His conscience to the public mart;
But lived himself the truth he taught,
    White-souled, clean-handed, pure of heart.

What if he felt the natural pride
    Of power in noble use, too true
With thin humilities to hide
    The work he did, the lore he knew?

Was he not just? Was any wronged
    By that assured self-estimate?
He took but what to him belonged,
    Unenvious of another's state.

Well might he heed the words he spake,
    And scan with care the written page
Through which he still shall warm and wake
    The hearts of men from age to age.

Ah! who shall blame him now because
    He solaced thus his hours of pain!
Should not the o'erworn thresher pause,
    And hold to light his golden grain?

No sense of humor dropped its oil
    On the hard ways his purpose went;
Small play of fancy lightened toil;
    He spake alone the thing he meant.

He loved his books, the Art that hints
    A beauty veiled behind its own,
The graver's line, the pencil's tints,
    The chisel's shape evoked from stone.

He cherished, void of selfish ends,
    The social courtesies that bless
And sweeten life, and loved his friends
    With most unworldly tenderness.

But still his tired eyes rarely learned
    The glad relief by Nature brought:
Her mountain ranges never turned
    His current of persistent thought.

The sea rolled chorus to his speech
   Three-banked like Latium's tall trireme,
With laboring oars ; the grove and beach
   Were Forum and the Academe.

The sensuous joy from all things fair
   His strenuous bent of soul repressed,
And left from youth to silvered hair
   Few hours for pleasure, none for rest.

For all his life was poor without ;
   O Nature, make the last amends ;
Train all thy flowers his grave about,
   And make thy singing-birds his friends !

Revive again, thou summer rain,
   The broken turf upon his bed !
Breathe, summer wind, thy tenderest strain
   Of low, sweet music overhead !

With calm and beauty symbolize
   His peace which follows long annoy,
And lend our earth-bent, mourning eyes
   Some hint of his diviner joy.

For safe with right and truth he is,
   As God lives he must live alway ;
There is no end for souls like his,
   No night for children of the day !

Nor cant nor poor solicitudes
   Made weak his life's great argument ;
Small leisure his for frames and moods
   Who followed duty where she went.

The broad, fair fields of God he saw
   Beyond the bigot's narrow bound ;
The truths he moulded into law,
   In Christ's beatitudes he found.

His State-craft was the Golden Rule,
   His right of vote a sacred trust;
Clear, over threat and ridicule,
   All heard his challenge: "Is it just?"

And when the hour supreme had come,
   Not for himself a thought he gave;
In that last pang of martyrdom,
   His care was for the half-freed slave.

Not vainly dusky hands upbore,
   In prayer, the passing soul to heaven
Whose mercy to His suffering poor
   Was service to the Master given.

Long shall the good State's annals tell,
   Her children's children long be taught,
How, praised or blamed, he guarded well
   The trust he neither shunned nor sought.

If for one moment turned thy face,
   O Mother, from thy son, not long
He waited calmly in his place
   The sure remorse which follows wrong.

Forgiven be the State he loved
   The one brief lapse, the single blot;
Forgotten be the stain removed,
   Her righted record shows it not!

The lifted sword above her shield
   With jealous care shall guard his fame;
The pine-tree on her ancient field
   To all the winds shall speak his name.

The marble image of her son
   Her loving hands shall yearly crown,
And from her pictured Pantheon
   His grand, majestic face look down.

O State so passing rich before,
   Who now shall doubt thy highest claim?
The world that counts thy jewels o'er
   Shall longest pause at SUMNER's name!

Miss ADELAIDE PHILLIPS then sang Mendelssohn's Aria:—

"O rest in the Lord—wait patiently for Him and He shall give thee thy heart's desires.

"Commit thy way unto Him, and trust in Him, and fret not thyself because of evil-doers."

At the close of the Eulogy the Quartette sang:—

"Cast thy burden upon the Lord, and He shall sustain thee: He never will suffer the righteous to fall; He is at thy right hand. Thy mercy, Lord, is great, and far above the heavens. Let none be made ashamed that wait upon Thee!"

The Introductory Remarks by Hon. ALEXANDER H. BULLOCK were as follows:—

In the train of those paying mournful tribute to CHARLES SUMNER most fit is the presence of the Legislature of Massachusetts. By their act, twenty-four years ago, the gate was opened through which he passed to the Senate of the United States for life. And now, after this lapse of time and the close of his career, the Government and the people of this Commonwealth contemplate with just and solemn satisfaction the contribution they then made to the higher sphere of statesmanship. They recall his first appearance there, seemingly lost amidst a majority who were the embodiment and type of ideals so much less heroic and elevated than his own; with what masterly unreserve he began and continued his great mission, abating nothing, disguising nothing, sweeping in his perspective many of the vast results which have since been attained; how he lived to see his grand central aspirations realized, his main purposes accomplished, at his death leaving as a truth, never before so well illustrated at the Capital, that the character of statesman and senator derives added strength and lustre from the character of scholar and philanthropist, liberator and reformer.

At the moment of the greatest triumph of Wilberforce, on the passage of his bill abolishing the slave trade, Sir Samuel Romilly, amid the ringing acclamations of the House of Commons, called upon the younger members to observe how superior were the rewards of virtue to all the vulgar conceptions of ambition. In the hour of the greatest triumph of Sumner—the hour of his death—a like admonition arose from his vacant chair, calling upon American public life to mark the lofty exemplar, by whom, amid abounding corruption, comparative poverty had been held as honor; to whom artifice and intrigue had been an abhorrence; who, in the long practice of official transactions and official manners, had never acquired an official heart; who had guarded his conscience against every assault, and always kept that vessel pure; upon whose headstone the whole Republic inscribes for its souvenance, " Incorruptible and unapproachable."

With one mind the Senators and Representatives of Massachusetts, successors to those who, nearly a quarter of a century since, sent him forth with the seal of his great commission, are present by these final and august ceremonies to deliver him over to history. In selecting their orator for this tender office, they could not fail to call for him who best would give voice to their Eulogy. As our lamented Senator was a master in all the art of letters, it is fitting that he should be embalmed by the art of another and similar master and personal friend. I introduce to you Mr. George William Curtis.

Mr. Curtis then rose and began the Eulogy.

14

EULOGY BY GEORGE WILLIAM CURTIS.

THE EULOGY.

THE prayer is said—the dirge is sung; from the waters of the Bay to the hills of Berkshire the funeral bells of the Commonwealth have tolled; the Congress of the United States, of which he was the oldest member in continuous service, has in both Houses spoken his praises— no voice more eloquent than that of his opponents; the race to whose elevation his life was consecrated has bewailed him with filial gratitude; this city, his birthplace and his home, has proudly mourned its illustrious citizen; the pulpit and the press everywhere in the land have blended sorrow and admiration; and now his native State, with all its honored magistracy— the State which gave him his great opportunity, clothing his words with the majesty of Massachusetts, so that when he spoke it was not the voice of a man, but of a Commonwealth—lamenting a son so beloved, a servant so faithful, a friend so true, comes last of all to say farewell,

and to deliver the character and career of
CHARLES SUMNER to history and the judgment
of mankind. I know how amply, how eloquently,
how tenderly, the story of his life has been told.
In this place you heard it in words that spoke
for the culture and the conscience of the country
—for the prosperous and happy. And yonder
in Faneuil Hall his eulogy fell from lips that
must always glow when they mention him—lips
that spoke for the most wronged and most
unfortunate in the land, who never saw the face
of SUMNER, but whose children's children will
bless his name forever. I might well hesitate
to stand here if I did not know that, enriched
by your sympathy, my words, telling the same
tale, will seem to your generous hearts to pro-
long for a moment the requiem that you would
not willingly let die.

Nor think the threefold strain superfluous.
How well this universal eulogy—these mingling
voices of various nativity, but all American—
befits a man whose aims and efforts were universal; whom neither a city, nor a State, nor
a party, nor a nation, nor a race, bound with
any local limitation! On a lofty hill overlooking
the lake of Cayuga, in New York, stands a

noble tree, in the grounds of the Cornell University, under which an Oxford scholar, choosing America for his home because America is the home of Liberty, has placed a seat upon which he has carved, "Above all nations is Humanity." That is the legend which CHARLES SUMNER carved upon his heart, and sought to write upon the hearts of his fellow-citizens and of the world. And if at this moment my voice should suddenly sink into silence, I can believe that this hall would thrill and murmur with the last words he ever publicly spoke in Massachusetts, standing on this very spot: "Nor would I have my country forget at any time, in the discharge of its transcendent duties, that, since the rule of conduct and of honor is the same for nations as for individuals, the greatest nation is that which does most for humanity."

Amidst the general sorrow, Massachusetts mourns him by the highest right, for with all the grasp of his hope and his cosmopolitan genius, perhaps for those very reasons, he was essentially a Massachusetts man. And here I touch the first great influence that moulded your Senator. This is the Puritan State, and the greatness of SUMNER was the greatness of the

Puritan genius—the greatness of moral power. Learning and culture and accomplishment; aesthetic taste and knowledge; the grace of society; the scholar's rich resource in travel; illustrious friendships in every land; the urbanity and charm of a citizen of the world—all these he had; all these you know; yet all these were but the velvet in which the iron Puritan hand was clad—the Puritan hand which in other days had smitten kings and dynasties hip and thigh; had saved civil and religious liberty in England; had swept the Mediterranean of pirates; had avenged the Lord's

"slaughtered saints, whose bones
Lie scattered on the Alpine mountains cold;"

the Puritan hand which, reaching out across the sea, sterner than the icy sternness of the New England shore, grasped a new continent, and wrought the amazing miracle of America.

The Puritan spirit, in the larger sense, enriched with many nationalities, broader, more generous, more humane, is the master influence of American civilization, and among all our public men it has no type so satisfactory and complete as CHARLES SUMNER. He was the son of Massachusetts. By the fruit let the tree be judged. The State to whose hard coast the Mayflower came, and upon whose rocks it dropped its seed—the State in which the mingled Puritan and Pilgrim spirit has been most active —is to-day the chief of Commonwealths. It is the community in which the average of well-being is higher than in any State we know in history. Puritan in origin though it be, it is more truly liberal and free than any similar community in the world. The fig and the pome-granate and the almond will not grow there, nor the nightingale sing, but nobler blossoms of the old human stock than its most famous children, the sun never shone upon; nor has the liberty-loving heart of man heard sweeter music than the voices of JAMES OTIS and SAMUEL ADAMS, of JOHN ADAMS and JOSEPH WARREN, of JOSIAH QUINCY and CHARLES SUMNER. Surely I may say so, born in the State that ROGER WILLIAMS founded—ROGER WILLIAMS, the prophet whom Massachusetts stoned.

Into this State and these influences CHARLES SUMNER was born sixty-three years ago, while as yet the traditions of colonial New England were virtually unchanged. Here were the town-meeting, the constable, the common school, the

15

training-day, the general intelligence, the morality, the habit of self-government, the homogeneity
of population, the ample territory, the universal
instinct of law. Here was the full daily practice
of what De Tocqueville afterward called the
two or three principal ideas which form the
basis of the social theory of the United States,
and which seemed to make a Republic possible,
practicable, and wise. It was one of the good
fortunes of Sumner's life that, born amidst these
influences, he used to the utmost the advantage
of school and college. To many men youth
itself is so sweet a siren that in hearing her
song they forget all but the pleasure of listening
to it. But the sibyl saved no scroll from Sumner; he had the wisdom to seize them all. His
classmates, gayly returning late at night, saw
the studious light shining in his window. The
boy was hard at work, already in those plastic
years storing his mind and memory, which
seemed indeed an "inability to forget," with the
literature and historic lore which gave his later
discourse such amplitude and splendor of illustration that, like a royal robe, it was stiff and
cumbrous and awkward with exaggerated richness of embroidery. He never lost this vast

capacity of work, and his life had no idle hours. Long afterward, when he was in Paris, recovering from the blow in the Senate, ordered not to think or read, and daily, as his physician lately tells us, undergoing a torture of treatment which he refused to mitigate by anæsthetics, simply unable to do nothing, he devoted himself to the study and collection of engravings, in which he became an expert. And I remember in the midsummer of 1871, when he remained, as was his custom, in Washington, after the city was deserted by all but its local population, and when I saw him daily, that he rose at seven in the morning, and with but a slight breakfast at nine, sat at his desk in the library hard at work until five in the afternoon. It was his vacation: the weather was tropical; and he was sixty years old. The renowned Senator at his post was still the solitary midnight student of the college.

But other influences mingled in his education, and helped to mould the man. While his heart burned with the tale of Plutarch's heroes, with the story of ancient states, and the politics of Greece and Rome and modern Europe, he lived in this historic city, and was therefore familiar with many of the most inspiring scenes of our

American story. I know not if the people of this neighborhood are always conscious of the hallowed ground upon which they daily tread. We who come hither from other States, pilgrims to the cradle of American independence, are moved by emotions such as we cannot elsewhere feel. Here is the "Old South" Meetinghouse—and here may it long remain!—where, however changed, still in imagination Sam Adams calls the Sons of Liberty to their duty. There is the old State-house, where James Otis, with electric eloquence, brings a continent to its feet. Beneath is the ground where Crispus Attucks fell. Beyond is Faneuil Hall, the plainest and most reverend political temple now standing in the world, and upon the principles which are its inseparable traditions has been founded the most humane republic in history. There is the Old North steeple, on which Paul Revere's lantern lights the land to independence. Below is the water on which the scarlet troops of Percy and of Howe glitter in the June sunshine of ninety-nine years ago; and lo! memorial of a battle lost and a cause won, the tall, gray, melancholy shaft on Bunker Hill rises—rises "till it meets the sun in his coming, while the earliest light of morning gilds it, and parting day lingers and plays on its summit."

These scenes, as well as his books and college, were the school of SUMNER; and as the tall and awkward youth, dreaming of Marathon and Arbela, of Sempach and Morgarten, walked on Bunker Hill, and his eyes wandered over peaceful fields and happy towns to Concord and Lexington, doubt not that the genius of his native land whispered to him that all knowledge and the highest training and the purest purpose were but the necessary equipment of the ambition that would serve in any way a country whose cause in his own day, as in the day of Bunker Hill, was the cause of human nature. CHARLES SUMNER was an educated man, a college-bred man, as all the great revolutionary leaders of Massachusetts were; and he knew, as every intelligent man knows, that from the day when Themistocles led the educated Athenians at Salamis to that when Von Moltke marshalled the educated Germans against France, the sure foundations of states are laid in knowledge, not in ignorance, and that every sneer at education, at cultivation, at book-learning, which is the recorded wisdom of the experience of mankind, is the demagogue's sneer at intelligent liberty, inviting national degeneration and ruin.

SUMNER was soon at the Law School the favorite pupil of that accomplished magistrate Judge Story, the right-hand of Marshall, to whom in difficult moments the great Webster turned for law. But the character of his legal studies when, a little later, he was lecturing at the Law School—for he spoke chiefly of constitutional law and the law of nations—showed even then the bent of his feeling, the vague reaching out toward the future, the first faint hints and foreshowings of his own ultimate career. Could it have been revealed to him in that modest lecture-room at Cambridge as he was unfolding to a few students the principles of international law, which in its full glory he believed to be nothing less than the science of the moral relations of states to each other, that one day in the Senate of the United States, and in its chief and most honorable place, he should plead for the practical application of the principles which he cherished, a recognized authority, and himself one of the lawgivers whom he had described as the reformers of nations and the builders of human society, how well might he have seen that culmination of his career as the most secret hope of his heart fulfilled! But again, as he stood there, could he have seen as in a vision that one day also he should stand in that Senatorial arena in deadly conflict with crime against humanity—a conflict that shook the continent and arrested the world—and as a general upon the battle-field marshals all his forces, holding his swift and glittering lines in hand—his squadrons and regiments and artillery, his skirmishers and reserves, massing and dispersing at his supreme will, and at last, snatching all his force, hurls it at the foe in one blasting bolt of fire and victory—so he, in that other and greater field, should gather up all the accumulated resources of his learning, all the training of the law, all the deep instincts and convictions of his conscience, and hurl them in one blazing and resistless mass in the very forefront of that mighty debate that flamed into civil war, melting four millions of chains, and regenerating a nation—could all this have been revealed to him, I doubt if he could have prepared himself for the great part that he was to play with more conscience or more care.

Then to the influences that made the man

was added a residence in Europe. He returned
a polished cosmopolitan; a learned youth who
had sat upon the bench in Westminster Hall,
and taught the judges the rulings of their own
courts; who had mingled on equal terms in the
bouts of lettered wit, no longer at the Mermaid,
but at Holland House, and the breakfast-rooms
of accomplished scholars in London and Paris
and Berlin and Rome. He returned knowing
almost every man and woman of renown in
Europe, and he brought back what he carried
away—a stainless purity of life and loftiness of
aim, the habit of incessant work, which was the
law of his being, and the tastes of a jurist, but
not those of a practising lawyer. His look, his
walk, his dress, his manner, were not those of
the busy advocate, but of the cultivated and
brilliant man of society—the Admirable Crichton
of the saloons. He was oftener seen in the
refined circles of the city, in the libraries and
dining-rooms of Prescott and Quincy, of Ban-
croft and Ticknor, than in the courts of law.
Distinguished foreigners, constantly arriving,
brought him letters, and he took them to the
galleries and the college. But while he saun-
tered, he studied. In his office he was diligently

editing great works of law; not practising at the bar, for, indeed, he was not formed for a jury lawyer, where the jury was less than a nation, or mankind. The electric agility, the consummate tact, the readiness for every resource, the humor that brightens or withers, the command of the opposite point of view, the superficial ardor, the facility of simulation that makes the worse appear the better reason, the passionate gust and sweep of eloquent appeal— these were lacking, and wanting these, he did not seek the laurels of the jury advocate. SUMNER's legal mind at this time, and throughout his life, was largely moulded, trained to the contemplation of great principles and to lofty research. As one of his admiring comrades, himself a renowned lawyer, says of him, "In sporting terms, he had a good eye for country, but no scent for a trail." The movement of his mind was grand and comprehensive. He spoke naturally, not in subtle and dextrous pleas, but in stately and measured orations.

When he returned from Europe he was thought to have been too much fascinated by England, and throughout his life it was sometimes said that he was still enthralled by his admiration for that country. But what is more natural to an American than love of England? Does not Hawthorne instinctively call it "Our Old Home"? The Pilgrims came to plant a purer England, and their children, the colonists, took up arms to maintain a truer England, but an England still. They became independent, but they did not renounce their race nor their language, and their victory left them the advanced outpost of English political progress and civilization. The principles that we most proudly maintain to-day, those to which SUMNER's whole life was devoted, are English traditions. The great muniments of individual liberty in every degree descended to us from our fathers. The Commonwealth, justice as the political corner-stone, the rule of the constitutional majority, the habeas corpus, the trial by jury, freedom of speech and of the press— these are English, and they are ours. I do not agree with the melancholy Fisher Ames that "the immortal spirit of the wood-nymph Liberty dwells only in the English oak"; but the most patriotic American may well remember that individual freedom sometimes seems almost surer and sturdier in England than here, and may wisely repair to drink at those elder fountains.

No Englishman in this generation has more influenced the thought of his country than John Stuart Mill, and the truest American will find upon his heroic pages gleams of a fairer and ampler America than ever in vision even Samuel Adams saw. No, no. Plymouth Rock was but a stepping-stone from one continent to another in the great march of the same historic development, and to-day, with electric touch, we grasp the hand of England under the sea, that the tumult of the ocean may not toss us further asunder, but throb as the beating of one common heart. Is it strange, then, that the young lawyer, whose deepest instinct was love of freedom, and whose youth had been devoted to the study of that noble science whose highest purpose is the defence of individual right, after long residence in the land of John Selden, of Coke, of Mansfield, of Blackstone, of Romilly, as well as of Shakespeare and Bacon, of Newton and Jeremy Taylor—a land which had appealed in every way to his heart, his mind, his imagination, whose history had inspired, whose learning had armed him to be a liberator of the oppressed— should always have turned with admiration to the country "Where," as her laureate sings—

"Where freedom broadens slowly down
From precedent to precedent"?

Such were the general influences that moulded
the young SUMNER. But to what a situation in
his own country he returned!—a situation neither
understood nor suspected by the fastidious and
elegant circles which received him. The man
never lived who enjoyed more or was more fitted
to enjoy the higher delights of human society
than SUMNER, or who might have seemed to
those who scanned his habits and his tastes so
little adapted for the heroic part. Could the
scope and progress and culmination of the great
contest which had already begun have been
foreseen and measured, CHARLES SUMNER would
probably have been selected as the type of the
cultivated and scholarly gentleman who would
recoil from the conflict as Sir Thomas Browne
shunned the stern tumult of the Great Rebellion.

In speaking of that conflict I shall speak
plainly; I hope to speak truly. To turn to Mr.
SUMNER's public career is to open a chapter of
our history written in fire and closed in blood,
but which we must be willing to recall if we
would justly measure the man. Trained in his
own expectation for other ends, framed for

friendship, for gentleness, for professional and social ease, and the placid renown of letters, he was suddenly caught up into the stormy cloud, and his life became a strife that filled a generation. But during all that tremendous time, on the one hand enthusiastically trusted, on the other contemptuously scorned and hated, his heart was that of a little child. He said no unworthy word, he did no unmanly deed; dishonor fled his face; and to-day those who so long and so naturally but so wrongfully believed him their enemy strew rosemary for remembrance upon his grave.

Down to the year 1830 the moral agitation against slavery in this country smouldered. But in that year Benjamin Lundy touched with fire the soul of William Lloyd Garrison, and that agitation burst out again irrepressibly. You remember—who can forget?—the passionate onset of the Abolitionists. It was conscience rising in insurrection. They made their great appeal with the ardor of martyrs and the zeal of primitive Christians. Fifth-monarchy men, ranters, Anabaptists, were never more repugnant to their times than they, and they became the prey of the worst and most disorderly passions. The abolition missionaries were mobbed, imprisoned, maimed, murdered, but still, as in the bitter days of Puritan persecution in Scotland, the undaunted voices of the Covenanters were heard singing hymns that echoed and re-echoed from peak to peak of the barren mountains until the great dumb wilderness was vocal with praise, so the solemn appeal of the Abolitionists to the Golden Rule and the Declaration of Independence echoed from solitary heart to heart until the land rang with the litany of liberty. In politics the discussion had been stamped out like a threatening fire upon the prairie whenever it arose. But soon after Mr. SUMNER's return from Europe this, too, flamed out afresh in the attempted annexation of Texas. Early in 1845 the plan was consummated. Mr. SUMNER was a Whig, but then and always he was above all a man. He was too well versed in the history of freedom not to know that the great victories over despotism and slavery in every form had been won by united action, and he knew that united action implies organization and a party. But while great political results are to be gained by means of great parties, he knew that a party which is too blind to see or too cowardly to acknowledge the real issue, which pursues its ends, however noble, by ignoble means, which tolerates corruption, which trusts unworthy men, which suffers the public service to be prostituted to personal ends, defies reason and conscience, and summons all honest men to oppose it. When conscience goes, all goes; and wherever conscience went, CHARLES SUMNER followed. It took him out of those delightful drawing-rooms and tranquil libraries; it drew him away from old companions and cherished friends; it exposed him to their suspicion, their hostility, their scorn; it forbade him the peaceful future of his dreams and expectations; it placed him at the fiery heart of the fiercest conflict of the century; it hedged his life with insults and threats and plots of assassination; it bared his head to the dreadful blow that struck him senseless to the Senate floor, and sent him a tortured wanderer beyond the sea; later it separated him from the co-operation of colleagues, and severed him from his party; and at last it exposed him, sick in body and in mind, to the blow that wounded his soul, the censure of his beloved Massachusetts. But he did not quail; he did not falter; he showed himself still to be her worthy son.

Wherever conscience went, CHARLES SUMNER followed. "God help me!" cried Martin Luther, "I can no other." "God help me!" said CHARLES SUMNER, "I must do my duty."

The Whigs are, or ought to be, he said, in 1845, the party of freedom. But when they refused to recognize the real contest in the country by rejecting in their National Convention of 1848 the Wilmot Proviso, Mr. SUMNER went with the other Conscience Whigs to Worcester, and organized the Free-soil party; and when, in the winter of 1850-51, the Legislature of Massachusetts was to elect the successor of DANIEL WEBSTER in the Senate of the United States, the Free-soil chiefs—as upright, able, and patriotic a body of political leaders as ever Massachusetts had—deliberately selected Mr. SUMNER as their candidate—a selection which showed the estimate of the man by those who knew him most intimately, and who most thoroughly understood the times. He was young, strong, learned, variously accomplished, a miracle of industry, zealous, pure, of indomitable courage, and of supreme moral energy. But he had little political ambition, and in 1846 had peremptorily declined to be a candidate for Congress. He was not a member of either of the great parties. He would not make any pledge of any kind, or move his tongue, or wink his eye, to secure success. He was pledged then and always and only to his sense of right. He stood for no partisan end whatever, but simply and solely for uncompromising resistance to slavery. The contest of the election was long; it lasted for three months, and on the 24th of April, 1851, he was elected. "I accept," he said, "as the servant of Massachusetts, mindful of the sentiments uttered by her successive Legislatures, of the genius which inspires her history, and of the men, her perpetual pride and ornament, who breathed into her that breath of liberty which early made her an example to her sister States." How these lofty words lift us out of the grossness of public corruption and incapacity into the air of ideal states and public men! What a stately summons are they to his beloved Massachusetts once more to take the lead, and again to guide her sister States to greater political purity and the ancient standards of public character and service!

The hour in which Mr. SUMNER wrote those

words—the hour of his entrance upon public life—was the darkest of our history. But if his mind had turned regretfully to that tranquil career of his earlier anticipation, how well might his good genius have whispered to him what the flower of English gentlemen and scholars had written three hundred years before, "To what purpose should our thoughts be directed to various kinds of knowledge unless room be afforded for putting it into practice, so that public advantage may be the result?" Or that other strain, full of the music of a consecrated soul, in which Philip Sidney writes to his father-in-law, Walsingham, "I think a wise and constant man ought never to grieve while he doth play, as a man may say, his own part truly."

What, then, was the political situation when Mr. SUMNER entered the Senate? Slavery had apparently subdued the country. Grand Juries in the Northern States presented citizens who, in time of peace, wished to discuss vital public questions as guilty of sedition. The Legislatures were summoned to make their speeches indictable offences. In the Legislature of Rhode Island such a bill was reported. The Governor of New York favored such a law. The Governor of Ohio delivered a citizen of that State to the authorities of another to be tried for helping a slave to escape. The Governor of Massachusetts said that all discussion of the subject which tended to incite insurrection had been held to be indictable. Every great national office was then, and long had been, held by the ministers of slavery. The American embassadors in Europe were everywhere silent, or smoothly apologized. Every Committee in Congress was the servant of slavery, and when the Vice-President left his seat in the Senate it was filled by another like himself. All the attendants who stood around him, the door-keepers, messengers, sergeants-at-arms, down to the very pages who noiselessly skimmed the floor, were selected by its agents. Beyond the superb walls of the Capitol, which Senator Benton had long solemnly warned the country was built by permission of that Supreme Power which would seize and occupy it when the time came, the whole vast system of national offices was within the patronage of slavery. Every little Post-Office, every Custom-House clerkship, was a bribe to silence, while the Postmaster-

General of the United States robbed the mails
at its bidding. When Sumner entered the Senate the most absolute subserviency to slavery
was decreed as the test of nationality, and that
power did not hesitate to declare that any serious effort, however lawfully made, to change its
policy would strike the tocsin of civil war.
Meanwhile, at the very moment of his election,
the horrors of the Fugitive Slave Law had
burst upon thousands of innocent homes.
Mothers snatched their children and fled, they
knew not whither. Brave men, long safe in
recovered liberty, were seized for no crime but
misfortune, and hurried to their doom. Young
men and girls who had been always free,
always residents of their own States, were kid-
napped and sold. The anguish, the sublime
heroism, of this ghastly persecution fills one of
the most tragical and most inspiring epochs of
our story. Even those who publicly sustained
the law from a sense of duty secretly helped
the flying fugitives upon their way. The
human heart is stronger than sophistry. The
man who impatiently exclaimed that of course
the law was hard, but it was the law, and
must be obeyed, suddenly felt the quivering,

panting fugitive clinging to his knees, guilty of no crime, and begging only the succor which no honest heart would refuse a dog cowering upon his threshold; and as he heard the dread power thundering at the door, "I am the Law, give me my prey!" in the same moment he heard God knocking at his heart, "Inasmuch as ye have done it unto the least of these my little ones, ye have done it unto me!"

Those days are passed. That fearful conflict is over; and the flowers just strewn all through these sorrowing States, indiscriminately upon the graves of the blue and the gray, show how truly it is ended. Heaven knows I speak of it with no willingness, with no bitterness; but how can I show you CHARLES SUMNER if I do not show you the time that made him what he was? This was the political and moral situation of the country when he took the oath as Senator, on the first of December, 1851. The famous political triumvirate of the former generation was gone. Mr. Calhoun, the master-will of the three, had died in the previous year. Mr. Webster was Secretary of State; and Henry Clay, with fading eye, and bowed frame, and trembling voice—Henry Clay, Compromise incar-

nate—feebly tottered out of the chamber as
CHARLES SUMNER, Conscience incarnate, came
in. As he took the oath the new triumvirate
was complete, for Mr. Seward and Mr. Chase
had taken their seats two years before. For
some months Mr. SUMNER did not speak upon
the great topic, and many of his friends at
home thought him keeping silence too long,
half fearing that he, too, had been enchanted
by the woeful Circe of the South. They did not
know how carefully slavery prevented him from
finding an opportunity. A month before he
could get the floor for his purpose, Theodore
Parker said, in a public speech, "I wish he
had spoken long ago. . . . But it is for
him to decide, not for us. 'A fool's bolt is
soon shot,' while a wise man often reserves his
fire." At length, on the 26th of August, 1852,
after many efforts to be heard, Mr. SUMNER
obtained the floor, saying as he arose, "The
subject is at last broadly before the Senate,
and by the blessing of God it shall be discussed."

The first great speech upon the repeal of the
Fugitive Slave Law was the most significant
event in the Senate since Mr. Webster's reply

to Hayne, and an epitome of Mr. SUMNER's whole public career. It was one of the words that are events, and from which historical epochs take their departure. These are strong words. See if they are justified. The slavery debate was certainly the most momentous that had ever occurred in the country, and brave words had been already uttered for freedom. The subtle, and sanguine, and sagacious Seward had spoken often and wisely. The passionless Chase, with massive and Websterian logic, had pressed his solid reasoning home; and the gay humor of Hale had irradiated his earnest and strenuous appeals. But all of these men were known to their colleagues as members of parties, as politicians, as men of political ambition. With such elements and men slavery was accustomed to deal. Carefully studying the Senator from New York, it saw, with the utmost purity of character, trained ability, acute political instinct, and partisan habit, the intellectual optimist who grasped the situation with his brain rather than with his heart and conscience. It tested him by its own terrible earnestness. It weighed him in the balance of its own unquailing and uncompromising resolution, and found

him wanting. Do not misunderstand me. Mr.
Seward was the only political leader for whom
I have ever felt the admiring loyalty which
older men felt for Webster, and Calhoun, and
Clay. His career has been nobly set forth by
your own distinguished citizen (Mr. Adams) in
his discourse before the Legislature of New
York. And as he went to Albany to say what
he believed to be the truth, so have I come
hither. Slavery knew Mr. Seward to be accustomed to political considerations, to party necessities, to the claims of compromise. It knew
the scope of his political philosophy, the bright-
ness of his hope of American glory under the
Union, the steady certainty of his trust that all
would be well. Even if, like Webster, and
Calhoun, and Clay, he saw the gathering storm,
he thought—and he did not conceal his thought
—that he had the confidence of his opponents,
and could avert or control the tempest. Slavery knew that he could not. If he proudly
declared the higher law, slavery knew that he
did it, as Plato announced the Golden Rule, as
a thinker, not as an actor; as a philosopher,
not as the founder of a religion ready to be
sealed with fire and blood. But this was the

very spirit of slavery, and it did not see it to be his.

In the midst of a speech which logically cut the ground from beneath the slave interest, and calmly foretold the blessing of the emancipation that was unavoidable, Mr. Seward would sometimes turn and hold out his fingers for a pinch of snuff toward some Southern Senator, who, turning away his face, offered him the box. When the Senate adjourned, Mr. Seward would perhaps join the same colleague to stroll home along the Avenue as if they had been country lawyers coming from a court where they had been arguing a dry point of law. It showed how imperfectly he felt or how inadequately he measured the sullen intensity and relentless purpose of the spirit which dominated our politics, and would pause at nothing in its course. In a word, that spirit was essentially revolutionary, and Mr. Seward had not a revolutionary fibre in his being. Long afterward, when the movement of secession had begun, as he walked with a fellow-Senator to the Capitol on the morning of Washington's birthday, he saw on all sides the national flags fluttering in the sun, and exclaimed to his companion, with triumphant incredulity,

"Look there! see those flags! and yet they talk
of disunion!"

Up to the moment of Mr. SUMNER's appearance in the Senate Mr. Seward had been the
foremost anti-slavery leader in public life. But
slavery, carefully studying him, believed, as I
think, that he would compromise. That was the
test. If he would compromise, he might annoy,
but he was not to be feared. If he would compromise, he might melodiously sing the glory of
the Union at his pleasure. If he would compromise, he would yield. If he were not as
invincibly resolute as slavery, he was already
conquered; and he was the leader of the North.
There sat Seward in the Senate—yes, and there
Webster had sat, there Clay had sat, with all
their great and memorable service; there in its
presiding chair Millard Fillmore had sat; and
over them all slavery had stalked straight on in
its remorseless imperial career. And if, as Mr.
Seward's most able eulogist mournfully remarks,
he was permitted at last to leave public life
"with fewer marks of recognition of his brilliant
career than he would have had if he had been
the most insignificant of our Presidents," may it
not be that, without questioning his generous

character, his lofty ability, and his illustrious service, there was a general feeling that in the last administration under which he served he had seemed in some degree to justify the instinct of slavery, that his will was not as sternly inexorable as its own?

I do not, of course, forget that compromise makes government possible, and that the Union was based upon it. "All government," says Burke, "is founded upon compromise and barter. . . . But," he adds, "in all fair dealing the thing bought must bear some proportion to the purchase paid. None will barter away the immediate jewel of the soul." So Sir James Mackintosh said of Lord Somers, whom he described as the perfect model of a wise statesman in a free community, that "to be useful he submitted to compromise with the evil that he could not extirpate." But it is the instinct of the highest statesmanship to know when the jewel of which Burke speaks is demanded, and to resolve that at any cost it shall not be sold. John Pym had it when he carried up to the Lords the impeachment of Strafford. John Adams had it when he lifted the Continental Congress in his arms and hurled it over the irrevocable line of independ-

ence. CHARLES SUMNER had it when, at the
close of his first great speech in the Senate, he
exclaimed, in the face of slavery in its highest
seat, "By the Constitution which I have sworn
to support, I am bound to disobey this act."
Until that moment slavery had not seen in public
life the man whom it truly feared. But now,
amazed, incredulous, appalled, it felt that it had
met its master. Here was a spirit as resolute
and haughty as its own, with resources infinitely
richer. Here at last was the North, the American conscience, the American will—the heir of
the traditions of English Magna Charta, and,
far beyond them, of the old Swiss cantons high
on the heaven-kissing Alps—the spirit that would
not wince, nor compromise, nor bend, but which,
like a cliff of adamant, said to the furious sea,
"Here shall thy proud waves be stayed."

Ten years afterward, when States were seced-
ing and preparing to secede—when the reluctant mind of the North began to see that war
was possible—when even many of Mr. Sumner's and Mr. Seward's party friends trembled
in dismay, Mr. Seward ended his last speech in
the Senate—a guarded plea for the Union—by
concessions which amazed many of his most

earnest friends. I know that he thought it the part of a wise statesmanship that he who was to be the head of the new administration should retain, if possible, the support of the opposition of the North by shunning everything like menace, and by speaking in the most temperate and conciliatory tone. But his mournful concluding words, "I learned early from Jefferson that, in political affairs, we cannot always do what seems to us absolutely best," sounded at that time, and under those circumstances, like a mortal cry of defeat and surrender. And at the very time that Mr. Seward was speaking those words, Mr. SUMNER was one evening surprised by a visit in Washington from a large number of the most conspicuous citizens of Boston, all of whom had been among his strongest and most positive political opponents. He welcomed them gravely, seeing that their purpose was very serious, and after a few moments, the most distinguished member of the party made an impassioned appeal to the Senator. "You know us all," he said, "as fellow-citizens of yours who have always and most strongly regretted and opposed your political course. But at this awful moment, when the country hangs upon the edge of civil war—and what civil war means you know—we believe that there is one man only who can avert the threatening calamity, one man whom the North really trusts, and by whose counsels it will be guided. We believe that you are that man. The North will listen to you and to no other, and we are here in the name of humanity and civilization, to implore you to save your country." The speaker was greatly affected, and after a moment Mr. SUMNER said, "Sir, I am surprised that you attribute to me such influence. I will, however, assume it. Be it so. What, then, is it that you would have me do?" "We implore you, Mr. SUMNER, as you love your country and your God, to vote for the Critten-den compromise." "Sir," said CHARLES SUM-NER, rising to his lofty height, and never more CHARLES SUMNER than in that moment, "if what you say is indeed true, and if at this moment the North trusts me, as you think, beyond all others, it is because the North knows that under no circumstances whatever would I compromise."

It was precisely because slavery recognized

this when he made his first important speech, and felt for the first time the immense force behind his words, that I call that speech so significant an event. I do not claim for SUMNER deeper convictions or a sterner will than those of many of his associates. But the Abolitionists, however devoted and eloquent, were only private citizens and agitators who abjured political methods. They seemed to the supreme influence in the government a band of pestilent fanatics. But CHARLES SUMNER in the Senate, CHARLES SUMNER in the seat of Daniel Webster, saying that the Constitution forbade him to obey the Fugitive Slave Law, was not an individual; he was a representative man. No meeting of enthusiastic men and women in a school-house had sent him to the Senate, but the Legislature of a State. Nor that alone, for that Legislature had not sent him as the representative of a party, but of an idea—an idea which had been powerful enough to hold its friends close together through a contest of three months, and at last defeating the influences which had so long controlled unquestioned the politics of the State, had lifted_into the Senate a man pledged only to cry *Delenda est Carthago,* and who, by the law of his mental and moral structure, could no more compromise the principle at stake than he could tell a lie. Still further, slavery heard the young Senator proudly assert that the Constitution did not recognize slavery, except in the slave-trade clause, whose force was long since spent; that the clause upon which the Fugitive Law was grounded was a mere compact conferring no power, and that every detail of the process provided was flagrantly and palpably unconstitutional. Slavery, he insisted, was sectional, liberty was national; and throwing this popular cry to the country, he irradiated his position with so splendid an illumination of illustration, precedent, argument, appeal, that it shone all over the land. How like a sunrise it strengthened and stimulated and inspired the North! It furnished the quiver of a thousand orators and newspapers, and was an exhaustless treasury of resources for the debate. Above all it satisfied men bred in reverence of law that their duty as citizens was coincident with the dictates of their consciences, and that the Constitution justified them in withstanding the statute which their souls loathed.

This was the very service that the country

needed at that time; and that no dramatic effect should be wanting, as Henry Clay had left the Senate for the last time on the day that Mr. SUMNER was sworn in, so, as he was making his first great plea for justice under the Constitution, his predecessor, Daniel Webster, then Secretary of State, came into the Chamber, and also for the last time. I know no more impressive scene. There is the old Senator, then the chief figure in America, who, a year before, on the 7th of March, had made his last speech supporting the policy of the Fugitive Slave Bill, and against the Wilmot Proviso. Worn, wasted, sad, with powers so great and public service so renowned, the Olympian man who had sought so long, so ably, so vainly, to placate the implacable, his seventy years ending in baffled hopes and bitter disappointment and a broken heart, gazed with those eyes of depthless melancholy upon his successor. And here stands that successor, with the light of spotless youth upon his face, towering, dauntless, radiant; the indomitable Puritan, speaking as a lawyer, a statesman, and a man, not for his State alone, nor for his country only, but for human rights everywhere and always, forecasting the future, heralding the new Amer-

13

ica. As Webster looked and listened, did he recall the words of that younger man seven years before in Faneuil Hall, when he prayed the party that Webster led to declare for emancipation? Did he remember the impassioned appeal to himself, that as he had justly earned the title of Defender of the Constitution, so now he should devote his marvellous powers to the overthrow of slavery, and thereby win a nobler name? Alas! It was demanding dawn of the sunset! It was beseeching yesterday to return to-morrow. It was imploring Daniel Webster to be CHARLES SUMNER. No, fellow-citizens, in that appeal SUMNER forecast his own glory. "Assume, then," cried he, "these unperformed duties. The aged shall bear witness to you; the young shall kindle with rapture as they repeat the name of Webster; the large company of the ransomed shall teach their children and their children's children to the latest generation to call you blessed, and you shall have yet another title, never to be forgotten on earth or in heaven, Defender of Humanity."

I dwell upon this first great speech of Mr. SUMNER's in the Senate, because it illustrates his own public qualities and character, his aims

and his methods. He began to take an official
part in affairs when all questions were determined by a single interest, a single policy, and
all issues grew out of that. His nature was so
transparent and simple, and the character of his
relation to his time so evident, that there is
but one story to tell. All his greater speeches
upon domestic topics after that of August,
1852, were but amplifications of the theme.
The power that he had defied did not relax,
but redoubled its efforts to subdue the country
to its will, and every new attempt found SUM-
NER with more practised powers, with more
comprehensive resources, ready and eager for
the battle. For the whole of his active career,
before, during, and after the war, his work was
substantially the same. He was essentially an
orator and a moral reformer, and with unsurpassed earnestness of appeal, emphasized from
first to last by the incalculable weight of his
commanding character, his work was to rouse,
and kindle, and inspire the public opinion of the
country to his own uncompromising hostility to
slavery. In this crusade he traversed the land,
as it were, by his speeches, a new Peter the
Hermit, and by his sincerity, his unconquerable

zeal, his affluent learning, making history, and
literature, and art, tributary to his purpose, he
entered the houses, and hearts, and minds of
the people of the Northern States, and fanned
the flame of a holy hatred of the intolerable
and audacious wrong. It was indispensable to
this work that he should not be able to admit
any qualification of its absorbing necessity, or
any abatement of the urgency with which it
must be pursued. Once, in later days, when I
argued with him that opponents might be sincere, and that there was some reason on the
other side, he thundered in reply, "Upon such
a question there *is* no other side!" The time
required such a leader—a man who did not
believe that there was another side to the
question; who would treat difference of opinion
almost as moral delinquency; and the hour
found the man in SUMNER.

For see what the leadership of opinion in this
country then demanded. In the first place, and
for the reasons I have mentioned—the instinct,
traditions, and habits of the dominant race in
our civilization—such a leader must be a man
who showed that the great principles of liberty,
but of liberty under law, of what we call regu-

lated liberty, were on his side; whose familiarity
with the Constitution and with constitutional
interpretation, and whose standing among lawyers who dealt with the comprehensive spirit
and purpose of the law, were recognized and
commanding, so that, instructed by him, the
farmer in the field, the mechanic in the shop,
the traveller by the way—all law-loving Americans everywhere, could maintain the contest
with their neighbors point by point upon the
letter of the Constitution, and show, or think
they showed, that the supreme law in its inten-
tion, in the purpose of its authors, by the
unquestionable witness of the time, demanded an
interpretation and a statute in favor of liberty.
Then, in the second place, this leader must be
identified with a political party, for the same
instinct which seeks the law and leans upon
precedent acts through the organization of parties. The Free-soil sentiment that sent SUMNER
to the Senate was the real creative force in our
politics at that time. It had a distinct organization in several States. It had nominated Presidential candidates at Buffalo; and although the
Whig and Democratic were still the great parties, the Free-soil principle was necessarily the

nucleus around which a new and truly national
party must presently gather. In 1852 the common enemy silenced the Whig party, which
almost instantly dissolved as a powerful element
in politics, and the Republican party arose. No
man had done more to form the opinion and
deepen the conviction from which it sprang than
SUMNER; no man accepted its aid with more
alacrity, or saw more clearly its immense opportunity. As early as September, 1854, he declared
in the State Convention of his political friends,
"As Republicans we go forth to encounter the
oligarchs of slavery"; and eighteen years afterward, in warning the party against what he
thought to be a fatal course, he said that he had
been one of the straitest of the sect, who had
never failed to sustain its candidates or to advance its principles. He was indeed one of its
fathers. No citizen who has acted with that
party will question the greatness of his service
to it; no citizen who opposed that party will
deny it. The personal assault upon him in the
Senate, following his prodigious defence of the
Republican position and policy, and soon after
the first national nominations of the party, made
him throughout the inspiring summer of 1856,

to the imagination of the twelve hundred thousand men who voted for its candidates, the very type and illustration of their hope and purpose. Nothing less than such humanity in the national policy and such lofty character in public life as were expressed by the name of CHARLES SUMNER was the aim of the great political awakening of that time. The rank and file of the party, to borrow a military phrase, dressed upon SUMNER; and long afterward, when party differences had arisen, I am sure that I spoke for the great body of his political associates when I said to one who indignantly regretted his course, that while at that time and under those circumstances we could not approve his judgment, yet there were thousands and thousands of men who would be startled and confused to find themselves marching in a political campaign out of step with CHARLES SUMNER. Thus he satisfied the second imperative condition of leadership of which I speak as a conspicuous and decided party chief.

But there were certain modifications of these conditions essential to the position, and these also were found in SUMNER. Such was the felicity of his career that even his defects of

constitution served to equip him more fully for
his task. Thus, while it was indispensable under
the circumstances that he should be a constitutional and international lawyer, it was no less
essential that his mind should deal more with
principles than with details, and with the spirit
rather than the letter. He saw so clearly the
great end to be achieved that he seemed sometimes almost to assume the means. Like an
Alpine guide leading his company of travellers
toward the pure and awful heights, with his eye
fixed upon their celestial beauty, and his soul
breathing an

" Ampler ether, a diviner air,"

he moved straight on, disdaining obstacles that
would have perplexed a guide less absolutely
absorbed, and who by moments of doubt and
hesitation would have imperilled everything.

Thus his legal mind, in the pursuit of a
moral end, had sometimes what I may call a
happy lack of logic; for it enabled him to
throw the whole force of his nature unreserv-
edly upon a good purpose. Sure of his end,
and that everything ought to make for it, he
felt that everything did make for it. For

instance, his first great public oration upon the "True Grandeur of Nations," was a most powerful presentation of the glory and beauty of peace, and a mighty denunciation of the horrors and wrongs of war. It was an intrepid and impressive discourse, and its influence will be deep and lasting. But it overstated its own case. It exposed the citizen soldier not only to ridicule, but to moral aversion. And yet the young men who sat in martial array before the orator had not submitted to military discipline merely for the splendor of a parade, but that in the solemn and exigent hour they might the more effectively defend the public safety and private honor, the school and the hospital, and social order itself, the only guarantee of peace, and all this not at the arbitrary command of their own will, but by the lawful and considered word of the civil power. What is military force which he derided but, in the last resort, the law which he revered, in execution? As a friend asked him, Are the judgments of Story and of Shaw advice merely? Do they not, if need be, command every bayonet in the State? Is force wrong, and must the policeman not only be prohibited from carrying a pistol or a

club, but must he be forbidden to lay his hand
upon the thief in the act to compel him to the
station? The young citizen soldiers who sat
before the orator were simply the ultimate
police. To decry to them with resounding and
affluent power the practice which covered war
with a false lustre was a noble service, but to
do it in a way that would forbid the just and
lawful punishment of a murderer disclosed a
defective logic. His argument logically seemed
to imply that he was an absolute non-resistant.
But he was not so; nor was there any incon-
sistency in his firm support of the war sixteen
years later. In the instances that I mention, he
used arguments that were two-edged swords,
apt to wound the wielder as well as the enemy.
And so he sometimes adopted propositions of
constitutional or international law which led
straight to his moral end, but which would
hardly have endured the legal microscope. Yet
he maintained them with such fervor of conviction, such an array of precedent, such amplitude of illustration, that to the great popular
mind, morally exalted like his own, his statements had the majesty and the conclusiveness
of demonstrations.

And this, again, was what the time needed. The debate was essentially, although under the forms of law, revolutionary. It aimed at the displacement not only of an administration, but of a theory of the government, and of traditional usage that did not mean to yield without a struggle. It required, therefore, not the judicially logical mind, nor the fine touch of casuistry that splits, and halts, and defers until the cause is lost, but the mind so absolutely alive with the idea and fixed upon the end that it compels the means. John Pym was resolved that Strafford should be impeached, and he found the law for it. CHARLES SUMNER was resolved that slavery should fall, and he found the Constitution for it. When the great debate ended, and there was the moment of dread silence before the outburst of civil war, the legal casuistry which had found the terrors of the Fugitive Slave Law constitutional could see no power in the Constitution to coerce States, CHARLES SUMNER, who had found in the Constitution no authority for slave-hunting, answered the furious cannonade at Fort Sumter by declaring that slavery had legally destroyed itself, and by demanding immediate emancipation.

And as the crisis in which SUMNER lived
required that, in a leader, the qualities of a
lawyer should be modified by those of the patriot and the moralist, so it demanded that the
party man should be more than a partisan. He
never forgot that a party is a means, not an
end. He knew the joy and the power of association—no man better. He knew the history
of parties everywhere—in Greece and Rome,
in England and France, and in our own earlier
day; and he knew how insensibly a party
comes to resemble an army, and an army to
stand for the country and cause which it has
defended. But he knew above all that parties
are kept pure and useful only by the resolute
independence of their members, and that those
leaders whom, from their lofty principle and
uncompromising qualities, parties do not care to
nominate, are the very leaders who make parties able to elect their candidates. The Republican party was organized to withstand slavery
when slavery dared all. It needed, therefore,
one great leader at least who was not merely a
partisan; who did not work for party ends but
for the ends of the party. It needed a man
absorbed and mastered by hostility to slavery;

a man of one idea, like Columbus, with his whole soul trembling ever to the west, wearying courts, and kings, and councils, with his single, incessant and importunate plea, until he sailed over the horizon and gave a New World to the Old; a man of one idea, like Luther, pleading his private conscience against the ancient hierarchy, and giving both worlds religious liberty. Yes, a man of one idea. This was what the time demanded in public and party life, and this it found in CHARLES SUMNER; not an anti-slavery man only, but a man in whose soul, for thirty years, the sigh of the slave never ceased, and whose dying words were a prayer to save the bill that made that slave wholly an equal citizen.

When the Republican party came into power it was forced to conduct a war in which the very same qualities were demanded. The public mind needed constantly to be roused and sustained by the trumpet-note of an ever higher endeavor, and from no leader did it hear that tone more steadily and clearly than from SUMNER. When the most radical, which in such a moment is the wisest, policy came to be discussed in detailed measures, he had already

robbed it of its terrors by making it familiar.
While Congress declared by a vote almost unanimous that emancipation was not a purpose or
an element of the war, SUMNER proclaimed to
the country that slavery was perpetual war, and
that emancipation only was peace. Like Nelson
in the battle of the Baltic—when the admiral
signaled to stop fighting he put the glass to his
blind eye and shouted, "I don't see the admiral's
signal; nail my own colors to the mast for closer
battle!" As before the war, so while it raged,
he felt the imperial necessity of the conclusion
so strongly that he made all arguments serve,
and forced all facts into line. He was alive
with the truth that Dryden nobly expresses: "I
have heard, indeed, of some virtuous persons
who have ended unfortunately, but never of
any virtuous nation. Providence is engaged too
deeply when the cause becomes so general."
Mr. Lincoln, who was a natural diplomatist, for-
tunately understood Mr. SUMNER. The President knew as well as the Senator that the war
sprang from slavery. He had already said that
the house of the Union divided against itself
could not stand. He knew as well as SUMNER
that slavery must be smitten. But he knew

also that in his position he could not smite until
public opinion lifted his arm. To stimulate that
opinion, therefore, was the most precious service
to the President, to the country, and the world.
Thus it was not the appeal to Lincoln, it was
the appeal to public opinion, that was demanded.
It was not SUMNER's direct but his reflected
light that was so useful. And when the President at last raised his arm—for he pulled no
unripe fruit, and he did nothing until he thought
the time had fully come—he knew that the
country was ready, and that no man more than
SUMNER had made it so. When the Assistant
Secretary of State carried the engrossed copy of
the Emancipation Proclamation to Mr. Lincoln
to sign, he had been shaking hands all the
morning, so that his writing was unsteady. He
looked at it for a moment with his sadly humor-
ous smile, and then said, " When people see that
shaky signature they will say, ' See how uncertain he was.' But I was never surer of anything in my life."

But while SUMNER righteously stimulated public opinion during the war, not less on one memorable occasion did he righteously moderate it.
I once ventured to ask Mr. Seward what in his

judgment was the darkest hour of the war. He answered instantly, "The time that elapsed between my informally sending to Lord Lyons a draft of my reply in the *Trent* case and my hearing from him that it would be satisfactory." He thought it the darkest hour, because he knew that in that reply he had made the utmost concession that public opinion would tolerate, and if it were not satisfactory, nothing remained but war with England—a war which Mr. Adams tells us, he thinks that the British government expected, and for which it had already issued naval instructions. Mr. SUMNER, who was most friendly with Mr. Seward, was chairman of the Senate Committee of Foreign Relations, and, next to his constant and inspiring consciousness that he was a Senator of Massachusetts, his position as the head of that committee was the pride and glory of his official life. Few men in the country have ever been so amply fitted for it as he. From his youth he had been a student of international law. He was master of its history and literature. It was his hope—surely a noble ambition—to contribute to it something that might still further humanize the comity of nations. He was familiar with the current poli-

tics of the world, and he personally knew most
of the distinguished foreign statesmen of his
time. Above all, he brought to his chair the
lofty conviction expressed by another master of
international law, that "the same rules of morality
which hold together men in families, and which
form families into commonwealths, also link
together those commonwealths as members of
the great society of mankind." He was very
proud of that chairmanship; and when, in the
spring of 1871, upon the annual renewal of the
committees of the Senate, his Republican colleagues decided not to restore him to his chair,
he felt degraded and humiliated before the country and foreign powers. He had held it for ten
years. His party was still in the ascendant.
His qualifications were undeniable. And he felt
that the refusal to restore him implied some
deep distrust or dissatisfaction, for which, whatever good reasons existed, none but the pleasure of the Senate has yet been given to the
country.

While he was still chairman, and at a critical
moment, the seizure of the *Trent* was hailed
with frantic applause. Nothing seemed less likely
than that an administration could stand which

should restore the prisoners, and Mr. Seward's
letter was one of the ablest and most skilful
that he ever wrote. Mr. Adams says frankly
that in his judgment it saved the unity of the
nation. But the impressive fact of the moment
was the acquiescence of the country in the surrender, and that in great degree was due to the
conclusive demonstration made by Mr. SUMNER
that fidelity to our own principles required the
surrender. It was precisely one of the occasions
when his value as a public man was plainly evident. From the crowded diplomatic gallery in
the Senate, attentive Europe looked and listened.
His words were weighed one by one by men
whom sympathy with his cause did not seduce,
nor a too susceptible imagination betray, and who
acknowledged when he ended, not only that the
nation had escaped war and that the action of
the administration had been vindicated, but that
the renown of the country had been raised by
the clear and luminous statement of its humane
and peaceful traditions of neutrality. "Until
to-day," said one of the most accomplished of
those diplomatists, "I have considered Mr. SUM-
NER a doctrinaire; henceforth I recognize him as
a statesman." He had silenced England by her

historic self. He had justified America by her own honorable precedent. The country knew that he spoke from the fullest knowledge, and with the loftiest American and humane purpose. and his service in promoting national acquiescence in the surrender of the captives was as characteristic as in nerving the public mind to demand emancipation.

But while Mr. SUMNER's public career was chiefly a relentless warfare with slavery, it was only because slavery was the present and palpable form of that injustice with which his nature was at war. The spring of his public life was that overpowering love of peace and justice and equality which spoke equally in his early Prison Discipline debates; in the Fourth of July oration in Boston; in his literary addresses; in the powerful anti-slavery speeches in the Senate; in his advocacy of emancipation as the true policy of the war, and of equal civil and political rights as the guarantee of its results; in his Senatorial efforts to establish arbitration; in his condemnation of privateering, prize-money, and letters of marque; in his arraignment of Great Britain for a policy which favored slavery; in his unflinching persistence for the Civil Rights

Bill; in his last great protest against the annexation of San Domingo, and his denunciation of
what he thought a cruel and un-American hostility to the republic of Hayti. He was a born
warrior with public injustice.

Many public men permit their hostility to a
wrong to be modified in its expression by personal feeling, and to reflect that good men, from
the influence of birth and training, may sometimes
support a wrong system. But SUMNER saw in
his opponents not persons, but a cause, and, like
Socrates in the battle he smote to the death, but
with no personal hostility. In turn he was so
identified with his own cause, that he seemed to
his opponents to be the very spirit with which
they contended,—visible, aggressive, arrogant.
His tone in debate when he arraigned slavery,
although he arraigned slavery alone, was so
unsparing that all his supporters felt themselves
to be personally insulted. After the war began
I heard his speech in the Senate for the expulsion
of Mr. Bright, of Indiana, for commerce with the
enemy. It was a lash of scorpions. Mr. Bright
sat in his place, pale and livid by turns, and
gazing at Mr. SUMNER as if he could scarce
restrain himself from springing at his throat.

Yet when the orator shook his lifted finger at his colleague, and hurled at him his scathing sentences, it was not the man that he saw before him: he saw only the rebellion, only slavery in arms, with Catalinian audacity proudly thrusting itself into the Capitol, and daring to sit in the very Senate-chamber. But Mr. SUMNER's attitude and tone that day, with a vast majority at his side, with a friendly army in the city, were no bolder, no more resolutely defiant, than when he stood in the same chamber demanding the expulsion of slavery from the statute-book, while the majority of his colleagues would fain have silenced him, and the city was a camp of his enemies.

It was often said that it was impossible he should know the peril of his position. It was not that. He did know it. But he saw and feared a greater peril—that of not doing his duty. He often stood practically alone among responsible public men. The spirit which begged Abraham Lincoln to strike out of his Springfield speech, in 1858, the words "a house divided against itself cannot stand," a request which Mr. Lincoln said that he would carefully consider, and having considered, spoke the words, and went straight on to the Presidency

and a glorious renown—this spirit censured
Sumner's fanaticism, his devotion to one idea;
derided his rhetoric, his false taste, his want of
logic; ridiculed his want of tact, his ignorance
of men, his visionary views, his impracticabil-
ity. Indeed, there were times when it almost
seemed that friends joined with foes to shear
Samson's flowing hair while Samson was smit-
ing the Philistines. If friends remonstrated he
replied, "I am a public servant. I am a sentinel of my country. I must cry 'halt,' though
it be only a shadow that passes, and not bring
my piece to a rest until I know who goes
there." It was an ideal vigilance—an ideal
sense of duty. I grant it. He was an ideal
character. He loved duty more than friendship, and he had that supreme quality of manhood, the power to go alone. I am not anxious
to call him a statesman, but he seems to have
measured more accurately than others the real
forces of his time. Miss Martineau, in the
remarkable paper published at the beginning of
the war, says that every public man in the
country with whom she talked, agreed that
silence upon slavery was the sole condition of
preserving the Union. Sumner was the man

who saw that silence would make the Union only the stately tomb of liberty; and that speech, constant, unsparing, unshrinking—speech ringing over a cowering land like an alarm-bell at midnight—was the only salvation of the Union as the home of freedom.

If now for a moment we turn to survey that public career, extending over the thirty stormiest years of our history, the one clear, conspicuous fact that appears in it, after the single devotion to one end, is that Mr. SUMNER lived to see that end accomplished. He began by urging the Whig party to raise the anti-slavery standard. It refused. He left the party, and presently it perished. He entered the Senate denouncing slavery in a manner that roused and strengthened the public mind for the contest that soon began. With the first gun of the war he demanded emancipation as the way of victory; and when victory with emancipation came, he advocated equal suffrage as the security of liberty. What public man has seen more glorious fulfilments of his aims and efforts? He did not, indeed, originate the laws that enacted the results, but he developed the spirit and the conviction that made the results possible. William the Third won few battles, but he gained his cause; Thomas Jefferson wrote the Declaration, but John Adams is the hero of American independence. SUMNER was more a moral reformer than a statesman, and to a surprising degree events were his allies. But no man of our first great period, not Otis or Patrick Henry, nor Jefferson or Adams, nor Hamilton or Jay, is surer of his place, than in the second great period CHARLES SUMNER is sure of his.

As his career drew to an end, events occurred without which his life would not have been wholly complete, and the most signal illustration of the power of personal character in politics would have been lost. He was, as I have said, a party man. Although always in advance, and by his genius a moral leader, he had yet always worked with and by his party. But as the main objects of his political activity were virtually accomplished, he came to believe that his party, reckless in absolute triumph, was ceasing to represent that high and generous patriotism to which his life was consecrated, that its moral tone was sensibly declining, that it defended policies hostile to public faith and human rights, trusting leaders who should not be trusted, and tolerating practices that honest men should spurn. Believing that his party was forfeiting the confidence of the country, he reasoned with it and appealed to it, as more than twenty years before he had reasoned with the Whig party in Faneuil Hall. His hope was by his speeches on the San Domingo treaty and the French arms and the Presidential nomination to shake what he thought to be the fatal apathy of the party, and to stimulate it once more to resume its leadership of the conscience and the patriotism of the country. It was my fortune to see him constantly and intimately during those days, to know the persuasions and flatteries lavished upon him to induce him to declare openly against the party, and his resolution not to leave it until he had exhausted every argument and prayer, and conscience forbade him to remain. That summons came, in his judgment, when a nomination was made which seemed to him the conclusive proof of a fatal party infatuation. "Anything else," he said to me, vehemently, a hundred times—"any other candidacy I can support, and it would save the party and the country." The nomination was made. He did not hesitate. He was sixty years old; smitten with sorrows that were not known; suffering at times acute agony from the disease of which he died; his heart heavy with the fierce strife of a generation, and longing for repose. But the familiar challenge of duty found him alert and watchful at his post, and he advanced without a doubt or a fear to what was undoubtedly the greatest trial of his life.

The anti-slavery contest, indeed, had closed many a door and many a heart against him; it had exposed him to the sneer, the hate, the ridicule, of opposition; it had threatened his life and assailed his person. But the great issue was clearly drawn; his whole being was stirred to its depths; he was in the bloom of youth, the pride of strength; history and reason, the human heart and the human conscience, were his immortal allies, and around him were the vast, increasing hosts of liberty; the men whose counsels he approved; the friends of his heart; the multitude that thought him only too eager for unquestionable right; the prayer of free men and women sustaining, inspiring, blessing him. But here was another scene, a far fiercer trial. His old companions in the Free-soil days, the great abolition leaders, most of his warmest personal friends, the great body of the party whom his words had inspired, looked at him with sorrowful surprise. Ah! no one who did not know that proud and tender heart, trusting, simple, almost credulous as that of a boy, could know how sore the trial was. He stood, among his oldest friends, virtually alone; with inexpressible pain they parted, each to his own duty. "Are you willing," I said to him one day, when he had passionately implored me to agree with him —and I should have been unworthy his friendship had I been silent—"is CHARLES SUMNER willing at this time, and in the circumstances of to-day, to intrust the colored race in this country, with all their rights, their liberty newly won and yet flexile and nascent, to a party, however fair its profession, which comprises all who have hated and despised the negro? The slave of yesterday in Alabama, in Carolina, in Mississippi, will his heart leap with joy or droop dismayed when he knows that CHARLES SUMNER has given his great name as a club to smite the party that gave him and his children their liberty?" The tears started to his eyes, that good gray head bowed down, but he answered,

sadly, "I must do my duty." And he did it.
He saw the proud, triumphant party that he had
led so often, men and women whom his heart
loved, the trusted friends of a life, the sympathy
and confidence and admiration upon which, on
his great days and after his resounding words,
he had been joyfully accustomed to lean—he
saw all these depart, and he turned to go alone
and do his duty.

Yet, great as was his sorrow, still greater, as
I believe, was his content in doing that duty.
His State, indeed, could not follow him. For
the first time in his life, he went one way, and
Massachusetts went the other. But Massachusetts was as true to her convictions of duty in
that hour as he was to his own. It was her
profound belief that the result he sought would
be perilous if not fatal to the welfare of the
country. But the inspiring moral of these events
is this, that while deploring his judgment in this
single case, and while, later, the Legislature,
misconceiving his noble and humane purpose,
censured him for the resolutions which the people
of the State did not understand, and which they
believed, most unjustly to him, to be somehow a
wrong to the precious dead, the flower of a

thousand homes—yet, despite all this, the great heart of Massachusetts never swerved from CHARLES SUMNER. It was grieved and amazed, and could not forego its own duty because he saw another. But I know that when in that year I spoke in rural Massachusetts, whether in public or in private, to those who, with me, could not follow him, nothing that I said was heard with more sympathy and applause than my declaration of undying honor and gratitude to him. "I seem to lean on the great heart of Massachusetts," he said, in the bitterest hour of the conflict of his life. And it never betrayed him. In that heart not the least suspicion of a mean or selfish motive ever clouded his image— not a doubt of his absolute fidelity to his conscience disturbed its faith; and had he died a year ago, while yet the censure of the Legislature was unrepealed, his body would have been received by you with the same affectionate reverence; here, and in Faneuil Hall, and at the State-house, all honor that boundless gratitude and admiration could lavish would have been poured forth, and yonder in Mount Auburn he would have been laid to rest with the same immense tenderness of sorrow.

This is the great victory, the great lesson, the great legacy of his life, that the fidelity of a public man to conscience, not to party, is rewarded with the sincerest popular love and confidence. What an inspiration to every youth longing with generous ambition to enter the great arena of the State, that he must heed first and always the divine voice in his own soul, if he would be sure of the sweet voices of good fame! Living, how SUMNER served us! and dying, at this moment how he serves us still! In a time when politics seem peculiarly mean and selfish and corrupt, when there is a general vague apprehension that the very moral foundations of the national character are loosened, when good men are painfully anxious to know whether the heart of the people is hardened, CHARLES SUMNER dies; and the universality and sincerity of sorrow, such as the death of no man left living among us could awaken, show how true, how sound, how generous, is still the heart of the American people. This is the dying service of CHARLES SUMNER, a revelation which inspires every American to bind his shining example as a frontlet between the eyes, and never again to despair of the higher and more glorious destiny of his country.

And of that destiny what a foreshowing was he! In that beautiful home at the sunny and leafy corner of the national city, where he lived among books, and pictures, and noble friendships, and lofty thoughts—the home to which he returned at the close of each day in the Senate, and to which the wise and good from every land naturally came—how the stately, and gracious, and all-accomplished man seemed the very personification of that new union for which he had so manfully striven, and whose coming his dying eyes beheld—the union of ever wider liberty and juster law, the America of comprehensive intelligence, and of moral power! For that he stands; up to that, his imperishable memory, like the words of his living lips, forever lifts us—lifts us to his own great faith in America and in man. Suddenly from his strong hand—my father, my father, the chariot of Israel, and the horsemen thereof!—the banner falls. Be it ours to grasp it and carry it still forward, still higher! Our work is not his work, but it can be well done only in his spirit. And as in the heroic legend of your

western valley the men of Hadley, faltering in
the fierce shock of Indian battle, suddenly saw
at their head the lofty form of an unknown
captain, with white hair streaming on the wind,
by his triumphant mien strengthening their
hearts and leading them to victory, so, men
and women of Massachusetts, of America, if in
that national conflict already begun, as vast and
vital as the struggle of his life, the contest
which is beyond that of any party, or policy,
or measure—the contest for conscience, intelligence and morality as the supreme power in
our politics and the sole salvation of America—
you should falter or fail, suddenly your hearts
shall see once more the towering form, shall
hear again the inspiring voice, shall be exalted
anew with the moral energy and faith of
CHARLES SUMNER, and the victories of his
immortal example shall transcend the triumphs
of his life.

A P P E N D I X.

23

EULOGY BY CARL SCHURZ,

DELIVERED BY INVITATION OF THE

CITY GOVERNMENT OF BOSTON,

IN THE

BOSTON MUSIC HALL,

APRIL 29, 1874.

EULOGY.

WHEN the news went forth, "CHARLES SUMNER is dead," a tremor of strange emotion was felt all over the land. It was as if a magnificent star, a star unlike all others, which the living generation had been wont to behold fixed and immovable above their heads, had all at once disappeared from the sky, and the people stared into the great void darkened by the sudden absence of the familiar light.

On the 16th of March a funeral procession passed through the streets of Boston. Uncounted thousands of men, women and children had assembled to see it pass. No uncommon pageant had attracted them; no military parade with glittering uniforms and gay banners; no pompous array of dignitaries in official robes; nothing but carriages and a hearse with a coffin, and in it the corpse of CHARLES SUMNER. But there they stood—a multitude immeasurable to the eye, rich and poor, white and black, old and young—in grave and mournful silence, to bid a last sad farewell to him who was being borne to his grave. And every breeze from every point of the compass came loaded with a sigh of sorrow. Indeed, there was not a city or town in this great republic which would not have surrounded that funeral procession with the same spectacle of a profound and universal sense of great bereavement.

Was it love? Was it gratitude for the services rendered to the people? Was it the baffled expectation of greater service still to come? Was it admiration of his talents or his virtues that inspired so general an emotion of sorrow?

He had stood aloof from the multitude; the friendship of his heart had been given to but few; to the many he had appeared distant, self-satisfied and cold. His public life had been full of bitter conflicts. No man had aroused against himself fiercer animosities. Although warmly recognized by many, the public services of no man had been more acrimoniously questioned by opponents. No statesman's motives, qualities of heart and mind, wisdom and character, except his integrity, had been the subject of more heated controversy; and yet, when sudden death snatched him from us, friend and foe bowed their heads alike.

Every patriotic citizen felt poorer than the day before. Every true American heart trembled with the apprehension that the republic had lost something it could ill spare.

Even from far distant lands, across the ocean, voices came, mingling their sympathetic grief with our own.

When you, Mr. Mayor, in the name of the City Government of Boston, invited me to interpret that which millions think and feel, I thanked you for the proud privilege you had conferred upon me, and the invitation appealed so irresistibly to my friendship for the man we had lost, that I could not decline it.

And yet, the thought struck me that you might have prepared a greater triumph to his memory, had you summoned not me, his friend, but one of those who had stood against him in the struggles of his life, to bear testimony to CHARLES SUMNER's virtues.

There are many among them to-day, to whose sense of justice you might have safely confided the office, which to me is a task of love.

Here I see his friends around me, the friends of his youth, of his manhood, of his advancing age; among them, men whose illustrious names are household words as far as the English tongue is spoken, and far beyond. I saw them standing round his open grave, when it received the flower-decked coffin, mute sadness heavily clouding their brows. I understood their grief, for nobody could share it more than I.

In such a presence, the temptation is great to seek that consolation for our loss which bereaved friendship finds in the exaltation of its bereavement. But not to you or me belonged this man while he lived; not to you or me belongs his memory now that he is gone. His deeds, his example, and his fame, he left as a legacy to the American people and to mankind; and it is my office to speak of this inheritance. I cannot speak of it without affection. I shall endeavor to do it with justice.

Among the public characters of America, CHARLES SUMNER stands peculiar and unique. His senatorial career is a conspicuous part of our political history. But in order to appreciate the man in the career, we must look at the story of his life.

The American people take pride in saying that almost
all their great historic characters were self-made men,
who, without the advantages of wealth and early opportunities, won their education, raised themselves to usefulness and distinction, and achieved their greatness
through a rugged hand-to-hand struggle with adverse
fortune. It is indeed so. A log cabin; a ragged little
boy walking barefooted to a lowly country school-house,
or sometimes no school-house at all;—a lad, after a
day's hard toil on the farm, or in the workshop, poring
greedily, sometimes stealthily, over a volume of poetry,
or history, or travels;—a forlorn-looking youth, with
elbows out, applying at a lawyer's office for an opportunity to study;—then the young man a successful
practitioner attracting the notice of his neighbors;—
then a member of a State Legislature, a representative
in Congress, a Senator, maybe a Cabinet Minister, or
even President. Such are the pictures presented by
many a proud American biography.

And it is natural that the American people should
be proud of it, for such a biography condenses in the
compass of a single life the great story of the American nation, as from the feebleness and misery of early
settlements in the bleak solitude it advanced to the
subjugation of the hostile forces of nature; plunged
into an arduous struggle with dangers and difficulties
only known to itself, gathering strength from every
conflict and experience from every trial; with undaunted
pluck widening the range of its experiments and creative action, until at last it stands there as one of the
greatest powers of the earth. The people are fond of

seeing their image reflected in the lives of their foremost representative men.

But not such a life was that of CHARLES SUMNER.
He was descended from good old Kentish yeomanry
stock, men stalwart of frame, stout of heart, who used
to stand in the front of the fierce battles of Old England; and the first of the name who came to America
had certainly not been exempt from the rough struggles
of the early settlements. But already from the year
1723 a long line of Sumners appears on the records of
Harvard College, and it is evident that the love of
study had long been hereditary in the family. Charles
Pinckney Sumner, the Senator's father, was a graduate
of Harvard, a lawyer by profession, for fourteen years
high sheriff of Suffolk County. His literary tastes and
acquirements, and his stately politeness are still remembered. He was altogether a man of high respecta-
bility.

He was not rich, but in good circumstances; and
well able to give his children the best opportunities
to study, without working for their daily bread.

CHARLES SUMNER was born in Boston, on the 6th
of January, 1811. At the age of ten he had received
his rudimentary training; at fifteen, after having gone
through the Boston Latin School, he entered Harvard
College, and plunged at once with fervor into the classics, polite literature and history. Graduated in 1830,
he entered the Cambridge Law School. Now life began
to open to him. Judge Story, his most distinguished
teacher, soon recognized in him a young man of uncommon stamp; and an intimate friendship sprang up

24

between teacher and pupil, which was severed only by
death.

He began to distinguish himself not only by the most
arduous industry and application, pushing his researches
far beyond the text-books—indeed, text-books never satisfied him—but by a striking eagerness and faculty to
master the original principles of the science, and to
trace them through its development.

His productive labor began, and I find it stated that
already then, while he was yet a pupil, his essays,
published in the "American Jurist," were "always characterized by breadth of view and accuracy of learning,
and sometimes by remarkably subtle and ingenious
investigations."

Leaving the Law School he entered the office of a
lawyer in Boston, to acquire a knowledge of practice,
never much to his taste. Then he visited Washington
for the first time, little dreaming what a theatre of
action, struggle, triumph and suffering the national
city was to become for him; for then he came only
as a studious, deeply interested looker-on, who merely
desired to form the acquaintance of the justices and
practicing lawyers at the bar of the Supreme Court.
He was received with marked kindness by Chief-Justice
Marshall, and in later years he loved to tell his friend-
how he had sat at the feet of that great magistrate,
and learned there what a judge should be.

Having been admitted to the bar in Worcester in
1834, when twenty-three years old, he opened an office
in Boston, was soon appointed reporter of the United
States Circuit Court, published three volumes con-

taining Judge Story's decisions, known as "Sumner's Reports," took Judge Story's place from time to time as lecturer in the Harvard Law School; also Professor Greenleaf's, who was absent, and edited during the years 1835 and 1836 Andrew Dunlap's Treatise on Admiralty Practice. Beyond this, his studies, arduous, incessant and thorough, ranged far and wide.

Truly a studious and laborious young man, who took the business of life earnestly in hand, determined to know something, and to be useful to his time and country.

But what he had learned and could learn at home did not satisfy his craving. In 1837 he went to Europe, armed with a letter from Judge Story's hand to the law magnates of England, to whom his patron introduced him as "a young lawyer giving promise of the most eminent distinction in his profession, with truly extraordinary attainments, literary and judicial, and a gentleman of the highest purity and propriety of character."

This was not a mere complimentary introduction; it was the conscientious testimony of a great judge, who well knew his responsibility, and who afterwards, when his death approached, adding to that testimony, was frequently heard to say, "I shall die content, as far as my professorship is concerned, if CHARLES SUMNER is to succeed me."

In England, young SUMNER, only feeling himself standing on the threshold of life, was received like a man of already achieved distinction. Every circle of a society, ordinarily so exclusive, was open to him.

Often, by invitation, he sat with the judges in Westminster Hall. Renowned statesmen introduced him on
the floor of the Houses of Parliament. Eagerly he followed the debates, and studied the principles and practice of parliamentary law on its maternal soil, where
from the first seed-corn it had grown up into a magnificent tree, in whose shadow a great people can dwell
in secure enjoyment of their rights. Scientific associations received him as a welcome guest, and the learned
and great willingly opened to his winning presence their
stores of knowledge and statesmanship.

In France he listened to the eminent men of the
Law School in Paris, at the Sorbonne and the College
de France, and with many of the statesmen of that
country he maintained instructive intercourse. In Italy
he gave himself up to the charms of art, poetry, history and classical literature. In Germany he enjoyed
the conversation of Humboldt, of Ranke the historian,
of Ritter the geographer, and of the great jurists, Sa-
vigny, Thibaut and Mittermaier.

Two years after his return the "London Quarterly
Review" said of his visit to England, "He presents in
his own person a decisive proof that an American gentleman, without official rank or wide-spread reputation,
by mere dint of courtesy, candor, an entire absence of
pretension, an appreciating spirit and a cultured mind,
may be received on a perfect footing of equality in the
best circles, social, political and intellectual."

It must have been true, for it came from a quarter
not given to the habit of flattering Americans beyond
their deserts. And CHARLES SUMNER was not then the

senator of power and fame; he was only the young
son of a late sheriff of Suffolk County in Massachusetts, who had neither riches nor station, but who possessed that most winning charm of youth—purity of
soul, modesty of conduct, culture of mind, an earnest
thirst of knowledge, and a brow bearing the stamp of
noble manhood and the promise of future achievements.

He returned to his native shores in 1840, himself
like a heavily freighted ship, bearing a rich cargo of
treasures collected in foreign lands.

He resumed the practice of law in Boston; but, as I
find it stated, "not with remarkable success in a financial point of view." That I readily believe. The
financial point of view was never to him a fruitful
source of inspiration. Again he devoted himself to the
more congenial task of teaching at the Cambridge Law
School, and of editing an American edition of "Vesey's
Reports," in twenty volumes, with elaborate notes con-
tributed by himself.

But now the time had come when a new field of
action was to open itself to him. On the 4th of July,
1845, he delivered before the City Authorities of Boston, an address on "The True Grandeur of Nations."
So far he had been only a student—a deep and arduous one, and a writer and a teacher, but nothing more.
On that day his public career commenced. And his
first public address disclosed at once the peculiar impulse
and inspirations of his heart, and the tendencies of his
mind. It was a plea for universal peace,—a poetic rhap-
sody on the wrongs and horrors of war and the beauties
of concord; not, indeed, without solid argument, but

that argument clothed in all the gorgeousness of historical illustration, classic imagery and fervid effusion, rising
high above the level of existing conditions, and pictur-
ing an ideal future,—the universal reign of justice and
charity,—not far off to his own imagination, but far
beyond the conceptions of living society; but to that
society he addressed the urgent summons, to go forth at
once in pursuit of this ideal consummation; to transform all swords into ploughshares, and all war-ships into
peaceful merchantmen, without delay; believing that thus
the nation would rise to a greatness never known before,
which it could accomplish if it only willed it.

And this speech he delivered while the citizen soldiery
of Boston in festive array were standing before him,
and while the very air was stirred by the premonitory
mutterings of an approaching war.

The whole man revealed himself in that utterance; a
soul full of the native instinct of justice; an overpowering sense of right and wrong, which made him look
at the problems of human society from the lofty plane
of an ideal morality, which fixed for him, high beyond
the existing condition of things, the aims for which he
must strive, and inspired and fired his ardent nature for
the struggle. His education had singularly favored and
developed that ideal tendency. It was not that of the
self-made man in the common acceptation of the word.
The distracting struggles for existence, the small, harass-
ing cares of every-day life, had remained foreign to him.
His education was that of the favored few. He found
all the avenues of knowledge wide open to him. All
that his country could give he had: the most renowned

schools; the living instruction of the most elevating personal associations. It was the education of the typical young English gentleman. Like the English gentleman, also, he travelled abroad to widen his mental horizon. And again, all that foreign countries could give he had: the instruction of great lawyers and men of science, the teachings and example of statesmen, the charming atmosphere of poetry and art, which graces and elevates the soul. He had also learned to work, to work hard and with a purpose, and at thirty-four, when he first appeared conspicuously before the people, he could already point to many results of his labors.

But his principal work had been an eager accumulation of knowledge in his own mind, an accumulation most extraordinary in its scope and variety. His natural inclination to search for fundamental principles and truths had been favored by his opportunities, and all his industry in collecting knowledge became subservient to the building up of his ideals. Having not been tossed and jostled through the school of want and adversity, he lacked, what that school is best apt to develop,—keen, practical instincts, sharpened by early struggles, and that sober appreciation of the realities and possibilities of the times which is forced upon men by a hard contact with the world. He judged life from the stillness of the student's closet and from his intercourse with the refined and elevated, and he acquired little of those experiences which might have dampened his zeal in working for his ideal aims, and staggered his faith in their realization. His mind loved to move and operate in the realm of ideas, not of things; in

fact, it could scarcely have done otherwise. Thus
nature and education made him an idealist,—and, indeed,
he stands as the most pronounced idealist among the
public men of America.

He was an ardent friend of liberty, not like one of
those who have themselves suffered oppression and felt
the galling weight of chains; nor like those who in the
common walks of life have experienced the comfort of
wide elbow-room and the quickening and encouraging
influence of free institutions for the practical work of
society. But to him liberty was the ideal goddess
clothed in sublime attributes of surpassing beauty and
beneficence, giving to every human being his eternal rights, showering around her the treasures of her
blessings, and lifting up the lowly to an ideal existence.

In the same ethereal light stood in his mind the
Republic, his country, the law, the future organization
of the great family of nations.

That idealism was sustained and quickened, not merely
by his vast learning and classical inspirations, but by
that rare and exquisite purity of life, and high moral
sensitiveness, which he had preserved intact and fresh
through all the temptations of his youth, and which
remained intact and fresh down to his last day.

Such was the man, when, in the exuberant vigor of
manhood, he entered public life. Until that time he
had entertained no aspirations for a political career.
When discussing with a friend of his youth,—now a
man of fame,—what the future might have in store for
them, he said: " You may be a Senator of the United

States some day; but nothing would make me happier than to be President of Harvard College."

And in later years he publicly declared: "With the ample opportunities of private life I was content. No tombstone for me could bear a fairer inscription than this: 'Here lies one who, without the honors or emoluments of public station, did something for his fellowmen.'" It was the scholar who spoke, and no doubt he spoke sincerely. But he found the slavery question in his path; or, rather, the slavery question seized upon him. The advocate of universal peace, of the eternal reign of justice and charity, could not fail to see in slavery the embodiment of universal war of man against man, of absolute injustice and oppression. Little knowing where the first word would carry him, he soon found himself in the midst of the struggle.

The idealist found a living question to deal with, which, like a flash of lightning, struck into the very depth of his soul, and set it on fire. The whole ardor of his nature broke out in the enthusiasm of the anti-slavery man. In a series of glowing addresses and letters he attacked the great wrong. He protested against the Mexican War; he assailed with powerful strokes the Fugitive Slave Law; he attempted to draw the Whig party into a decided anti-slavery policy; and when that failed, he broke through his party affiliations, and joined the small band of Free-Soilers. He was an abolitionist by nature, but not one of those who rejected the Constitution as a covenant with slavery. His legal mind found in the Constitution no express recognition of slavery, and he consistently construed it as a warrant of

25

freedom. This placed him in the ranks of those who were called "political abolitionists."

He did not think of the sacrifices which this obedience to his moral impulses might cost him. For, at that time, abolitionism was by no means a fashionable thing. An anti-slavery man was then, even in Boston, positively the horror of a large portion of polite society. To make anti-slavery speeches was looked upon, not only as an incendiary, but a vulgar occupation. And that the highly refined SUMNER, who was so learned and able, who had seen the world and mixed with the highest social circles in Europe; who knew the classics by heart, and could deliver judgment on a picture or a statue like a veteran connoisseur; who was a favorite with the wealthy and powerful, and could, in his aspirations for an easy and fitting position in life, count upon their whole influence, if he only would not do anything foolish,—that such a man should go among the abolitionists, and not only sympathize with them, but work with them, and expose himself to the chance of being dragged through the streets by vulgar hands with a rope round his neck, like William Lloyd Garrison,—that was a thing at which the polite society of that day would revolt, and which no man could undertake without danger of being severely dropped. But that was the thing which the refined SUMNER actually did, probably without giving a moment's thought to the possible consequences.

He went even so far as openly to defy that dictatorship which Daniel Webster had for so many years been exercising over the political mind of Massachusetts, and which then was about to exert its power in favor of a compromise with slavery.

But times were changing, and only six years after the delivery of his first popular address he was elected to the Senate of the United States by a combination of Democrats and Free-Soilers.

CHARLES SUMNER entered the Senate on the first day of December, 1851. He entered as the successor of Daniel Webster, who had been appointed Secretary of State. On that same first of December Henry Clay spoke his last word in the Senate, and then left the chamber, never to return.

A striking and most significant coincidence: Henry Clay disappeared from public life; Daniel Webster left the Senate, drawing near his end; CHARLES SUMNER stepped upon the scene. The close of one and the setting in of another epoch in the history of the American Republic were portrayed in the exit and entry of these men.

Clay and Webster had appeared in the councils of the nation in the early part of this century. The Republic was then still in its childhood, in almost every respect still an untested experiment, an unsolved problem. Slowly and painfully had it struggled through the first conflicts of constitutional theories, and acquired only an uncertain degree of national consistency. There were the somewhat unruly democracies of the States, with their fresh revolutionary reminiscences, their instincts of entirely independent sovereignty, and their now and then seemingly divergent interests; and the task of binding them firmly together in the bonds of common aspirations, of national spirit and the authority of national law, had, indeed, fairly progressed, but was far from being entirely accomplished. The United States, not yet compacted by the means of rapid locomotion which to-day make every inhabitant of the land a neighbor of the national capital, were then still a straggling confederacy; and the members of that confederacy had, since the triumphant issue of the Revolution, more common memories of severe trials, sufferings, embarrassments, dangers and anxieties together, than of cheering successes and of assured prosperity and well-being.

The great powers of the Old World, fiercely contending among themselves for the mastery, trampled, without remorse, upon the neutral rights of the young and feeble Republic. A war was impending with one of them, bringing on disastrous reverses and spreading alarm and discontent over the land. A dark cloud of financial difficulty hung over the nation. And the danger from abroad and embarrassments at home were heightened by a restless party spirit, which former disagreements had left behind them, and which every newly arising question seemed to embitter. The outlook was dark and uncertain. It was under such circumstances that Henry Clay first, and Daniel Webster shortly after him, stepped upon the scene, and at once took their station in the foremost rank of public men.

The problems to be solved by the statesmen of that period were of an eminently practical nature. They had to establish the position of the young Republic among the powers of the earth; to make her rights as a neutral respected; to secure the safety of her maritime interests. They had to provide for national defence. They had to set the interior household of the Republic in working order.

They had to find remedies for a burdensome public debt and a disordered currency. They had to invent and originate policies, to bring to light the resources of the land, sleeping unknown in the virgin soil: to open and make accessible to the husbandman the wild acres yet untouched; to protect the frontier settler against the inroads of the savage; to call into full activity the agricultural, commercial and industrial energies of the people; to develop and extend the prosperity of the nation so as to make even the discontented cease to doubt that the National Union was, and should be maintained as, a blessing to all.

Thus we find the statesmanship of those times busily occupied with practical detail of foreign policy, national defence, financial policy, tariffs, banks, organization of governmental departments, land policy, Indian policy, internal improvements, settlements of disputes and difficulties among the States, contrivances of expediency of all sorts, to put the Government firmly upon its feet, and to set and keep in orderly motion the working of the political machinery, to build up and strengthen and secure the framework in which the mighty developments of the future were to take place.

Such a task, sometimes small in its details, but difficult and grand in its comprehensiveness, required that creative, organizing, building kind of statesmanship, which to large and enlightened views of the aims and ends of political organization and of the wants of society must add a practical knowledge of details, a skillful handling of existing material, a just understanding of causes and effects, the ability to compose distracting conflicts and to bring the social forces into fruitful co-operation.

On this field of action Clay and Webster stood in the front rank of an illustrious array of contemporaries: Clay, the originator of measures and policies, with his inventive and organizing mind, not rich in profound ideas or in knowledge gathered by book-study, but learning as he went; quick in the perception of existing wants and difficulties and of the means within reach to satisfy the one and overcome the other; and a born captain also,—a commander of men, who appeared as if riding through the struggles of those days mounted on a splendidly caparisoned charger, sword in hand, and with waving helmet and plume, leading the front;— a fiery and truly magnetic soul, overawing with his frown, enchanting with his smile, flourishing the weapon of eloquence like a wizard's wand, overwhelming opposition and kindling and fanning the flame of enthusiasm; —a marshaller of parties, whose very presence and voice like a signal-blast created and wielded organization.

And by his side Daniel Webster, with that awful vastness of brain, a tremendous storehouse of thought and knowledge, which gave forth its treasures with ponderous majesty of utterance; he not an originator of measures and policies, but a mighty advocate, the greatest advocate this country ever knew,—a king in the realm of intellect, and the solemn embodiment of authority,—a huge Atlas, who carried the Constitution on his shoulders. He could have carried there the whole moral grandeur of the nation, had he never compromised his own.

Such men filled the stage during that period of construction and conservative national organization, devoting the best efforts of their statesmanship, the statesmanship of the political mind, to the purpose of raising their country to greatness in wealth and power, of making the people proud of their common nationality, and of imbedding the Union in the contentment of prosperity, in enlightened patriotism, national law, and constitutional principle.

And when they drew near their end, they could boast of many a grand achievement, not indeed exclusively their own, for other powerful minds had their share in the work. The United States stood there among the great powers of the earth, strong and respected. The Republic had no foreign foe to fear; its growth in population and wealth, in popular intelligence and progressive civilization, the wonder of the world. There was no visible limit to its development; there seemed to be no danger to its integrity.

But among the problems which the statesmen of that period had grappled with, there was one which had eluded their grasp. Many a conflict of opinion and interest they had succeeded in settling, either by positive decision, or by judicious composition. But one conflict had stubbornly baffled the statesmanship of expedients, for it was more than a mere conflict of opinion and

interest. It was a conflict grounded deep in the moral
nature of men—the slavery question.

Many a time had it appeared on the surface during the
period I have described, threatening to overthrow all
that had been ingeniously built up, and to break asunder
all that had been laboriously cemented together. In
their anxiety to avert every danger threatening the
Union, they attempted to repress the slavery question
by compromise, and, apparently, with success, at least
for awhile.

But however firmly those compromises seemed to
stand, there was a force of nature at work which, like a
restless flood, silently but unceasingly and irresistibly
washed their foundation away, until at last the towering
structure toppled down.

The anti-slavery movement is now one of the great
chapters of our past history. The passions of the struggle having been buried in thousands of graves, and the
victory of Universal Freedom standing as firm and
unquestionable as the eternal hills, we may now look
back upon that history with an impartial eye. It may
be hoped that even the people of the South, if they do
not yet appreciate the spirit which created and guided
the anti-slavery movement, will not much longer misunderstand it. Indeed, they grievously misunderstood
it at the time. They looked upon it as the offspring
of a wanton desire to meddle with other people's affairs,
or as the product of hypocritical selfishness assuming
the mask and cant of philanthropy, merely to rob the
South and to enrich New England; or as an insidious

contrivance of criminally reckless political ambition, striving to grasp and monopolize power at the risk of destroying a part of the country or even the whole.

It was, perhaps, not unnatural that those interested in slavery should have thought so; but from this great error arose their fatal miscalculation as to the peculiar strength of the anti-slavery cause.

No idea ever agitated the popular mind to whose origin calculating selfishness was more foreign. Even the great uprising which brought about the War of Independence was less free from selfish motives, for it sprang from resistance to a tyrannical abuse of the taxing power. Then the people rose against that oppression which touched their property; the anti-slavery movement originated in an impulse purely moral.

It was the irresistible breaking out of a trouble of conscience,—a trouble of conscience which had already disturbed the men who made the American Republic. It found a voice in their anxious admonitions, their gloomy prophecies, their scrupulous care to exclude from the Constitution all forms of expression which might have appeared to sanction the idea of property in man.

It found a voice in the fierce struggles which resulted in the Missouri Compromise. It was repressed for a time by material interest, by the greed of gain, when the peculiar product of slave labor became one of the principal staples of the country and a mine of wealth. But the trouble of conscience raised its voice again, shrill and defiant as when your own John Quincy Adams stood in the halls of Congress, and when devoted advocates of the rights of man began and carried on, in the face of ridicule and brutal persecution, an agitation seemingly hopeless. It cried out again and again, until at last its tones and echoes grew louder than all the noises that were to drown it.

The anti-slavery movement found arrayed against itself all the influences, all the agencies, all the arguments which ordinarily control the actions of men.

Commerce said,—Do not disturb slavery, for its products fill our ships and are one of the principal means of our exchanges. Industry said,—Do not disturb slavery, for it feeds our machinery and gives us markets. The greed of wealth said,—Do not disturb slavery, for it is an inexhaustible fountain of riches. Political ambition said,—Do not disturb slavery, for it furnishes us combinations and compromises to keep parties alive and to make power the price of shrewd management. An anxious statesmanship said,—Do not disturb slavery, for you might break to pieces the union of these States.

There never was a more formidable combination of interests and influences than that which confronted the anti-slavery movement in its earlier stages. And what was its answer? "Whether all you say be true or false, it matters not, but slavery is wrong."

Slavery is wrong! That one word was enough. It stood there like a huge rock in the sea, shivering to spray the waves dashing upon it. Interest, greed, argument, vituperation, calumny, ridicule, persecution, patriotic appeal,—it was all in vain. Amidst all the storm and assault that one word stood there unmoved, intact and impregnable : Slavery is wrong.

Such was the vital spirit of the anti-slavery movement in its early development. Such a spirit alone could inspire that religious devotion which gave to the believer all the stubborn energy of fanaticism; it alone could kindle that deep enthusiasm which made men willing to risk and sacrifice everything for a great cause; it alone could keep alive that unconquerable faith in the certainty of ultimate success which boldly attempted to overcome seeming impossibilities.

It was indeed a great spirit, as, against difficulties which threw pusillanimity into despair, it painfully struggled into light, often baffled and as often pressing forward with devotion always fresh; nourished by nothing but a profound sense of right; encouraged by nothing but the cheering sympathy of liberty-loving mankind the world over, and by the hope that some day the conscience of the American people would be quickened by a full understanding of the dangers which the existence of the great wrong would bring upon the Republic. No scramble for the spoils of office then, no expectation of a speedy conquest of power,—nothing but that conviction, that enthusiasm, that faith in the breasts of a small band of men, and the prospect of new uncertain struggles and trials.

At the time when Mr. Sumner entered the Senate, the hope of final victory appeared as distant as ever; but it only appeared so. The statesmen of the past period had just succeeded in building up that compromise which admitted California as a free State, and imposed upon the Republic the Fugitive Slave Law. That compromise, like all its predecessors, was consid-

ered and called a final settlement. The two great political parties accepted it as such. In whatever they might
differ, as to this they solemnly proclaimed their agree-
ment. Fidelity to it was looked upon as a test of true
patriotism, and as a qualification necessary for the
possession of political power. Opposition to it was
denounced as factious, unpatriotic, revolutionary demagogism, little short of treason. An overwhelming
majority of the American people acquiesced in it.
Material interest looked upon it with satisfaction, as a
promise of repose; timid and sanguine patriots greeted
it as a new bond of union; politicians hailed it as an
assurance that the fight for the public plunder might
be carried on without the disturbing intrusion of a
moral principle in politics. But, deep down, men's conscience like a volcanic fire was restless, ready for a
new outbreak as soon as the thin crust of compromise
should crack. And just then the day was fast approaching when the moral idea, which so far had only broken
out sporadically, and moved small numbers of men
to open action, should receive a reinforcement strong
enough to transform a forlorn hope into an army of
irresistible strength. One of those eternal laws which
govern the development of human affairs asserted itself,
—the law that a great wrong, which has been maintained in defiance of the moral sense of mankind, must
finally, by the very means and measures necessary for
its sustenance, render itself so insupportable as to insure
its downfall and destruction.

So it was with slavery. I candidly acquit the American slave-power of willful and wanton aggression upon

the liberties and general interests of the American people.   If slavery was to be kept alive at all, its supporters could not act otherwise than they did.

Slavery could not live and thrive in an atmosphere of free inquiry and untrammelled discussion.   Therefore free inquiry and discussion touching slavery had to be suppressed.

Slavery could not be secure, if slaves, escaping merely across a State line, thereby escaped the grasp of their masters.   Hence an effective Fugitive Slave Law was imperatively demanded.

Slavery could not protect its interests in the Union unless its power balanced that of the free States in the national councils.   Therefore by colonization or conquest the number of slave States had to be augmented.   Hence the annexation of Texas, the Mexican war, and intrigues for the acquisition of Cuba.

Slavery could not maintain the equilibrium of power, if it permitted itself to be excluded from the national Territories.   Hence the breaking down of the Missouri Compromise and the usurpation in Kansas.

Thus slavery was pushed on and on by the inexorable logic of its existence; the slave masters were only the slaves of the necessities of slavery, and all their seeming exactions and usurpations were merely a struggle for its life.

Many of their demands had been satisfied, on the part of the North, by submission or compromise.   The Northern people, although with reluctant conscience, had acquiesced in the contrivances of politicians, for the sake of peace.   But when the slave-power went so far

as to demand for slavery the great domain of the nation
which had been held sacred to freedom forever, then
the people of the North suddenly understood that the
necessities of slavery demanded what they could not
yield. Then the conscience of the masses was relieved
of the doubts and fears which had held it so long in
check; their moral impulses were quickened by practical perceptions; the moral idea became a practical
force, and the final struggle began. It was made inevitable by the necessities of slavery; it was indeed an
irrepressible conflict.

These things were impending when Henry Clay and
Daniel Webster, the architects of the last compromise,
left the Senate. Had they, with all their far-seeing
statesmanship, never understood this logic of things?
When they made their compromises, did they only
desire to postpone the final struggle until they should
be gone, so that they might not witness the terrible
concussion? Or had their great and manifold achievements with the statesmanship of organization and expediency so deluded their minds, that they really hoped
a compromise which only ignored, but did not settle,
the great moral question, could furnish an enduring
basis for future developments?

One thing they and their contemporaries had indeed
accomplished; under their care the Republic had grown
so great and strong, its vitality had become so tough,
that it could endure the final struggle without falling
to pieces under its shocks.

Whatever their errors, their delusions, and, perhaps,
their misgivings may have been, this they had accom-

plished; and then they left the last compromise tottering behind them, and turned their faces to the wall and died.

And with them stepped into the background the statesmanship of organization, expedients and compromises; and to the front came, ready for action, the moral idea which was to fight out the great conflict, and to open a new epoch of American history.

That was the historic significance of the remarkable scene which showed us Henry Clay walking out of the Senate Chamber never to return, when CHARLES SUMNER sat down there as the successor of Daniel Webster.

No man could, in his whole being, have more strikingly portrayed that contrast. When CHARLES SUMNER had been elected to the Senate, Theodore Parker said to him, in a letter of congratulation, "You told me once that you were in morals, not in politics. Now I hope you will show that you are still in morals, although in politics. I hope you will be the Senator with a conscience." That hope was gratified. He always remained in morals while in politics. He never was anything else but the Senator with a conscience. CHARLES SUMNER entered the Senate not as a mere advocate, but as the very embodiment of the moral idea. From this fountain flowed his highest aspirations. There had been great anti-slavery men in the Senate before him; they were there with him, men like Seward and Chase. But they had been trained in a different school. Their minds had ranged over other political fields. They understood politics. He did not. He knew but one political object,—to combat and over-

throw the great wrong of slavery; to serve the ideal
of the liberty and equality of men; and to establish
the universal reign of "peace, justice and charity."
He brought to the Senate a studious mind, vast learning, great legal attainments, a powerful eloquence, a
strong and ardent nature; and all this he vowed to
one service. With all this he was not a mere expounder
of a policy; he was a worshipper, sincere and devout,
at the shrine of his ideal. In no public man had the
moral idea of the anti-slavery movement more overruling strength. He made everything yield to it. He did
not possess it; it possessed him. That was the secret
of his peculiar power.

He introduced himself into the debates of the Senate,
the slavery question having been silenced forever, as
politicians then thought, by several speeches on other
subjects,—the reception of Kossuth, the Land Policy,
Ocean Postage; but they were not remarkable, and
attracted but little attention.

At last he availed himself of an appropriation bill to
attack the Fugitive Slave Law, and at once a spirit
broke forth in that first word on the great question
which startled every listener.

Thus he opened the argument:—

"Painfully convinced of the unutterable wrong and
woe of slavery,—profoundly believing that according to
the true spirit of the Constitution and the sentiments
of the fathers, it can find no place under our National
Government,—I could not allow this session to reach
its close without making or seizing an opportunity to

declare myself openly against the usurpation, injustice, and cruelty of the late intolerant enactment for the recovery of fugitive slaves."

Then this significant declaration :—

"Whatever I am or may be, I freely offer to this cause. I have never been a politician. The slave of principles, I call no party master. By sentiment, education, and conviction, a friend of Human Rights in their utmost expansion, I have ever most sincerely embraced the Democratic idea—not, indeed, as represented or professed by any party, but according to its real significance, as transfigured in the Declaration of Independence, and in the injunctions of Christianity. In this idea I see no narrow advantage merely for individuals or classes, but the sovereignty of the people, and the greatest happiness of all secured by equal laws."

A vast array of historical research and of legal argument was then called up to prove the sectionalism of slavery, the nationalism of freedom, and the unconstitutionality of the Fugitive Slave Act, followed by this bold declaration : "By the Supreme Law, which commands me to do no injustice, by the comprehensive Christian Law of Brotherhood, by the Constitution have sworn to support, I am bound to disobey this law." And the speech closed with this solemn quotation : "Beware of the groans of wounded souls, since the inward sore will at length break out. Oppress not

27

to the utmost a single heart; for a solitary sigh has power to overturn a whole world."

The amendment to the appropriation bill moved by Mr. SUMNER received only four votes of fifty-one. But every hearer had been struck by the words spoken as something different from the tone of other anti-slavery speeches delivered in those halls. Southern Senators, startled at the peculiarity of the speech, called it, in reply, "the most extraordinary language they had ever listened to." Mr. Chase, supporting SUMNER in debate, spoke of it, "as marking a new era in American history, when the anti-slavery idea ceased to stand on the defensive and was boldly advancing to the attack."

Indeed, it had that significance. There stood up in the Senate a man who was no politician; but who, on the highest field of politics, with a concentrated intensity of feeling and purpose never before witnessed there, gave expression to a moral impulse, which, although sleeping perhaps for a time, certainly existed in the popular conscience, and which, once become a political force, could not fail to produce a great revolution.

CHARLES SUMNER possessed all the instincts, the courage, the firmness and the faith of the devotee of a great idea. In the Senate he was a member of a feeble minority, so feeble, indeed, as to be to the ruling power a mere subject of derision; and for the first three years of his service without organized popular support. The slaveholders had been accustomed to put the metal of their Northern opponents to a variety of tests. Many a

hot anti-slavery zeal had cooled under the social blandishments with which the South knew so well how to
impregnate the atmosphere of the national capital, and
many a high courage had given way before the haughty
assumption and fierce menace of Southern men in Congress. Mr. SUMNER had to pass that ordeal. He was
at first petted and flattered by Southern society, but,
fond as he was of the charms of social intercourse, and
accessible to demonstrative appreciation, no blandishments could touch his convictions of duty.

And when the advocates of slavery turned upon him
with anger and menace, he hurled at them with prouder
defiance his answer, repeating itself in endless varia-
tions: "You must yield, for young are wro."

The slave-power had so frequently succeeded in
making the North yield to its demands, even after the
most formidable demonstrations of reluctance, that it
had become a serious question whether there existed
any such thing as Northern firmness. But it did exist,
and in CHARLES SUMNER it had developed its severest
political type. The stronger the assault, the higher rose
in him the power of resistance. In him lived that spirit
which not only would not yield, but would turn upon
the assailant. The Southern force, which believed itself
irresistible, found itself striking against a body which
was immovable. To think of yielding to any demand
of slavery, of making a compromise with it, in however
tempting a form, was, to his nature, an absolute impossibility.

Mr. SUMNER's courage was of a peculiar kind. He
attacked the slave-power in the most unsparing manner,

when its supporters were most violent in resenting
opposition, and when that violence was always apt to
proceed from words to blows. One day, while SUMNER
was delivering one of his severest speeches, Stephen
A. Douglas, walking up and down behind the President's chair in the old Senate Chamber, and listening to
him, remarked to a friend: "Do you hear that man?
He may be a fool, but I tell you that man has pluck.
I wonder whether he knows himself what he is doing.
I am not sure whether I should have the courage to
say those things to the men who are scowling around
him."

Of all men in the Senate Chamber, SUMNER was probably least aware that the thing he did required pluck. He
simply did what he felt it his duty to his cause to do.
It was to him a matter of course. He was like a soldier
who, when he has to march upon the enemy's batteries,
does not say to himself, "Now I am going to perform an
act of heroism," but who simply obeys an impulse of
duty, and marches forward without thinking of the bullets
that fly around his head. A thought of the boldness of
what he has done may then occur to him afterwards, when
he is told of it. This was one of the striking peculiari-
ties of Mr. SUMNER's character, as all those know who
knew him well.

Neither was he conscious of the stinging force of the
language he frequently employed. He simply uttered,
what he felt to be true, in language fitting the strength of
his convictions. The indignation of his moral sense at
what he felt to be wrong was so deep and sincere that he
thought everybody must find the extreme severity of his

expressions as natural as they came to his own mind. And he was not unfrequently surprised, greatly surprised, when others found his language offensive.

As he possessed the firmness and courage, so he possessed the faith of the devotee. From the beginning, and through all the vicissitudes of the anti-slavery movement, his heart was profoundly assured that his generation would see slavery entirely extinguished.

While travelling in France to restore his health, after having been beaten down on the floor of the Senate, he visited Alexis de Tocqueville, the celebrated author of "Democracy in America." Tocqueville expressed his anxiety about the 'issue of the anti-slavery movement, which then had suffered defeat by the election of Buchanan. "There can be no doubt about the result," said SUMNER. "Slavery will soon succumb and disappear." "Disappear! In what way, and how soon?" asked Tocqueville. "In what manner I cannot say," replied SUMNER. "How soon I cannot say. But it will be soon; I feel it; I know it. It cannot be otherwise." That was all the reason he gave. "Mr. SUMNER is a remarkable man," said De Tocqueville afterwards to a friend of mine. "He says that slavery will soon entirely disappear in the United States. He does not know how, he does not know when; but he feels it, he is perfectly sure of it. The man speaks like a prophet." And so it was.

What appeared a perplexing puzzle to other men's minds was perfectly clear to him. His method of reasoning was simple; it was the reasoning of religious faith. Slavery is wrong,—therefore it must and will perish;

freedom is right,—therefore it must and will prevail. And by no power of resistance, by no difficulty, by no disappointment, by no defeat, could that faith be shaken. For his cause, so great and just, he thought nothing impossible, everything certain. And he was unable to understand how others could fail to share his faith.

In one sense he was no party leader. He possessed none of the instinct or experience of the politician, nor that sagacity of mind which appreciates and measures the importance of changing circumstances, or the possibilities and opportunities of the day. He lacked, entirely, the genius of organization. He never understood, nor did he value, the art of strengthening his following by timely concession, or prudent reticence, or advantageous combination and alliance. He knew nothing of management and party manœuvre. Indeed, not unfrequently he alarmed many devoted friends of his cause by bold declarations, for which, they thought, the public mind was not prepared, and by the unreserved avowal and straightforward advocacy of ultimate objects, which, they thought, might safely be left to the natural development of events. He was not seldom accused of doing things calculated to frighten the people and to disorganize the anti-slavery forces.

Such was his unequivocal declaration in his first great anti-slavery speech in the Senate, that he held himself bound by every conviction of justice, right and duty, to disobey the Fugitive Slave Law, and his ringing answer to the question put by Senator Butler of South Carolina, whether, without the Fugitive Slave Law, he would, under the Constitution, consider it his duty to aid the surrender of fugitive slaves, "Is thy servant a dog, that he should do this thing?"

Such was his speech on the "Barbarism of Slavery," delivered on a bill to admit Kansas immediately under a free State Constitution;—a speech so unsparing and vehement in the denunciation of slavery in all its political, moral and social aspects, and so direct in its prediction of the complete annihilation of slavery, that it was said such a speech would scarcely aid the admission of Kansas.

Such was his unbending and open resistance to any plan of compromise calculated to preserve slavery, when after Mr. Lincoln's election the Rebellion first raised its head, and a large number of Northern people, even anti-slavery men, frightened by the threatening prospect of civil war, cast blindly about for a plan of adjustment, while really no adjustment was possible.

Such was, early in the war, and during its most doubtful hours, his declaration, laid before the Senate in a series of resolutions, that the States in rebellion had destroyed themselves as such by the very act of rebellion; that slavery, as a creation of State law, had perished with the States, and that general emancipation must immediately follow,—thus putting the programme of emancipation boldly in the foreground, at a time when many thought, that the cry of union alone, union with or without slavery, could hold together the Union forces.

Such was his declaration, demanding negro suffrage even before the close of the war, while the public opinion at the North, whose aid the Government needed, still recoiled from such a measure.

Thus he was apt to go rough-shod over the considerations of management, deemed important by his co-workers. I believe he never consulted with his friends around him, before doing those things, and when they afterwards remonstrated with him, he ingenuously asked : "Is it not right and true, what I have said? And if it is right and true, must I not say it?"

And yet, although he had no organizing mind, and despised management, he was a leader. He was a leader as the embodiment of the moral idea, with all its uncompromising firmness, its unflagging faith, its daring devotion. And in this sense he could be a leader only because he was no politician. He forced others to follow, because he was himself impracticable. Simply obeying his moral impulse, he dared to say things which in the highest legislative body of the Republic nobody else would say; and he proved that they could be said, and yet the world would move on. With his wealth of learning and his legal ability, he furnished an arsenal of arguments, convincing more timid souls that what he said could be sustained in repeating. And presently the politicians felt encouraged to follow in the direction where the idealist had driven a stake ahead. Nay, he forced them to follow, for they knew that the idealist, whom they could not venture to disown, would not fall back at their bidding. Such was his leadership in the struggle with slavery.

Nor was that leadership interrupted when, on the 22d of May, 1856, Preston Brooks of South Carolina, maddened by an arraignment of his State and its Senator, came upon CHARLES SUMNER in the Senate, struck him down with heavy blows and left him on the ground bleeding and insensible. For three years SUMNER's voice was not heard, but his blood marked the vantage ground from which his party could not recede; and his Senatorial chair, kept empty for him by the noble people of Massachusetts, stood there in most eloquent silence, confirming, sealing, inflaming all he had said with terrible illustration,—a guide-post to the onward march of freedom.

When, in 1861, the Republican party had taken the reins of government in hand, his peculiar leadership entered upon a new field of action. No sooner was the victory of the anti-slavery cause in the election ascertained, than the Rebellion raised its head. South Carolina opened the secession movement. The portentous shadow of an approaching civil war spread over the land. A tremor fluttered through the hearts even of strong men in the North,—a vague fear such as is produced by the first rumbling of an earthquake. Could not a bloody conflict be averted? A fresh clamor for compromise arose. Even Republicans in Congress began to waver. The proposed compromise involved new and express constitutional recognitions of the existence and rights of slavery, and guarantees against interference with it by constitutional amendment or national law. The pressure from the country, even from Massachusetts, in favor of the scheme, was extraordinary, but a majority of the anti-slavery men in the Senate, in their front Mr. SUMNER, stood firm, feeling that a compromise, giving express constitutional sanction and an indefi-

nite lease of life to slavery, would be a surrender, and
knowing, also, that even by the offer of such a surrender, secession and civil war would still be insisted
on by the Southern leaders. The history of those days,
as we now know it, confirms the accuracy of that judgment. The war was inevitable. Thus the anti-slavery
cause escaped a useless humiliation, and retained intact
its moral force for future action.

But now the time had come when the anti-slavery
movement, no longer a mere opposition to the demands
of the slave-power, was to proceed to positive action.
The war had scarcely commenced in earnest, when Mr.
SUMNER urged general emancipation. Only the great
ideal object of the liberty of all men could give sanction to a war in the eyes of the devotee of universal
peace. To the end of stamping upon the war the character of a war of emancipation all his energies were
bent. His unreserved and emphatic utterances alarmed
the politicians. Our armies suffered disaster upon disaster in the field. The managing mind insisted that
care must be taken, by nourishing the popular enthusiasm for the integrity of the Union,—the strictly
national idea alone,—to unite all the social and political elements of the North for the struggle; and that so
bold a measure as immediate emancipation might reani-
mate old dissensions, and put hearty co-operation in
jeopardy.

But Mr. SUMNER's convictions could not be repressed.
In a bold decree of universal liberty he saw only a
new source of inspiration and strength. Nor was his
impulsive instinct unsupported by good reason. The

distraction produced in the North by an emancipation measure could only be of short duration. The moral spirit was certain, ultimately, to gain the upper hand.

But in another direction a bold and unequivocal anti-slavery policy could not fail to produce most salutary effects. One of the dangers threatening us was foreign interference. No European powers gave us their expressed sympathy except Germany and Russia. The governing classes of England, with conspicuous individual exceptions, always gratefully to be remembered, were ill-disposed towards the Union cause. The permanent disruption of the Republic was loudly predicted, as if it were desired, and intervention—an intervention which could be only in favor of the South—was openly spoken of. The Emperor of the French, who availed himself of our embarrassments to execute his ambitious designs in Mexico, was animated by sentiments no less hostile. It appeared as if only a plausible opportunity had been wanting, to bring foreign intervention upon our heads. A threatening spirit, disarmed only by timely prudence, had manifested itself in the Trent case. It seemed doubtful whether the most skillful diplomacy, unaided by a stronger force, would be able to avert the danger.

But the greatest strength of the anti-slavery cause had always been in the conscience of mankind. There was our natural ally. The cause of slavery as such could have no open sympathy among the nations of Europe. It stood condemned by the moral sentiment of the civilized world. How could any European gov-

ernment, in the face of that universal sentiment, undertake openly to interfere against a power waging war
against slavery? Surely, that could not be thought of.

But had the Government of the United States distinctly
professed that it was waging war against slavery, and
for freedom? Had it not been officially declared that
the war for the Union would not alter the condition of
a single human being in America? Why then not
arrest the useless effusion of blood; why not, by intervention, stop a destructive war, in which, confessedly,
slavery and freedom were not at stake? Such were the
arguments of our enemies in Europe; and they were
not without color.

It was obvious that nothing but a measure impressing
beyond dispute upon our war a decided anti-slavery
character, making it in profession what it was inevitably
destined to be in fact, a war of emancipation,—could
enlist on our side the enlightened public opinion of the
Old World so strongly as to restrain the hostile spirit
of foreign governments. No European government
could well venture to interfere against those who had
convinced the world that they were fighting to give
freedom to the slaves of North America.

Thus the moral instinct did not err. The emancipation policy was not only the policy of principle, but
also the policy of safety. Mr. SUMNER urged it with
impetuous and unflagging zeal. In the Senate he found
but little encouragement. The resolutions he introduced
in February, 1862, declaring State suicide as the consequence of Rebellion, and the extinction of slavery in

the insurrectionary States as the consequence of State suicide, were looked upon as an ill-timed and hazardous demonstration, disturbing all ideas of management.

To the President, then, he devoted his efforts. Nothing could be more interesting, nay, touching, than the peculiar relations that sprung up between Abraham Lincoln and CHARLES SUMNER. No two men could be more alike as to their moral impulses and ultimate aims; no two men more unlike in their methods of reasoning and their judgment of means.

Abraham Lincoln was a true child of the people. There was in his heart an inexhaustible fountain of tenderness, and from it sprung that longing to be true, just and merciful to all, which made the people love him. In the deep, large humanity of his soul had grown his moral and political principles, to which he clung with the fidelity of an honest nature, and which he defended with the strength of a vigorous mind.

But he had not grown great in any high school of statesmanship. He had, from the humblest beginnings, slowly and laboriously worked himself up, or rather he had gradually risen up without being aware of it, and suddenly he found himself in the foremost rank of the distinguished men of the land. In his youth and early manhood he had achieved no striking successes that might have imparted to him that overweening self-appreciation which so frequently leads self-made men to overestimate their faculties, and to ignore the limits of their strength. He was not a learned man, but he had learned and meditated enough to feel how much there was still for him to learn. His marvellous suc-

cess in his riper years left intact the inborn modesty
of his nature. He was absolutely without pretension.
His simplicity, which by its genuineness extorted
respect and affection, was wonderfully persuasive, and
sometimes deeply pathetic and strikingly brilliant.

His natural gifts were great; he possessed a clear
and penetrating mind, but in forming his opinions on
subjects of importance, he was so careful, conscientious
and diffident, that he would always hear and probe
what opponents had to say, before he became firmly
satisfied of the justness of his own conclusions,—not
as if he had been easily controlled and led by other
men, for he had a will of his own;—but his mental
operations were slow and hesitating, and inapt to
conceive quick resolutions. He lacked self-reliance.
Nobody felt more than he the awful weight of his
responsibilities. He was not one of those bold reformers who will defy the opposition of the world, and
undertake to impose their opinions and will upon a
reluctant age. With careful consideration of the possibilities of the hour he advanced slowly, but when he
had so advanced, he planted his foot with firmness, and
no power was strong enough to force him to a back-
ward step. And every day of great responsibility
enlarged the horizon of his mind, and every day he
grasped the helm of affairs with a steadier hand.

It was to such a man that SUMNER, during the most
doubtful days at the beginning of the war, addressed his
appeals for immediate emancipation,—appeals impetuous
and impatient, as they could spring only from his ardent
and overruling convictions.

The President at first passively resisted the vehement counsel of the Senator, but he bade the counsellor welcome. It was Mr. Lincoln's constant endeavor to surround himself with the best and ablest men of the country. Not only did the first names of the Republican party appear in his Cabinet, but every able man in Congress was always invited as an adviser, whether his views agreed with those of the President or not. But Mr. Sumner he treated as a favorite counsellor, almost like a Minister of State, outside of the Cabinet.

There were statesmen around the President who were also politicians, understanding the art of management. Mr. Lincoln appreciated the value of their advice as to what was prudent and practicable. But he knew also how to discriminate. In Mr. Sumner he saw a counsellor who was no politician, but who stood before him as the true representative of the moral earnestness, of the great inspirations of their common cause. From him he heard what was right, and necessary and inevitable. By the former he was told what, in their opinion, could prudently and safely be done. Having heard them both, Abraham Lincoln counselled with himself, and formed his resolution. Thus Mr. Lincoln, while scarcely ever fully and speedily following Sumner's advice, never ceased to ask for it, for he knew its significance. And Sumner, while almost always dissatisfied with Lincoln's cautious hesitation, never grew weary in giving his advice, for he never distrusted Lincoln's fidelity. Always agreed as to the ultimate end, they almost always differed as to times and means; but, while differing, they firmly trusted, for they understood one another.

And thus their mutual respect grew into an affectionate friendship, which no clash of disagreeing opinions could break. SUMNER loved to tell his friends, after Lincoln's death,—and I heard him relate it often, never without an expression of tenderness,—how at one time those who disliked and feared his intimacy with the President, and desired to see it disrupted, thought it was irreparably broken. It was at the close of Lincoln's first administration, in 1865, when the President had proposed certain measures of reconstruction, touching the State of Louisiana.

The end of the session of Congress was near at hand, and the success of the bill depended on a vote of the Senate before the hour of adjournment on the 4th of March. Mr. Lincoln had the measure very much at heart. But SUMNER opposed it, because it did not contain sufficient guarantees for the rights of the colored people, and by a parliamentary manœuvre, simply consuming time until the adjournment came, he with two or three other Senators succeeded in defeating it. Lincoln was reported to be deeply chagrined at SUMNER's action, and the newspapers already announced that the breach between Lincoln and SUMNER was complete, and could not be healed. But those who said so did not know the men. On the night of the 6th of March, two days after Lincoln's second inauguration, the customary inauguration ball was to take place. SUMNER did not think of attending it. But towards evening he received a card from the President, which read thus: "Dear Mr. SUMNER, unless you send me word to the contrary, I shall this evening call with my carriage at your house, to take you with me to the inauguration ball. Sincerely yours, ABRAHAM LINCOLN." Mr. SUMNER, deeply touched, at once made up his mind to go to an inauguration ball for the first time. Soon the carriage arrived, the President invited SUMNER to take a seat in it with him, and SUMNER found there Mrs. Lincoln and Mr. Colfax, the Speaker of the House of Representatives. Arrived at the ball-room, the President asked Mr. SUMNER to offer his arm to Mrs. Lincoln; and the astonished spectators, who had been made to believe that the breach between Lincoln and SUMNER was irreparable, beheld the President's wife on the arm of the Senator, and the Senator, on that occasion of state, invited to take the seat of honor by the President's side. Not a word passed between them about their disagreement.

The world became convinced that such a friendship between such men could not be broken by a mere honest difference of opinion. Abraham Lincoln, a man of sincere and profound convictions himself, esteemed and honored sincere and profound convictions in others. It was thus that Abraham Lincoln composed his quarrels with his friends, and at his bedside, when he died, there was no mourner more deeply afflicted than CHARLES SUMNER.

Let me return to the year 1862. Long, incessant and arduous was SUMNER's labor for emancipation. At last the great Proclamation, which sealed the fate of slavery, came, and no man had done more to bring it forth than he.

Still, CHARLES SUMNER thought his work far from

accomplished. During the three years of war that followed, so full of vicissitudes, alarms and anxieties, he stood in the Senate and in the President's closet as the ever-watchful sentinel of freedom and equal rights. No occasion eluded his grasp to push on the destruction of slavery, not only by sweeping decrees, but in detail, by pursuing it, as with a probing-iron, into every nook and corner of its existence. It was his sleepless care that every blow struck at the Rebellion should surely and heavily tell against slavery, and that every drop of American blood that was shed should surely be consecrated to human freedom. He could not rest until assurance was made doubly sure, and I doubt whether our legislative history shows an example of equal watchfulness, fidelity and devotion to a great object. Such was the character of Mr. SUMNER's legislative activity during the war.

As the Rebellion succumbed, new problems arose. To set upon their feet again States disorganized by insurrection and civil war; to remodel a society which had been lifted out of its ancient hinges by the sudden change of its system of labor; to protect the emancipated slaves against the old pretension of absolute control on the part of their former masters; to guard society against the possible transgressions of a large multitude long held in slavery and ignorance and now suddenly set free; so to lodge political power in this inflammable state of things as to prevent violent reactions and hostile collisions; to lead social forces so discordant into orderly and fruitful co-operation, and to infuse into communities, but recently rent by the most violent passions, a new spirit of loyal attachment to a common nationality,—this was certainly one of the most perplexing tasks ever imposed upon the statesmanship of any time and any country.

But to Mr. SUMNER's mind the problem of reconstruction did not appear perplexing at all. Believing, as he always did, that the Democratic idea, as he found it defined in the Declaration of Independence, "Human rights in their utmost expansion," contained an ultimately certain solution of all difficulties, he saw the principal aim to be reached by any reconstruction policy, in the investment of the emancipated slaves with all the rights and privileges of American citizenship. The complexity of the problem, the hazardous character of the experiment, never troubled him. And as, early in the war, he had for himself laid down the theory that, by the very act of rebellion, the insurrectionary States had destroyed themselves as such, so he argued now, with assured consistency, that those States had relapsed into a territorial condition; that the National Government had to fill the void by creations of its own, and that in doing so the establishment of universal suffrage there was an unavoidable necessity. Thus he marched forward to the realization of his ideal, on the straightest line, and with the firmness of profound conviction.

In the discussions which followed, he had the advantage of a man who knows exactly what he wants, and who is imperturbably, religiously convinced that he is right. But his constitutional theory, as well as the measures he proposed, found little favor in Congress.

The public mind struggled long against the results he
had pointed out as inevitable. The whole power of
President Johnson's administration was employed to
lead the development of things in another direction.
But through all the vacillations of public opinion,
through all the perplexities in which Congress entangled
itself, the very necessity of things seemed to press
toward the ends which SUMNER and those who thought
like him had advocated from the beginning.

At last, Mr. SUMNER saw the fondest dreams of his
life realized. Slavery was forever blotted out in this
Republic by the 13th Amendment to the Constitution.
By the 14th the emancipated slaves were secured in
their rights of citizenship before the law, and the 15th
guaranteed to them the right to vote.

It was, indeed, a most astonishing, a marvellous consummation. What ten years before not even the most
sanguine would have ventured to anticipate, what only
the profound faith of the devotee could believe possible, was done. And no man had a better right than
CHARLES SUMNER to claim for himself a pre-eminent
share in that great consummation. He had, indeed,
not been the originator of most of the practical measures of legislation by which such results were reached.
He had even combated some of them as in conflict
with his theories. He did not possess the peculiar ability of constructing policies in detail, of taking account
of existing circumstances and advantage of opportunities. But he had resolutely marched ahead of public
opinion in marking the ends to be reached. Nobody
had done more to inspire and strengthen the moral spirit

of the anti-slavery cause. He stood foremost among the propelling, driving forces which pushed on the great work with undaunted courage, untiring effort, irresistible energy and religious devotion. No man's singleness of purpose, fidelity and faith surpassed his, and when by future generations the names are called which are inseparably united with the deliverance of the American Republic from slavery, no name will be called before his own.

While the championship of human rights is his first title to fame, I should be unjust to his merit, did I omit to mention the services he rendered on another field of action. When, in 1861, the secession of the Southern States left the anti-slavery party in the majority in the Senate of the United States, CHARLES SUMNER was placed as chairman at the head of the Committee on Foreign Relations. It was a high distinction, and no selection could have been more fortunate. Without belittling others, it may be said that of the many able men then and since in the Senate, Mr. SUMNER was by far the fittest for that responsible position. He had ever since his college days made international law a special and favorite study, and was perfectly familiar with its principles, the history of its development, and its literature. Nothing of importance had ever been published on that subject in any language that had escaped his attention. His knowledge of history was uncommonly extensive and accurate; all the leading international law cases, with their incidents in detail, their theories and settlements, he had at his fingers' ends; and to his last day he remained indefatigable in inquiry. Moreover, he had seen the world; he had studied the institutions and policies of foreign countries, on their own soil, aided by his personal intercourse with many of their leading statesmen, not a few of whom remained in friendly correspondence with him ever since their first acquaintance.

No public man had a higher appreciation of the position, dignity, and interests of his own country, and no one was less liable than he to be carried away or driven to hasty and ill-considered steps, by excited popular clamor. He was ever strenuous in asserting our own rights, while his sense of justice did not permit him to be regardless of the rights of other nations. His abhorrence of the barbarities of war, and his ardent love of peace, led him earnestly to seek for every international difference a peaceable solution; and where no settlement could be reached by the direct negotiations of diplomacy, the idea of arbitration was always uppermost in his mind. He desired to raise the Republic to the high office of a missionary of peace and civilization in the world. He was, therefore, not only an uncommonly well-informed, enlightened and experienced, but also an eminently conservative, cautious and safe counsellor; and the few instances in which he appeared more impulsive than prudent will, upon candid investigation, not impugn this statement. I am far from claiming for him absolute correctness of view, and infallibility of judgment in every case; but taking his whole career together, it may well be doubted, whether in the whole history of the Republic, the Senate of the United States ever possessed a chairman of the Committee on Foreign Relations who united in himself, in such completeness, the qualifications necessary and desirable for the important and delicate duties of that position. This may sound like the extravagant praise of a personal friend; but it is the sober opinion of men most competent to judge, that it does not go beyond his merits.

His qualities were soon put to the test. Early in the war one of the gallant captains in our navy arrested the British mail steamer Trent, running from one neutral port to another, on the high seas, and took from her by force Mason and Slidell, two emissaries of the Confederate Government, and their despatches. The people of the North loudly applauded the act. The Secretary of the Navy approved it. The House of Representatives commended it in resolutions. Even in the Senate a majority seemed inclined to stand by it. The British Government, in a threatening tone, demanded the instant restitution of the prisoners, and an apology. The people of the North responded with a shout of indignation at British insolence. The excitement seemed irrepressible. Those in quest of popularity saw a chance to win it easily by bellicose declamation.

But among those who felt the weight of responsibility more moderate counsels prevailed. The Government wisely resolved to surrender the prisoners, and peace with Great Britain was preserved.

It was Mr. SUMNER who threw himself into the breach against the violent drift of public opinion. In a speech in the Senate, no less remarkable for patriotic spirit than legal learning and ingenious and irresistible argument, he justified the surrender of the prisoners, not on the ground that during our struggle with the Rebellion we were not in a condition to go to war with Great Britain, but on the higher ground that the surrender, demanded by Great Britain in violation of her own traditional pretensions as to the rights of belligerents, was in perfect accord with American precedent, and the advanced principles of our Government concerning the rights of neutrals, and that this very act, therefore, would for all time constitute an additional and most conspicuous precedent, to aid in the establishment of more humane rules for the protection of the rights of neutrals and the mitigation of the injustice and barbarity attending maritime war.

The success of this argument was complete. It turned the tide of public opinion. It convinced the American people that this was not an act of pusillanimity, but of justice; not a humiliation of the Republic, but a noble vindication of her time-honored principles, and a service rendered to the cause of progress.

Other complications followed. The interference of European powers in Mexico came. Excited demands for intervention on our part were made in the Senate, and Mr. SUMNER, trusting that the victory of the Union over the Rebellion would bring on the deliverance of Mexico in its train, with signal moderation and tact prevented the agitation of so dangerous a policy. It is needless to mention the many subsequent instances in which his wisdom and skill rendered the Republic similar service.

Only one of his acts provoked comment in foreign countries calculated to impair the high esteem in which his name was universally held there. It was his speech on the Alabama case, preceding the rejection by the Senate of the Clarendon-Johnson treaty. He was accused of having yielded to a vulgar impulse of demagogism in flattering and exciting, by unfair statements and extravagant demands, the grudge the American people might bear to England. No accusation could possibly be more unjust, and I know whereof I speak. Mr. SUMNER loved England—had loved her as long as he lived—from a feeling of consanguinity, for the treasures of literature she had given to the world, for the services she had rendered to human freedom, for the blows she had struck at slavery, for the sturdy work she had done for the cause of progress and civilization, for the many dear friends he had among her citizens. Such was his impulse, and no man was more incapable of pandering to a vulgar prejudice.

I will not deny that as to our differences with Great Britain he was not entirely free from personal feeling. That the England he loved so well,—the England of Clarkson and Wilberforce, of Cobden and Bright; the England to whom he had looked as the champion of the anti-slavery cause in the world,—should make such hot haste to recognize, nay, as he termed it, to set up, on the seas, as a belligerent, that Rebellion, whose avowed object it was to found an empire of slavery, and to aid that Rebellion by every means short of open war against the Union,—that was a shock to his feelings which he felt like a betrayal of friendship. And

yet while that feeling appeared in the warmth of his
language, it did not dictate his policy. I will not discuss here the correctness of his opinions as to what he
styled the precipitate and unjustifiable recognition of
Southern belligerency, or his theory of consequential
damages. What he desired to accomplish was, not to
extort from England a large sum of money, but to put
our grievance in the strongest light; to convince England of the great wrong she had inflicted upon us, and
thus to prepare a composition, which, consisting more
in the settlement of great principles and rules of international law to govern the future intercourse of nations,
than in the payment of large damages, would remove
all questions of difference, and serve to restore and confirm a friendship which ought never to have been interrupted.

When, finally, the Treaty of Washington was nego-
tiated by the Joint High Commission, Mr. SUMNER,
although thinking that more might have been accomplished, did not only not oppose that treaty, but ac-
tively aided in securing for it the consent of the Senate.
Nothing would have been more painful to him than a
continuance of unfriendly relations with Great Britain.
Had there been danger of war, no man's voice would
have pleaded with more fervor to avert such a calamity. He gave ample proof that he did not desire any
personal opinions to stand in the way of a settlement,
and if that settlement, which he willingly supported,
did not in every respect satisfy him, it was because he
desired to put the future relations of the two countries
upon a still safer and more enduring basis.

No statesman ever took part in the direction of our foreign affairs who so completely identified himself with the most advanced, humane and progressive principles. Ever jealous of the honor of his country, he sought to elevate that honor by a policy scrupulously just to the strong, and generous to the weak. A profound lover of peace, he faithfully advocated arbitration as a substitute for war. The barbarities of war he constantly labored to mitigate. In the hottest days of our civil conflict he protested against the issue of letters of marque and reprisal; he never lost an opportunity to condemn privateering as a barbarous practice, and he even went so far as to designate the system of prize-money as inconsistent with our enlightened civilization. In some respects, his principles were in advance of our time; but surely the day will come when this Republic, marching in the front of progress, will adopt them as her own, and remember their champion with pride.

I now approach the last period of his life, which brought to him new and bitter struggles.

The work of reconstruction completed, he felt that three objects still demanded new efforts. One was that the colored race should be protected by national legislation against degrading discrimination, in the enjoyment of facilities of education, travel and pleasure, such as stand under the control of law; and this object he embodied in his Civil Rights Bill, of which he was the mover and especial champion. The second was, that generous reconciliation should wipe out the lingering animosities of past conflicts and reunite in new bonds of brotherhood all those who had been divided. And the third was, that the government should be restored to the purity and high tone of its earlier days, and that from its new birth the Republic should issue with a new lustre of moral greatness, to lead its children to a higher perfection of manhood, and to be a shining example and beacon-light to all the nations of the earth.

This accomplished, he often said to his friends he would be content to lie down and die; but death overtook him before he was thus content, and before death came he was destined to taste more of the bitterness of life.

His Civil Rights Bill he pressed with unflagging perseverance, against an opposition which stood upon the ground that the objects his measure contemplated, belonged, under the Constitution, to the jurisdiction of the States; that the colored people, armed with the ballot, possessed the necessary means to provide for their own security, and that the progressive development of public sentiment would afford to them greater protection than could be given by national legislation of questionable constitutionality.

The pursuit of the other objects brought upon him experiences of a painful nature. I have to speak of his disagreement with the administration of President Grant and with his party. Nothing could be farther from my desire than to re-open, on a solemn occasion like this, those bitter conflicts which are still so fresh in our minds, and to assail any living man in the name of the dead. Were it my purpose to attack, I should do so in my own name and choose the place where I can be answered,—not this. But I have a duty to perform; it is to set forth in the light of truth the motives of the dead before the living. I knew CHARLES SUMNER'S motives well. We stood together shoulder to shoulder in many a hard contest. We were friends, and between us passed those confidences which only intimate friendship knows. Therefore I can truly say that I knew his motives well.

The civil war had greatly changed the country, and left many problems behind it, requiring again that building, organizing, constructive kind of statesmanship which I described as presiding over the Republic in its earlier history. For a solution of many of those problems Mr. SUMNER'S mind was little fitted, and he naturally turned to those which appealed to his moral nature. No great civil war has ever passed over any country, especially a republic, without producing widespread and dangerous demoralization and corruption, not only in the government, but among the people. In such times the sordid instincts of human nature develop themselves to unusual recklessness under the guise of patriotism. The ascendancy of no political party in a republic has ever been long maintained without tempting many of its members to avail themselves for their selfish advantage of the opportunities of power and party protection, and without attracting a horde of camp followers, professing principle, but meaning spoil. It has always been so, and the American Republic has not escaped the experience.

Neither Mr. SUMNER nor many others could in our

circumstances close their eyes to this fact. He recognized the danger early, and already, in 1864, he introduced in the Senate a bill for the reform of the civil
service, crude in its detail, but embodying correct
principles. Thus he may be said to have been the
earliest pioneer of the Civil Service Reform movement.

The evil grew under President Johnson's administration, and ever since it has been cropping out, not only
drawn to light by the efforts of the opposition, but
voluntarily and involuntarily, by members of the ruling
party itself. There were in it many men who confessed
to themselves the urgent necessity of meeting the growing danger.

Mr. SUMNER could not be silent. He cherished in
his mind a high ideal of what this Republic and its
government should be: a government composed of the
best and wisest of the land; animated by none but the
highest and most patriotic aspirations; yielding to no
selfish impulse; noble in its tone and character; setting
its face sternly against all wrong and injustice; presenting in its whole being to the American people a
shining example of purity and lofty public spirit. Mr.
SUMNER was proud of his country; there was no
prouder American in the land. He felt in himself the
whole dignity of the Republic. And when he saw anything that lowered the dignity of the Republic and the
character of its government, he felt it as he would have
felt a personal offence. He criticised it, he denounced
it, he remonstrated against it, for he could not do
otherwise. He did so, frequently and without hesitation
and reserve, when Mr. Lincoln was President. He

continued to do so ever since, the more loudly, the more difficult it was to make himself heard.   It was his nature; he felt it to be his right as a citizen; he esteemed it his duty as a Senator.

That, and no other, was the motive which impelled him.   The rupture with the administration was brought on by his opposition to the Santo Domingo Treaty. In the reasons upon which that opposition was based, I know that personal feeling had no share.   They were patriotic reasons, publicly and candidly expressed, and it seems they were appreciated by a very large portion of the American people.   It has been said that he provoked the resentment of the President by first promising to support that treaty and then opposing it, thus rendering himself guilty of an act of duplicity. He has publicly denied the justice of the charge and stated the facts as they stood in his memory.   I am willing to make the fullest allowance for the possibility of a misapprehension of words.   But I affirm, also, that no living man who knew Mr. SUMNER well, will hesitate a moment to pronounce the charge of duplicity as founded on the most radical of misapprehensions. An act of duplicity on his part was simply a moral impossibility.   It was absolutely foreign to his nature. Whatever may have been the defects of his character, he never knowingly deceived a human being.   There was in him not the faintest shadow of dissimulation, disguise or trickery.   Not one of his words ever had the purpose of a double meaning, not one of his acts a hidden aim.   His likes and dislikes, his approval and disapproval, as soon as they were clear to his own consciousness, appeared before the world in the open light of noonday. His frankness was so unbounded, his candor so entire, his ingenuousness so childlike, that he lacked even the discretion of ordinary prudence. He was almost incapable of moderating his feelings, of toning down his meaning in the expression. When he might have gained a point by indirection, he would not have done so, because he could not. He was one of those who, when they attack, attack always in front and in broad daylight. The night surprise and the flank march were absolutely foreign to his tactics, because they were incompatible with his nature. I have known many men in my life, but never one who was less capable of a perfidious act or an artful profession.

Call him a vain, an impracticable, an imperious man if you will, but American history does not mention the name of one, of whom with greater justice it can be said that he was a true man.

The same candor and purity of motives which prompted and characterized his opposition to the Santo Domingo scheme, prompted and characterized the attacks upon the administration which followed. The charges he made, and the arguments with which he supported them, I feel not called upon to enumerate. Whether and how far they were correct or erroneous, just or unjust, important or unimportant, the judgment of history will determine. May that judgment be just and fair to us all. But this I can affirm to-day, for I know it: CHARLES SUMNER never made a charge which he did not himself firmly, religiously believe to be true. Neither did he condemn those he attacked for anything he did not firmly, religiously believe to be wrong. And while attacking those in power for what he considered wrong, he was always ready to support them in all he considered right. After all he has said of the President, he would to-day, if he lived, conscientiously, cordially, joyously aid in sustaining the President's recent veto on an act of financial legislation which threatened to inflict a deep injury on the character, as well as the true interests of the American people.

But at the time of which I speak, all he said was so deeply grounded in his feeling and conscience, that it was for him difficult to understand how others could form different conclusions. When, shortly before the National Republican Convention of 1872, he had delivered in the Senate that fierce philippic for which he has been censured so much, he turned to me with the question, whether I did not think that the statements and arguments he had produced would certainly exercise a decisive influence on the action of that convention. I replied that I thought it would not. He was greatly astonished,—not as if he indulged in the delusion that his personal word would have such authoritative weight, but it seemed impossible to him that opinions which in him had risen to the full strength of overruling conviction, that a feeling of duty which in him had grown so solemn and irresistible as to inspire him to any risk and sacrifice, ever so painful, should fall powerless at the feet of a party which so long had followed inspirations kindred to his own. Such was the ingenuousness

31

of his nature ; such his faith in the rectitude of his own
cause. The result of his effort is a matter of history.
After the Philadelphia Convention, and not until then,
he resolved to oppose his party, and to join a movement
which was doomed to defeat. He obeyed his sense of
right and duty at a terrible sacrifice.

He had been one of the great chiefs of his party, by
many regarded as the greatest. He had stood in the
Senate as a mighty monument of the struggles and victories of the anti-slavery cause. He had been a martyr
of his earnestness. By all Republicans he had been
looked up to with respect, by many with veneration.
He had been the idol of the people of his State. All
this was suddenly changed. Already, at the time of
his opposition to the Santo Domingo scheme, he had
been deprived of his place at the head of the Senate
Committee on Foreign Relations, which he had held so
long, and with so much honor to the Republic and to
himself. But few know how sharp a pang it gave to
his heart, this removal, which he felt as the wanton
degradation of a faithful servant who was conscious of
only doing his duty.

But, when he had pronounced against the candidates
of his party, worse experiences were for him in store.
Journals which for years had been full of his praise now
assailed him with remorseless ridicule and vituperation,
questioning even his past services and calling him a
traitor. Men who had been proud of his acquaintance
turned away their heads when they met him in the
street. Former flatterers eagerly covered his name with
slander. Many of those who had been his associates

in the struggle for freedom sullenly withdrew from him their friendship. Even some men of the colored race, for whose elevation he had labored with a fidelity and devotion equalled by few and surpassed by none, joined in the chorus of denunciation. Oh, how keenly he felt it! And, as if the cruel malice of ingratitude and the unsparing persecution of infuriated partisanship had not been enough, another enemy came upon him, threatening his very life. It was a new attack of that disease which, for many years, from time to time, had prostrated him with the acutest suffering, and which shortly should lay him low. It admonished him that every word he spoke might be his last. He found himself forced to leave the field of a contest in which not only his principles of right, but even his good name, earned by so many years of faithful effort, was at stake. He possessed no longer the elastic spirit of youth, and the prospect of new struggles had ceased to charm him. His hair had grown gray with years, and he had reached that age when a statesman begins to love the thought of reposing his head upon the pillow of assured public esteem. Even the sweet comfort of that sanctuary was denied him, in which the voice of wife and child would have said: Rest here, for whatever the world may say, we know that you are good and faithful and noble. Only the friends of his youth, who knew him best, surrounded him with never-flagging confidence and love, and those of his companions-in-arms, who knew him also, and who were true to him as they were true to their common cause. Thus he stood in the presidential campaign of 1872.

It is at such a moment of bitter ordeal that an honest public man feels the impulse of retiring within himself; to examine with scrupulous care the quality of his own motives; anxiously to inquire whether he is really right in his opinions and objects when so many old friends say that he is wrong; and then, after such a review at the hand of conscience and duty, to form anew his conclusions without bias, and to proclaim them without fear. This he did.

He had desired, and as he wrote, "he had confidently hoped, on returning home from Washington, to meet his fellow-citizens in Faneuil Hall, that venerable forum, and to speak once more on great questions involving the welfare of the country, but recurring symptoms of a painful character warned him against such an attempt." The speech he had intended to pronounce, but could not, he left in a written form for publication, and went to Europe, seeking rest, uncertain whether he would ever return alive. In it he reiterated all the reasons which had forced him to oppose the administration and the candidates of his party. They were unchanged. Then followed an earnest and pathetic plea for universal peace and reconciliation. He showed how necessary the revival of fraternal feeling was, not only for the prosperity and physical well-being, but for the moral elevation of the American people and for the safety and greatness of the Republic. He gave words to his profound sympathy with the Southern States in their misfortunes. Indignantly he declared, that "second only to the wide-spread devastations of war were the robberies to which those States had been subjected,

under an administration calling itself Republican, and
with local governments deriving their animating impulse
from the party in power; and that the people in these
communities would have been less than men, if, sinking
under the intolerable burden, they did not turn for
help to a new party, promising honesty and reform."

He recalled the reiterated expression he had given to
his sentiments, ever since the breaking out of the war;
and closed the recital with these words: "Such is the
simple and harmonious record, showing how from the
beginning I was devoted to peace, how constantly I
longed for reconciliation; how, with every measure of
equal rights, this longing found utterance; how it
became an essential part of my life; how I discarded
all idea of vengeance and punishment; how reconstruction was, to my mind, a transition period, and how
earnestly I looked forward to the day when, after the
recognition of equal rights, the Republic should again
be one in reality as in name. If there are any who
ever maintained a policy of hate, I never was so
minded; and now in protesting against any such policy,
I act only in obedience to the irresistible promptings of
my soul."

And well might he speak thus. Let the people of
the South hear what I say. They were wont to see in
him only the implacable assailant of that peculiar institution, which was so closely interwoven with all their
traditions and habits of life, that they regarded it as
the very basis of their social and moral existence, as
the source of their prosperity and greatness; the unsparing enemy of the Rebellion, whose success was to realize

the fondest dreams of their ambition; the never-resting advocate of the grant of suffrage to the colored people, which they thought to be designed for their own degradation. Thus they had persuaded themselves that CHARLES SUMNER was to them a relentless foe.

They did not know, as others knew, that he whom they cursed as their persecutor had a heart beating warmly and tenderly for all the human kind; that the efforts of his life were unceasingly devoted to those whom he thought most in need of aid; that in the slave he saw only the human soul, with its eternal title to the same right and dignity which he himself enjoyed; that he assailed the slavemaster only as the oppressor who denied that right; and that the former oppressor ceasing to be such, and being oppressed himself, could surely count upon the fulness of his active sympathy freely given in the spirit of equal justice; that it was the religion of his life to protect the weak and oppressed against the strong, no matter who were the weak and oppressed, no matter who were the strong. They knew not, that while fiercely combating a wrong, there was not in his heart a spark of hatred even for the wrong-doer who hated him. They knew not how well he deserved the high homage involuntarily paid to him by a cartoon during the late presidential campaign —a cartoon, designed to be malicious, which represented CHARLES SUMNER strewing flowers on the grave of Preston Brooks. They foresaw not, that to welcome them back to the full brotherhood of the American people, he would expose himself to a blow, wounding him as cruelly as that which years ago levelled him to the ground in the Senate Chamber. And this new blow he received for them. The people of the South ignored this long. Now that he is gone, let them never forget it.

From Europe Mr. SUMNER returned late in the fall of 1872, much strengthened, but far from being well. At the opening of the session he reintroduced two measures which, as he thought, should complete the record of his political life. One was his Civil Rights Bill, which had failed in the last Congress, and the other, a resolution providing that the names of the battles won over fellow-citizens in the war of the Rebellion, should be removed from the regimental colors of the army, and from the army register. It was in substance only a repetition of a resolution which he had introduced ten years before, in 1862, during the war, when the first names of victories were put on American battle-flags. This resolution called forth a new storm against him. It was denounced as an insult to the heroic soldiers of the Union, and a degradation of their victories and well-earned laurels. It was condemned as an unpatriotic act.

CHARLES SUMNER insult the soldiers who had spilled their blood in a war for human rights! CHARLES SUMNER degrade victories and depreciate laurels won for the cause of universal freedom! How strange an imputation!

Let the dead man have a hearing. This was his thought: No civilized nation, from the republics of antiquity down to our days, ever thought it wise or patriotic to preserve in conspicuous and durable form

the mementos of victories won over fellow-citizens in
civil war. Why not? Because every citizen should
feel himself with all others as the child of a common
country, and not as a defeated foe. All civilized governments of our days have instinctively followed the
same dictate of wisdom and patriotism. The Irishman,
when fighting for old England at Waterloo, was not to
behold on the red cross floating above him the name
of the Boyne. The Scotch Highlander, when standing
in the trenches of Sebastopol, was not by the colors of
his regiment to be reminded of Culloden. No French
soldier at Austerlitz or Solferino had to read upon the
tricolor any reminiscence of the Vendée. No Hunga-
rian at Sadowa was taunted by any Austrian banner
with the surrender of Villagos. No German regiment,
from Saxony or Hanover, charging under the iron hail
of Gravelotte, was made to remember by words written
on a Prussian standard that the black eagle had conquered them at Koniggratz and Langensalza. Should
the son of South Carolina, when at some future day
defending the Republic against some foreign foe, be
reminded by an inscription on the colors floating over
him, that under this flag the gun was fired that killed
his father at Gettysburg? Should this great and
enlightened Republic, proud of standing in the front
of human progress, be less wise, less large-hearted,
than the ancients were two thousand years ago, and
the kingly governments of Europe are to-day? Let the
battle-flags of the brave volunteers, which they brought
home from the war with the glorious record of their
victories, be preserved intact as a proud ornament of

our State-houses and armories. But let the colors of
the army, under which the sons of all the States are
to meet and mingle in common patriotism, speak of
nothing but union,—not a union of conquerors and
conquered, but a union which is the mother of all,
equally tender to all, knowing of nothing but equality,
peace and love among her children. Do you want conspicuous mementos of your victories? They are written
upon the dusky brow of every freeman who was once a
slave; they are written on the gate-posts of a restored
Union; and the most glorious of all will be written on
the faces of a contented people, reunited in common
national pride.

Such were the sentiments which inspired that resolution. Such were the sentiments which called forth a
storm of obloquy. Such were the sentiments for which
the Legislature of Massachusetts passed a solemn resolution of censure upon CHARLES SUMNER,—Massachusetts, his own Massachusetts, whom he loved so ardently
with a filial love,—of whom he was so proud, who had
honored him so much in days gone by, and whom he
had so long and so faithfully labored to serve and to
honor! Oh, those were evil days, that winter; days
sad and dark, when he sat there in his lonesome chamber, unable to leave it, the world moving around him,
and in it so much that was hostile,—and he prostrated
by the tormenting disease, which had returned with
fresh violence,—unable to defend himself,—and with
this bitter arrow in his heart! Why was not that resolution held up to scorn and vituperation as an insult
to the brave, and an unpatriotic act—why was he not

attacked and condemned for it when he first offered it,
ten years before, and when he was in the fulness of
manhood and power? If not then, why now? Why
now? I shall never forget the melancholy hours I sat
with him, seeking to lift him up with cheering words,
and he,—his frame for hours racked with excruciating
pain, and then exhausted with suffering,—gloomily
brooding over the thought that he might die so!

How thankful I am, how thankful every human soul
in Massachusetts, how thankful every American must
be, that he did not die then!—and, indeed, more than
once, death seemed to be knocking at his door. How
thankful that he was spared to see the day, when the
people by striking developments were convinced that
those who had acted as he did, had after all not been
impelled by mere whims of vanity, or reckless ambition,
or sinister designs, but had good and patriotic reasons
for what they did;—when the heart of Massachusetts
came back to him full of the old love and confidence,
assuring him that he would again be her chosen son
for her representative seat in the House of States;—
when the lawgivers of the old Commonwealth, obeying
an irresistible impulse of justice, wiped away from the
records of the Legislature, and from the fair name of
the State, that resolution of censure which had stung
him so deeply,—and when returning vigor lifted him
up, and a new sunburst of hope illumined his life!
How thankful we all are that he lived that one year
longer!

And yet, have you thought of it, if he had died in
those dark days, when so many clouds hung over him,

—would not then the much vilified man have been the same CHARLES SUMNER, whose death but one year later afflicted millions of hearts with a pang of bereavement, whose praise is now on every lip for the purity of his life, for his fidelity to great principles, and for the loftiness of his patriotism? Was he not a year ago the same, the same in purpose, the same in principle, the same in character? What had he done then that so many who praise him to-day should have then disowned him? See what he had done. He had simply been true to his convictions of duty. He had approved and urged what he thought right, he had attacked and opposed what he thought wrong. To his convictions of duty he had sacrificed political associations most dear to him, the security of his position of which he was proud. For his convictions of duty he had stood up against those more powerful than he; he had exposed himself to reproach, obloquy and persecution. Had he not done so, he would not have been the man you praise to-day; and yet for doing so he was cried down but yesterday. He had lived up to the great word he spoke when he entered the Senate: "The slave of principle, I call no party master." That declaration was greeted with applause, and when, true to his word, he refused to call a party master, the act was covered with reproach.

The spirit impelling him to do so was the same conscience which urged him to break away from the powerful party which controlled his State in the days of Daniel Webster, and to join a feeble minority, which stood up for freedom; to throw away the favor and defy the power of the wealthy and refined, in order to plead the cause of the down-trodden and degraded; to stand up against the slave-power in Congress with a courage never surpassed; to attack the prejudice of birth and religion, and to plead fearlessly for the rights of the foreign-born citizen at a time when the know-nothing movement was controlling his State and might have defeated his own re-election to the Senate; to advocate emancipation when others trembled with fear; to march ahead of his followers, when they were afraid to follow; to rise up alone for what he thought right, when others would not rise with him. It was that brave spirit which does everything, defies everything, risks everything, sacrifices everything, comfort, society, party, popular support, station of honor, prospects, for sense of right and conviction of duty. That is it for which you honored him long, for which you reproached him yesterday, and for which you honor him again to-day, and will honor him forever.

Ah, what a lesson is this for the American people,— a lesson learned so often, and, alas! forgotten almost as often as it is learned! Is it well to discourage, to proscribe in your public men that independent spirit which will boldly assert a conscientious sense of duty, even against the behests of power or party? Is it well to teach them that they must serve the command and interest of party, even at the price of conscience, or they must be crushed under its heel, whatever their past service, whatever their ability, whatever their character may be? Is it well to make them believe that he who dares to be himself must be hunted as a political outlaw, who will find justice only when he is dead? That would have been the sad moral of his death, had CHARLES SUMNER died a year ago.

Let the American people never forget that it has always been the independent spirit, the all-defying sense of duty which broke the way for every great progressive movement since mankind has a history; which gave the American Colonies their sovereignty and made this great Republic; which defied the power of slavery, and made this a Republic of freemen; and which—who knows—may again be needed some day to defy the power of ignorance, to arrest the inroads of corruption, or to break the subtle tyranny of organization in order to preserve this as a Republic! And therefore let no man understand me as offering what I have said about Mr. SUMNER's course, during the last period of his life, as an apology for what he did. He was right before his own conscience, and needs no apology. Woe to the Republic when it looks in vain for the men who seek the truth without prejudice and speak the truth without fear, as they understand it, no matter whether the world be willing to listen or not! Alas for the generation that would put such men into their graves with the poor boon of an apology for what was in them noblest and best! Who will not agree that, had power or partisan spirit, which persecuted him because he followed higher aims than party interest, ever succeeded in subjugating and moulding him after its fashion, against his conscience, against his conviction of duty, against his sense of right, he would have sunk into his grave a miserable ruin of his great self, wrecked in his moral nature, deserving only a tear of pity? For he was great and useful only because he dared to be himself all the days of his life; and for this you have, when he died, put the laurel upon his brow!

From the coffin which hides his body, CHARLES SUM-NER now rises up before our eyes an historic character. Let us look at him once more. His life lies before us like an open book which contains no double meanings, no crooked passages, no mysteries, no concealments. It is clear as crystal.

Even his warmest friend will not see in it the model of perfect statesmanship; not that eagle glance which, from a lofty eminence, at one sweep surveys the whole field on which by labor, thought, strife, accommodation, impulse, restraint, slow and rapid movement, the destinies of a nation are worked out,—and which, while surveying the whole, yet observes and penetrates the fitness and working of every detail of the great machinery;—not that ever calm and steady and self-controlling good sense, which judges existing things just as they are, and existing forces just as to what they can accomplish, and while instructing, conciliating, persuading and moulding those forces, and guiding them on toward an ideal end, correctly estimates comparative good and comparative evil, and impels or restrains as that estimate may command. That is the true genius of statesmanship, fitting all times, all circumstances, and all great objects to be reached by political action.

Mr. SUMNER's natural abilities were not of the very first order; but they were supplemented by acquired

abilities of most remarkable power. His mind was not
apt to invent and create by inspiration; it produced by
study and work. Neither had his mind superior constructive capacity. When he desired to originate a
measure of legislation, he scarcely ever elaborated its
practical detail; he usually threw his idea into the form
of a resolution, or a bill giving in the main his purpose
only. and then he advanced to the discussion of the
principles involved. It was difficult for him to look at
a question or problem from more than one point of view,
and to comprehend its different bearings, its complex
relations with other questions or problems; and to that
one point of view he was apt to subject all other considerations. He not only thought, but he did not hesitate to say that all construction of the Constitution must
be subservient to the supreme duty of giving the amplest
protection to the natural rights of man by direct national
legislation. He was not free from that dangerous tendency to forget the limits which bound the legitimate
range of legislative and governmental action. On
economical questions his views were enlightened and
thoroughly consistent. He had studied such subjects
more than is commonly supposed. It was one of his
last regrets that his health did not permit him to make
a speech in favor of an early resumption of specie pay-
ments. On matters of international law and foreign
affairs he was the recognized authority of the Senate.

But some of his very shortcomings served to increase
that peculiar power which he exerted in his time. His
public life was thrown into a period of a revolutionary
character, when one great end was the self-imposed

subject of a universal struggle, a struggle which was not made, not manufactured by the design of men, but had grown from the natural conflict of existing things, and grew irresistibly on and on, until it enveloped all the thought of the nation; and that one great end appealing more than to the practical sense, to the moral impulses of men, making of them the fighting force. There Mr. SUMNER found his place and there he grew great, for that moral impulse was stronger in him than in most of the world around him; and it was in him not a mere crude, untutored force of nature, but educated and elevated by thought and study; and it found in his brain and heart an armory of strong weapons given to but few; vast information, legal learning, industry, eloquence, undaunted courage, an independent and iron will, profound convictions, unbounded devotion and sublime faith. It found there also a keen and just instinct as to the objects which must be reached and the forces which must be set in motion and driven on to reach them. Thus keeping the end steadily, obstinately, intensely in view, he marched ahead of his followers, never disturbed by their anxieties and fears, showing them that what was necessary was possible, and forcing them to follow him,—a great moving power, such as the struggle required.

Nor can it be said that this impatient, irrepressible propulsion was against all prudence and sound judgment, for it must not be forgotten, that, when Mr. SUMNER stepped into the front, the policy of compromise was exhausted; the time of composition and expedient was past. Things had gone so far, that the idea of reaching the end, which ultimately must be reached, by mutual concession and a gradual and peaceable process, was utterly hopeless. The conflicting forces could not be reconciled; the final struggle was indeed irrepressible and inevitable, and all that could then be done was to gather up all the existing forces for one supreme effort, and to take care that the final struggle should bring forth the necessary results.

Thus the instinct and the obstinate, concentrated, irresistible moving power which Mr. SUMNER possessed was an essential part of the true statesmanship of the revolutionary period. Had he lived before or after this great period, in quiet, ordinary times, he would perhaps never have gone into public life, or never risen in it to conspicuous significance. But all he was by nature, by acquirement, by ability, by moral impulse, made him one of the heroes of that great struggle against slavery, and in some respects the first. And then when the victory was won, the same moral nature, the same sense of justice, the same enlightened mind, impelled him to plead the cause of peace, reconciliation and brotherhood, through equal rights and even justice, thus completing the fulness of his ideal. On the pedestal of his time he stands one of the greatest of Americans.

What a peculiar power of fascination there was in him as a public man! It acted much through his eloquence, but not through his eloquence alone. His speech was not a graceful flow of melodious periods, now drawing on the listener with the persuasive tone of confidential conversation, then carrying him along

33

with a more rapid rush of thought and language, and
at last lifting him up with the peals of reason in passion. His arguments marched forth at once in grave
and stately array; his sentences like rows of massive
doric columns, unrelieved by pleasing variety, severe
and imposing. His orations, especially those pronounced in the Senate before the war, contain many
passages of grandest beauty. There was nothing kindly
persuasive in his utterance; his reasoning appeared in
the form of consecutive assertion, not seldom strictly
logical and irresistibly strong. His mighty appeals were
always addressed to the noblest instincts of human
nature. His speech was never enlivened by anything
like wit or humor. They were foreign to his nature.
He has never been guilty of a flash of irony or sar-
casm. His weapon was not the foil, but the battle-axe.

He has often been accused of being uncharitable to
opponents in debate, and of wounding their feelings
with uncalled for harshness of language. He was guilty
of that, but no man was less conscious of the stinging
force of his language than he. He was often sorry for
the effect his thrusts had produced, but being always so
firmly and honestly persuaded of the correctness of his
own opinions, that he could scarcely ever appreciate
the position of an opponent, he fell into the same fault
again. Not seldom he appeared haughty in his assump-
tions of authority; but it was the imperiousness of profound conviction, which, while sometimes exasperating
his hearers, yet scarcely ever failed to exercise over
them a certain sway. His fancy was not fertile, his
figures mostly labored and stiff. In his later years his

vast learning began to become an encumbering burden
to his eloquence. The mass of quoted sayings and historical illustrations, not seldom accumulated beyond
measure and grotesquely grouped, sometimes threatened
to suffocate the original thought and to oppress the
hearer. But even then his words scarcely ever failed
to chain the attention of the audience, and I have more
than once seen the Senate attentively listening while he
read from printed slips the most elaborate disquisition,
which, if attempted by any one of his colleagues, would
at once have emptied the floor and galleries. But there
were always moments recalling to our mind the days of
his freshest vigor, when he stood in the midst of the
great struggle, lifting up the youth of the country with
heart-stirring appeals, and with the lion-like thunder of
his voice shaking the Senate chamber.

Still there was another source from which that fascination sprung. Behind all he said and did there stood
a grand manhood, which never failed to make itself felt.
What a figure he was, with his tall and stalwart frame,
his manly face, topped with his shaggy locks, his noble
bearing, the finest type of American Senatorship, the
tallest oak of the forest! And how small they appeared
by his side, the common run of politicians, who spend
their days with the laying of pipe, and the setting up
of pins, and the pulling of wires; who barter an office
to secure this vote, and procure a contract to get that;
who stand always with their ears to the wind to hear
how the administration sneezes, and what their constituents whisper, in mortal trepidation lest they fail in being
all things to everybody! How he towered above them,

he whose aims were always the highest and noblest; whose very presence made you forget the vulgarities of political life; who dared to differ with any man ever so powerful, any multitude ever so numerous; who regarded party as nothing but a means for great ends, and for those ends defied its power; to whom the arts of demagogism were so contemptible, that he would rather have sunk into obscurity and oblivion than descend to them; to whom the dignity of his office was so sacred that he would not even ask for it for fear of darkening its lustre!

Honor to the people of Massachusetts who, for twenty-three years, kept in the Senate, and would have kept him there ever so long, had he lived, a man who never, even to them, conceded a single iota of his convictions in order to remain there! And what a life was his! A life so wholly devoted to what was good and pure! There he stood in the midst of the grasping materialism of our times, around him the eager chase for the almighty dollar, no thought of opportunity ever entering the smallest corner of his mind, and disturbing his high endeavors; with a virtue which the possession of power could not even tempt, much less debauch; from whose presence the very thought of corruption instinctively shrunk back; a life so spotless, an integrity so intact, a character so high, that the most daring eagerness of calumny, the most wanton audacity of insinuation, standing on tiptoe, could not touch the soles of his shoes!

They say that he indulged in overweening self-appreciation. Ay, he did have a magnificent pride, a lofty self-esteem. Why should he not? Let wretches despise themselves, for they have good reason to do so; not he. But in his self-esteem there was nothing small and mean; no man lived to whose very nature envy and petty jealousy were more foreign. Conscious of his own merit, he never depreciated the merit of others; nay, he not only recognized it, but he expressed that recognition with that cordial spontaneity which can only flow from a sincere and generous heart. His pride of self was like his pride of country. He was the proudest American; he was the proudest New Englander; and yet he was the most cosmopolitan American I have ever seen. There was in him not the faintest shadow of that narrow prejudice which looks askance at what has grown in foreign lands. His generous heart and his enlightened mind were too generous and too enlightened not to give the fullest measure of appreciation to all that was good and worthy, from whatever quarter of the globe it came.

And now his home! There are those around me who have breathed the air of his house in Washington, —that atmosphere of refinement, taste, scholarship, art, friendship, and warm-hearted hospitality; who have seen those rooms covered and filled with his pictures, his engravings, his statues, his bronzes, his books and rare manuscripts—the collections of a lifetime—the image of the richness of his mind, the comfort and consolation of his solitude. They have beheld his childlike smile of satisfaction when he unlocked the most precious of his treasures and told their stories.

They remember the conversations at his hospitable

board, genially inspired and directed by him, on art, and books, and inventions, and great times, and great men,—when suddenly sometimes, by accident, a new mine of curious knowledge disclosed itself in him, which his friends had never known he possessed; or when a sunburst of the affectionate gentleness of his soul warmed all hearts around him. They remember his craving for friendship, as it spoke through the far outstretched hand when you arrived, and the glad exclamation: "I am so happy you came,"—and the beseeching, almost despondent tone when you departed: "Do not leave me yet; do stay awhile longer, I want so much to speak with you!" It is all gone now. He could not stay himself, and he has left his friends behind, feeling more deeply than ever that no man could know him well but to love him.

Now we have laid him into his grave, in the motherly soil of Massachusetts, which was so dear to him. He is at rest now, the stalwart, brave old champion, whose face and bearing were so austere, and whose heart was so full of tenderness; who began his career with a pathetic plea for universal peace and charity, and whose whole life was an arduous, incessant, never-resting struggle, which left him all covered with scars. And we can do nothing for him but commemorate his lofty ideals of Liberty, and Equality, and Justice, and Reconciliation, and Purity, and the earnestness and courage and touching fidelity with which he fought for them; so genuine in his sincerity, so single-minded in his zeal, so heroic in his devotion!

Oh, that we could but for one short hour call him

up from his coffin, to let him see with the same eyes which saw so much hostility, that those who stood against him in the struggles of his life are his enemies no longer! That we could show him the fruit of the conflicts and sufferings of his last three years, and that he had not struggled and suffered in vain! We would bring before him, not only those who from offended partisan zeal assailed him, and who now with sorrowful hearts praise the purity of his patriotism; but we would bring to him that man of the South, a slaveholder and a leader of secession in his time, the echo of whose words spoken in the name of the South in the halls of the National Capitol we heard but yesterday; words of respect, of gratitude, of tenderness. That man of the South should then do what he deplored not to have done while he lived,—he should lay his hand upon the shoulders of the old friend of the human kind and say to him: "Is it you whom I hated, and who, as I thought, hated me? I have learned now the greatness and magnanimity of your soul, and here I offer you my hand and heart."

Could he but see this with those eyes, so weary of contention and strife, how contentedly would he close them again, having beheld the greatness of his victories!

People of Massachusetts! he was the son of your soil, in which he now sleeps; but he is not all your own. He belongs to all of us in the North and in the South, —to the blacks he helped to make free, and to the whites he strove to make brothers again. Let, on the grave of him whom so many thought to be their enemy, and found to be their friend, the hands be

clasped which so bitterly warred against each other.
Let upon that grave the youth of America be taught,
by the story of his life, that not only genius, power
and success, but more than these, patriotic devotion
and virtue, make the greatness of the citizen! If this
lesson be understood, followed, more than CHARLES
SUMNER's living word could have done for the glory of
America will then be done by the inspiration of his
great example. And it will truly be said, that although
his body lies mouldering in the earth, yet in the
assured rights of all, in the brotherhood of a reunited
people, and in a purified Republic, he still lives and
will live forever.

ORATION BY ROBERT B. ELLIOTT,

(Of South Carolina,)

DELIVERED BY INVITATION OF

THE COLORED CITIZENS OF BOSTON,

IN FANEUIL HALL,

APRIL 14, 1874.

34

ORATION.

The boon of a noble human life cannot be appropriated by any single nation or race. It is a part of the common wealth of the world; a treasure, a guide and an inspiration to all men, in all lands, and through all ages. The earthly activities of this life are circumscribed by time and space; but the divine and essential genius which informs and inspires that life is boundless in the sweep of its influence, and immortal in the energy of its activity. In the great All Hail Hereafter, in that mysterious and glorious Future, which the heart of man, touched, as I firmly believe, by a divine intimation, is ever painting with more or less of conscious fondness, those mighty spirits moving in new majesty and power on their great missions of Truth and Love, will have laid aside the limitations which fettered them here and become the apparent and acknowledged leaders and voices of humanity itself.

Charles Sumner, in his mortal limitations, was an American; more narrowly, he was a Massachusetts man; more narrowly still, he was a white man: but to-day what nation shall claim him, what State shall

appropriate him, what race shall boast him? He was
the fair consummate flower of humanity. He was the
fruit of the ages. He was the child of the Past and
the promise of the Future. The whole world, could it
but know its relations, would mourn his departure,
and mankind everywhere would join in his honors.

But, fellow-citizens, if any fraction of humanity may
claim a peculiar right to do honor to the memory of
this great common benefactor of the world, surely it is
the colored race in these United States. To other men
his services may seem only a vast accession of strength
to a cause already moving with steady and assured
advance; to us, to the colored race, he is and ever
will be the great leader in political life, whose ponderous and incessant blows battered down the walls of our
prison-house, and whose strong hand led us forth into
the sunlight of Freedom. I do not seek to appropriate
him to my race; but I do feel to-day that my race
might almost bid the race to which by blood he
belonged, to stand aside while we to whose welfare his
life was so completely given, advance to do grateful
honor to him who was *our* great Benefactor and Friend.
"To the illustrious the whole world is a sepulchre."
To CHARLES SUMNER the whole civilized world has paid
its honors, and now *we* meet to give some formal testimony of our profound reverence for the personal gifts
and powers, for the measure of unselfish devotion,
which he gave to *us*.

If I could on this occasion frame into articulate words
the feelings of our hearts, if I could but half express
the depth and sincerity of that gratitude which dwells

in all our hearts, I might hope to rise to the height of the feelings of this hour. But that may not be.

This is Faneuil Hall. Here, within this venerable shelter, so fitly styled "The Cradle of Liberty," a little more than twenty-eight years ago the voice of CHARLES SUMNER was first heard in that great warfare to which his after-life was so completely devoted. His tones were trumpet-like. Listen to them: "Let Massachusetts, then, be aroused. Let all her children be summoned to this holy cause. There are questions of ordinary politics in which men may remain neutral; but neutrality now is treason to liberty, to humanity, and to the fundamental principles of free institutions. . . . Massachusetts *must* continue foremost in the cause of Freedom."

Brave, glorious words! But how few then to echo them! Twenty-eight years only have passed, and here in that same Faneuil Hall, that prostrate race against whose further enslavement CHARLES SUMNER then thundered his protest and warning, have met beneath the protection of the laws, not only of Massachusetts, but of the American Republic, to do honor to that splendid career then and there begun, which witnessed the final overthrow of Slavery and the citizenship of its victims throughout the Republic.

From that hour, in this Hall, in November, 1845, CHARLES SUMNER may be said to have entered on his life-work. With what splendid equipments of mind, of heart, of body, did he advance to the conflict! No knightlier figure ever moved forth to ancient jousts.

No braver heart ever enlisted in Freedom's cause. No scholarship more complete and affluent, since Milton, has placed its gifts and graces at the shrine of Justice and public Honor.

He little dreamed, I have ventured to think, of the severity of the sacrifices or the glory of the achievements which lay in the pathway on which he then entered. The mad and remorseless spirit of Slavery which then aroused his courage and drew him to the conflict, moved steadily forward to its purposes. Texas was annexed; the whole North, the entire national domain, were converted into the hunting-ground of Slavery; but CHARLES SUMNER was lifted by Massachusetts into the Senate of the United States. The voice which had awakened the echoes of this historic Hall in November, 1845, was transferred to that central point to rouse the sleeping conscience of the whole nation. With these vows, uttered likewise in this Hall, he entered upon his august duties in the Senate, "To vindicate Freedom and oppose Slavery, so far as I may constitutionally—with earnestness, and yet, I trust, without personal unkindness on my part—is the object near my heart. Would that my voice, leaving this crowded hall to-night, could traverse the hills and valleys of New England, that it could run along the rivers and lakes of my country, lighting in every heart a beacon-flame to arouse the slumberers throughout the land! Others may become indifferent to these principles, bartering them for political success, vain and short-lived, or forgetting the visions of youth in the dreams of age. Whenever I forget them, whenever I

become indifferent to them, whenever I cease to be
constant in maintaining them, through good report and
evil report, in any future combinations of party, then
may 'my tongue cleave to the roof of my mouth, may
my right hand forget its cunning.'"

From the hour he entered the Senate the combat
narrowed and deepened.   The dreadful Fugitive Slave
Law hung its pall over the whole land.   The spirit of
Slavery was omnipresent, ruling Courts, Congress,
Churches.   In all this fierce conflict, above the loudest
din, ever sounded his courageous, clarion voice.   What
cause was ever honored by nobler efforts of research,
of argument, of historical illustration, of classical adorn-
ments, of strong-hearted, resounding and lofty eloquence?   But above all other utterances was the
constant and conspicuous enunciation of the highest
moral principles as applicable to all political action
and duty.   Hear him: "Sir, I have never been a politician.   The slave of principles, I call no party master.
By sentiment, education and conviction a friend of
Human Rights in their utmost expansion, I have ever
most sincerely embraced the Democratic Idea,—not,
indeed, as represented or professed by any party, but
according to its real significance, as transfigured in the
Declaration of Independence and in the injunctions of
Christianity.   Amidst the vicissitudes of public affairs,
I shall hold fast always to this idea, and to any political party that truly embraces it."

With such sentiments planted and cultivated into full
growth and vigor in the very soil of his moral nature,
he presented himself to the country and the world in

his first senatorial speech in August, 1852, upon the
repeal of the Fugitive Slave Law. Reading that massive
and noble argument again in the light of twenty years
of subsequent events, how difficult to realize the prodigious moral energy which it at once demanded and
displayed! The argument is ample and conclusive; the
historical proofs are abundant; the eloquence is noble
and affecting; but high above all rises the grandeur of
the moral convictions which underlie and inspire all its
wealth of argumentation and oratory. With proud and
undaunted spirit he thus denounces that wicked enactment: "Sir, the Slave Act violates the Constitution
and shocks the Public Conscience. With modesty, and
yet with firmness, let me add, sir, it offends against
the Divine Law.

"No such enactment is entitled to support. As the
throne of God is above every earthly throne, so are
his laws and statutes above all the laws and statutes
of men. The mandates of an earthly power are to be
discussed; those of Heaven must at once be performed; nor can we suffer ourselves to be drawn into
any compacts in opposition to God." Words worthy,
are they not, fellow-citizens, of the noblest of the
martyrs and confessors of any age? One year before,
his faithful friend, Theodore Parker, a name ever
sacred in the hearts of those who love Freedom and
Truth, had written him, "I hope you will build on the
Rock of Ages and look to Eternity for your justification." How truly did he build on the Rock of Ages!
Yet, while he looked to eternity, time has brought him
his abundant justification!

Upon the lofty arena of the Senate he now struggled incessantly with the intellectual gladiators whom Slavery ever had as her champions. The heat and din of the conflict grew greater at every step. Yet there he stood, proud, defiant, uncomplaining, aggressive. How heavy the strain on his great but sensitive nature, so finely cultured, his words of acknowledgment of the cordial support which Massachusetts ever gave him, will attest. Hear him at Worcester: "After months of constant, anxious service in another place, away from Massachusetts, I am permitted to stand among you again, my fellow-citizens, and to draw satisfaction and strength from your generous presence. Life is full of change and contrast. From slave soil I have come to free soil. From the tainted breath of Slavery I have passed into the bracing air of Freedom. And the heated antagonism of debate, shooting forth its fiery cinders, is changed into this brimming, overflowing welcome, while I seem to lean on the great heart of our beloved Commonwealth, as it palpitates audibly in this crowded assembly."

A little later, Slavery, in its rapid march, assailed the time-honored barrier which the compromise of a former generation had set up against its advance over our vast North-western territories. Mr. SUMNER was now at the height of his powers. His age was forty-three; his senatorial experience was such as to confirm his confidence in his own powers, and to concentrate upon him the confidence and admiration of the friends of Freedom. History has been to me the delight and study of my life, but I know of no figure in history

35

which commands more of my admiration than that of
CHARLES SUMNER in the Senate of the United States,
from the hour when Douglas presented his ill-omened
measure for the repeal of the Missouri Compromise
until the blow of the assassin laid him low. Here was
the perfection of moral constancy and daring. Here
was sleepless vigilance, unwearying labor, hopefulness
born only of deepest faith, buoyant resolution caring
nothing for human odds, but serenely abiding in the
perfect peace which the unselfish service of Truth
alone can bring. The issues then before the country
awakened his profoundest alarm. The balance seemed
to him to be about to pass from Freedom to Slavery.
The American Republic, so solemnly dedicated by the
Fathers to Freedom, seemed about to cut loose from
all her ancient moorings. The imminence and greatness of the danger oppressed him. Listen to these
words, opening that speech which seems to me perhaps
the most perfect of his life, in which he first opposed
the removal of the Landmark of Freedom: "Mr.
President, I approach this discussion with awe. The
mighty question, with untold issues, oppresses me.
Like a portentous cloud, surcharged with irresistible
storm and ruin, it seems to fill the whole heavens,
making me painfully conscious how unequal to the occasion I am,—how unequal, also, is all that I can say
to all that I feel." But listen, also, to these words of
lofty cheer which fitly close the same speech, in which,
rising on the wings of Faith, he looks beyond the
storm raging around him, and contemplates that purer
and final " UNION contemplated at the beginning,

against which the storms of faction and the assaults of foreign power shall beat in vain, as upon the Rock of Ages,—and LIBERTY, seeking a firm foothold, WILL HAVE AT LAST WHEREON TO STAND AND MOVE THE WORLD."

To such a man, to a faith so clear-sighted, to a spirit so faithful to God and His Truth, no disaster or defeat, my fellow-citizens, can ever come. Victory sits forever on his triumphant crest.

And in his last final protest against that measureless wrong, see how, from the oppression of temporary defeat, he rises to joyous heights of serene moral confidence: "Sir, more clearly than ever before, I now penetrate that great Future when Slavery must disappear. Proudly I discern the flag of my country, as it ripples in every breeze, at last in reality, as in name, the Flag of Freedom,—undoubted, pure and irresistible. Sorrowfully I bend before the wrong you commit. Joyfully I welcome the promises of the Future."

But the sacred Landmark of Freedom for which he pleaded was ruthlessly swept away, and two years later, the country was convulsed by the outrages of the Slave Power on the plains of Kansas. The conflict raged equally in the halls of Congress, where Slavery sought to gather the fruits of this great wrong, by the organization of the Territory of Kansas as a Slave State.

Against this measure, CHARLES SUMNER uttered the magnificent philippic entitled so aptly "The Crime against Kansas," thus expressing in a single phrase, the moral aspects and character of that whole passage of history.

In that speech he developed new powers of denunciation and invective. From the impressive exordium
beginning, "Mr. President, you are now called to
redress a great wrong,"— on through the ample statement, the exhaustive narrative, the irresistible argument, the fiery invective, the pathetic appeal, to those
last words of the memorable peroration,— "In the name
of the Heavenly Father, whose service is perfect Freedom, I make this last appeal," — he spoke with absolute fidelity to the convictions of his own heart, and of
the aroused conscience of the free North. It was the
full discharge, aye, the explosion, of the slumbering
volcano of moral indignation which Slavery had aroused
in thirty years of continuous and intolerable aggres-
sions. It was the voice of the Declaration of Independence calling back the recreant sons to the faith and
practice of the Fathers. It was, as Whittier said, "a
grand and terrible philippic, worthy of the great occasion; the severe and awful truth which the sharp agony
of the national crisis demanded." It was more than a
speech, it was an event. It was more than a half battle, it was a *battle* crowned with glorious victory. It
was a scene and a speech to be compared only with
the great triumphs of oratory, — Demosthenes pleading
for Athenian liberty, Cicero thundering against the
oppressor of Sicily, Burke arraigning the Scourge of
India.

But why do I thus characterize that great utterance?
Two days after its delivery it received a demonstration
of its quality and power, more impressive and startling
than any which attended the former masterpieces of

human speech.   Slavery, in the person of a Representative in Congress from South Carolina, struck him to the floor and covered him with murderous blows.   It was, as another has eloquently said, "our champion beaten to the ground for the noblest word Massachusetts ever spoke in the Senate."

The effect of this assault upon the fortunes of the two struggling Powers, — Freedom and Slavery, — was significant.   Each rushed to the support of its champion.   Brooks was hailed throughout the South as the chivalrous exponent of Slavery, while CHARLES SUMNER ceased to be the assailant merely of Slavery, and became the champion and martyr of free speech and the sacred right of parliamentary debate.

Alas, — do we not still say alas, — that "that noble head," as Emerson then said, "so comely and so wise, must be the target for a pair of bullies to beat with clubs!"   Yet that blood was precious testimony for Truth and Freedom.   In an instant the civilized world stood by the side of SUMNER.   What neither moral force, nor finished scholarship, nor commanding eloquence could do, this final brutality achieved; and from that day the hot and furious wrath of every freedom-loving heart, fell upon that institution whose agent and representative had thus outraged humanity itself.   America and Europe rang with a shout of horror.   This historic hall echoed with fitting words of indignant eloquence.   "It is," said one still living, "it is a blow not merely at Massachusetts, a blow not merely at the name and fame of our common country; it is a blow at constitutional liberty all the world over; it is a stab at the cause of Universal Freedom. It is aimed at all men, everywhere, who are struggling for what we now regard as our great birth-right, and which we intend to transmit unimpaired to our latest posterity. . . . Forever, forever and aye, that stain will plead in silence for liberty, wherever man is enslaved, for humanity all over the world, for truth and for justice, now and forever."

Months and years of bodily suffering followed this outrage, borne, as all his life's experiences were borne, with unsurpassed fortitude, but with longings inexpressible for a return to the activities and dangers of the conflict in which he was now the central figure. While recalling this devotion of her great Senator, let me not forget to pay a tribute to that generous and true Commonwealth which he so truly represented. If CHARLES SUMNER was faithful, so was Massachusetts. The proud State felt, and felt truly, that his vacant chair was her truest representative until he to whom it belonged should re-occupy it. While still prostrated and unable to resume his duties, Massachusetts by a vote approaching unanimity, re-elected him as her Senator, — State and Senator, true to each other, worthy of each other.

But while resting among the Alleghanies of our own country, or seeking health on foreign shores, his heart was never absent from the Great Cause. What tributes do his brief utterances bear to the unwavering fidelity of his soul! Speaking to a sympathizing friend, he says, " Oh, no. My suffering is little, in comparison with daily occurrences. The poorest slave is in danger of worse outrages every moment of his life." Again he writes to the young men of Fitchburg, "We have been told that the 'duties of life are more than life'; and I assure you that the hardest part of my present lot is the enforced absence from public duties, and especially from that seat, where, as Senator from Massachusetts, it is my right, and also my strong desire at this moment, to be heard."

Again he writes, "With sorrow inexpressible I am constrained to all the care and reserve of an invalid. More than four months have passed since you clasped my hand as I lay bleeding in the Senate chamber. This is hard, very hard, for me to bear, for I long to do something, at this critical moment, for the Cause. What is life worth without action?"

Again, while lingering at Savoy, subjected to daily treatment by fire, he writes, "It is with a pang unspeakable that I find myself thus arrested in the labors of life and in the duties of my position. This is harder to bear than the fire."

No testimonies of this noble life will be more precious than these longings of this great heart for the duties of his position.

At last on the 4th of June, 1860, he was permitted to re-enter upon those scenes of senatorial debate from which, four years before, he had been so cruelly withdrawn. Butler and Brooks were both dead. The memories of his outrage and sufferings must have filled his mind, yet see how he puts by all personal considerations, and remembers only the Cause for which he is to speak: "Mr. President, I have no personal griefs to utter,—only a vulgar egotism could intrude such into

this chamber; I have no personal wrongs to avenge,
— only a brutish nature could attempt to wield that
vengeance which belongs to the Lord. The years that
have intervened and the tombs that have opened since
I spoke, have their voices, which I cannot fail to hear.
Besides, what am I, what is any man among the living
or among the dead, compared with the question before
us?"

With these simple and yet pathetic allusions he commenced that most exhaustive delineation of the spirit,
methods and effects of Slavery, which, under its singularly felicitous title, "The Barbarism of Slavery," will
remain a monument of research, of invective, and of
impassioned eloquence.

From this time the great drama moved rapidly to its
catastrophe. The Slave Power writhed beneath the
effect of this awful arraignment at the bar of the
world's judgment. It saw in secession from the Union
and the establishment of a separate Slaveholding Confederacy, its only hope and safety. Abraham Lincoln
became President, and in April, 1861, the bombard-
ment of Fort Sumter in Charleston harbor, sounded the
tocsin of civil war throughout the land. Into that
struggle CHARLES SUMNER entered without hesitation
and without alarm. His only anxiety had been to keep
the North clear of the deadly spirit of Compromise.
Let justice be done him here. His moral equilibrium
and courage were never more conspicuous. Many had
joined him in his fierce assaults on Slavery, who now
shrunk back from the gulf of war and disunion which
seemed to open before them. Compromises were sug-

gested on all sides,—compromises, too, which would have robbed Freedom of all her advantage and left the Slave to his hopeless bondage. Let no negro forget,—nay, let no American forget,—that CHARLES SUMNER never sullied his lips with degrading compromise.

Duty was his master; Justice ruled him; and to every suggestion of compromise with Slavery he responded, "Get thee behind me, Satan!"

His inflexible spirit may be seen in these words to Governor Andrew: "*Timeo Danaos et dona ferentes.* Don't let these words be ever out of your mind, when you think of any proposition from the Slave Masters. *They are all essentially false, with treason in their hearts, if not on their tongues.* How can it be otherwise? Slavery is a falsehood, and its supporters are all perverted and changed. Punic in faith, Punic in character, you are to meet all that they do or say with denial or distrust. I know these men and see through their plot. The time has not yet come to touch the chords which I wish to awaken. *But I see my way clear.* O God! let Massachusetts keep true. It is all I ask."

Again, to the same friend he writes, "More than the loss of forts, arsenals, or the national capital, *I fear the loss of our principles. . . .* Keep firm, and do not listen to any proposition."

Fellow-citizens, I am a negro,—one of the victim race. My heart bows in gratitude to every man who struck a blow for the liberty of my race. But how can I fail to remember that alone, *alone*, of all the great leaders of our cause at Washington, CHARLES SUMNER kept his faith to Freedom, stern and true. What measure of honor shall we not pay to him whose only prayer, amidst the abounding dangers of that hour, was, "O God! let Massachusetts keep true"? Lincoln, Seward, Adams,—eulogy even cannot claim such absolute fidelity for either of them. History, I venture to predict, will point to this passage in the life of CHARLES SUMNER, as the highest proof of the superior and faultless tone of his moral nature. What a majestic moral figure! Let us bear it in our hearts as the crowning gift and glory of his life.

But humanity swept onward; timid compromisers were overwhelmed by the logic of events; and at last God held this great nation face to face with its duty. The death-grapple rocked and agonized the land. Released from the Delilah bands of compromise, the Samson of the North resumed and re-asserted his resistless strength. In the van of every effort and policy which sought the overthrow of Slavery or the triumph of Freedom, was CHARLES SUMNER. "EMANCIPATION, our best WEAPON," is the inspiring title of a speech bearing so early a date as October 1, 1861. "WELCOME TO FUGITIVE SLAVES," was a senatorial utterance of December 4, 1861. With tireless industry, working in all directions: in legislation for the support of our armies; for maintaining our public credit; in inspiring the President to his full duty; in guarding our relations with other nations; above all, in saving the nation from the fatal mistake of Mr. Lincoln's Louisiana scheme of reconstruction, he sustained, encouraged, vindicated, and ennobled the National Cause.

The triumph of the national arms in the spring of 1865, threw upon the National Government the unparalleled task of re-establishing civil government in the rebellious States. The work of destruction was ended, and the work of rebuilding must be begun. The ill-advised and ill-starred attempts of Andrew Johnson complicated the problem already bristling with difficulties, constitutional and legal, and beset with dangers, political and moral. The moral intrepidity and prescience of Mr. SUMNER, were earliest to detect the false political theories which then so widely prevailed. With wonted boldness he denounced the Presidential scheme of reconstruction, and summoned Congress and the country to its duty. In a series of senatorial efforts he proclaimed and emphasized in the ear of the nation, the paramount duty of guarding the results of the war by "irreversible constitutional guarantees." Especially did he denounce the injustice and wickedness of any settlement which left the colored race of the South under the hands of their former masters. This was an axiom in his arguments, the postulate of his reasonings. From this starting point he readily reached that conclusion, finally accepted by the country and enacted into our national laws and Constitution, that the colored race must be made citizens of the United States and voters in their respective States. The Declaration of Independence, with its lofty and immortal truth,—"ALL men are created FREE and EQUAL,"—was to him a clear and constant guide. In this grand, germinal truth, he saw the only true and final rule of government, and he pressed towards its practical realization with eager and unfaltering steps.

He had heard this sacred tenet of the Fathers flouted in the Senate as a "self-evident lie," but he only bore it the more proudly and conspicuously on his shield until he could gratefully say, "The Declaration of Independence, so lately a dishonored tradition, is now the rubric and faith of the Republic." God be praised! he found at last that " *Union, where Liberty, seeking a firm foothold, might have whereon to stand and move the world.*"

Once only in all this splendid and faithful career did CHARLES SUMNER part company with the great mass of the friends of Freedom, and on this he needs no silence.

Differing, as I could not but differ, from his judgment in the last national campaign, I point to it to-day as one of the highest proofs of his utter devotion to the call of duty. Still was he true, utterly true, to his convictions, to the commanding voice of Conscience. He had been faithful in defeat; could he be faithful in success? Draw no veil of silence over this passage; but write it high on his monument,—that in old age, when the weary frame longed for repose, he could again brace himself for the conflict in which nearly all of the friends of a lifetime stood arrayed against him.

> "Nothing is here for tears; nothing to wail
> Or knock the breast; no weakness, no contempt,
> Dispraise or blame; nothing but well and fair."

As his life was wholly consecrated to Duty, so his death was wanting in no element of moral grandeur. He fell with armor on, with face still inflexibly turned towards present duties, fronting eternity with the simple trust which God gives to his faithful servant. With no vague dread or anxiety concerning the Future, he bore his earthly cares and duties to the threshold of Eternity, and laid down the burdens of life only at the feet of his Divine Master. "Don't let my Civil Rights Bill fail," was his fitting adieu to Earth and greeting to Heaven.

Fellow-citizens, the life of CHARLES SUMNER needs no interpreter. It is an open, illuminated page. The ends he aimed at were always high; the means he used were always direct. Neither deception nor indirection, neither concealment nor disguise of any kind or degree, had place in his nature or methods. By open means he sought open ends. He walked in the sunlight, and wrote his heart's inmost purpose on his forehead.

His activity and capacity of intellectual labor were almost unequalled. Confined somewhat by the overshadowing nature of the Anti-Slavery cause in the range of his topics, he multiplied his blows and redoubled the energy of his assaults upon that great enemy of his country's peace. Here his vigor knew no bounds. He laid all ages and lands under contribution. Scholarship in all its walks—history, art, literature, science—all these he made his aids and servitors.

But who does not see that *these* are not his glory? He was a scholar among scholars; an orator of consummate power; a statesman familiar with the structure of governments and the social forces of the world. But he was greater and better than one or all of these; *he was a man of absolute moral rectitude of purpose and of life.* His personal purity was perfect, and unquestioned everywhere. He carried morals into politics. And this is the *greatness* of CHARLES SUMNER,—that by the power of his moral enthusiasm he rescued the nation from its shameful subservience to the demands of material and commercial interests, and guided it up to the high plane of Justice and Right. Above his other great qualities towers that moral greatness to which scholarship, oratory, and statesmanship are but secondary and insignificant. He was just because he *loved* Justice; he was right because he *loved* Right. Let this be his record and epitaph.

To have lived such a life were glory enough. Success was not needed to perfect its star-bright, immortal beauty. But success came. What amazing contrasts did his life witness! He heard the hundred guns which Boston fired for the passage of the Fugitive Slave Act; and he saw Boston sending forth, with honors and blessings, a regiment of fugitive slaves to save that Union which the crime of her Webster had imperilled. He saw Franklin Pierce employing the power of the nation to force back one helpless fugitive to the hell of Slavery; and he saw Abraham Lincoln write the edict of Emancipation. He heard Taney declare that "the black man had no rights which the white man was bound to respect"; and he welcomed Revels to his seat as a Senator of the United States.

But as defeat could not damp his ardor, so success could not abate his zeal. He fell while bearing aloft the same banner of Human Rights which, twenty-eight years before, he had unfurled and lifted in this hall.

The blessings of the poor are his laurels. One sacred

thought,—Duty,—presided over his life, inspiring him in youth, guiding him in manhood, strengthening him in age. Be it ours to walk by the light of this pure example. Be it ours to copy his stainless integrity, his supreme devotion to Humanity, his profound faith in Truth, and his unconquerable moral enthusiasm.

Adieu! great Servant and Apostle of Liberty! If others forget thee, thy fame shall be guarded by the millions of that emancipated race whose gratitude shall be more enduring than monumental marble or brass.

SERMON BY HENRY W. FOOTE,

PREACHED AT

KING'S CHAPEL,

SUNDAY, MARCH 22, 1874.

37

SERMON.

"Righteousness exalteth a nation: but sin is a reproach to any people."

"For, behold, the Lord, the Lord of hosts, doth take away from Jerusalem and from Judah the stay and the staff, the whole stay of bread and the whole stay of water, . . . the honorable man and the counsellor, . . . and the eloquent orator."

"I will make a man more precious than fine gold: even a man than the golden wedge of Ophir."—Prov. xiv: 34; Is. iii: 1, 3; xiii: 12.

THE Old Testament might be called the *New Test* (if we cared to play upon words),—the most modern touchstone to which we can bring character and duty, public or private. There are those, indeed, who deem it to be obsolete because it is old,—a method of reasoning which would banish the light of the solar system from the universe, nay, which would abolish the universe itself as utterly antediluvian. But the fathers of New England knew the rock on which they builded, when they strove to found their commonwealth on the eternal principles which they read on the ancient tables of stone; and the living waters of conscience and duty which have quickened the souls of their children, which are the hope of the Republic to-day, have flowed forth from those granitic summits of immemorial law, as the stream gushed forth from the rock which Moses smote.

There are those, too, who sometimes deem that religion belongs in a region apart from the strifes and questions of political life. And this is partly true. Religion is at home on the Mount of Transfiguration, above the smoke of the camp-fires and the noise of conflicts, where the heaven is nearer; but she does not take men up with her there unless she meets them in the plain, where in the dust and heat of conflict she is a light on their way and an inspiration in their spirit. We should all agree that questions of the day should not be made a *religion* of; that the church is no place for criminations or discords. But religion should be made a *question of the day,*—every day. And since she should be the most vital factor in every personal duty, and since no duty is more personal to every man and woman, under a system of government like ours, than that which concerns the public weal, it follows that the church has sometimes the necessity laid upon it of trying to show how religion bears on public duty and public service. And here, again, the Old Testament fairly blazes with light. It may almost be termed the great Manual of Political Duty; and we need ask no better test of its inspired power to mould humanity towards the ideal future than is afforded by comparing its starry words, glowing in the firmament of truth with the light of justice and freedom, with the wisest maxims of the masters in statecraft, from Machiavelli's Prince and the Testament of Peter the Great of Russia, to the Bismarckian theory of a diplomacy gangrened with falsehood, or the idea that a nation is to be ruled by packing a caucus. When you come to deal with any question of public morals, or when you seek for words with which to describe a faithful public servant, the difficulty is not how to find, but what to choose, out of the riches of this Old Testament, so New.

Our texts strike the chord to which our thoughts must perforce attune themselves to-day. A certain theme is laid down for us by the proud duty which fell to this church of being the voice of this dear old Commonwealth of Massachusetts in her public service of mourning for one who had served her so long in the highest office in her gift. I could not, if I would, put aside the task which seems to be written for me in the signs of public mourning which still remain on these walls.

The part which this church took in those solemn offices was due, as you know, not to our basing any claim upon the former connection of Senator SUMNER with this church, but to our placing the church at the service of the State government for the rites of honor which it sought to render; and these dark drapings still hang here, in sympathy with the legislative vote which retains them at the Capitol during the period of public mourning, because we were a part of the State and acted for the State. Yet there was a special fitness —a sort of family right—in our association in those memorable services when the streets of the city were like the aisles of a crowded church, and this house of prayer was as a central chapel. For many years of his life were rooted in this church; his father was its clerk during a part of the Senator's childhood; his mother I knew well, as her pastor, in the gentle loveliness of an old age, subdued by the chastening of many and singular sorrows; and we have a right to think that probably the clarion call of the Gospel wrought within him, more than he was himself aware, from the Christian teaching of those faithful men and lovers of truth and righteousness whose names are our heritage and our inspiration. Yet I do not propose to make this the occasion for a Commemorative Discourse of Eulogy: such a discourse will be given elsewhere, and by one qualified to speak. —as the Legislature may determine. Much has been already said by distinguished men in public places, and the time for Congressional Eulogy is still to come. My duty here is other than that,—very simple, yet very true. It is, to try to impress on ourselves, while the feeling of the hour is fresh, some of the principles which we need more than ever to insist on in our judgments of public duty and our actions as faithful citizens. I would say nothing to open old feuds or strifes, now forever silenced; nor is it needful to stir the embers of that fire of controversy which consumed the nation for so long,—now happily turned to ashes and as far back of us as the flood. I pray that no word of mine may bring us down from the high level of a common sympathy, in which, as at great moments of our war, the whole heart of this Commonwealth has been melted into one.

There is, indeed, something sublime in the healing and reconciling work which is wrought by death. Out of that silence comes to us a deeper lesson than all the voices of life have ever been able to bring home to us.

> " That which the open book could never teach
>   The closed one whispers."

We feel this when we stand beside the humblest and poorest clay that has enshrined an immortal spirit. But how much more when it is one who has been a power in the land, whose name has been a watchword of passionate admiration and of intensest opposition, who has been a factor in the history of a tremendous period, not to be left out in the tracing of causes and results! When sudden stillness falls on such a one, and all the tumult of tongues is quieted or turned to a rivalry in praise of things not always so greatly valued while they were with us, how falsely does it seem that we speak of him who brings this to pass as "the king of terrors"! Rather does he seem to come as the angel of peace. And we may well say, with Sir Walter Raleigh, "O eloquent, just, and mighty Death! whom none could advise, thou hast persuaded; what none hath dared, thou hath done; and whom all the world hath flattered, thou only hast cast out of the world and despised. Thou hast drawn together all the far-stretched greatness, all the pride and ambition of man, and covered it all over with these two narrow words, '*Hic jacet*.'" Yes! He covers over those things which partook of mortal weakness and infirmity; but the things which are immortal, great memories of great gifts, faithful thoughts of faithfulnesses to conscience, tried experience of long fidelity,—these are not covered, but now first begin to be revealed and fruitful in the fullest sense, as the seeds of a flower fall from the bursting capsule on fertile ground.

There is no higher calling in human society than that of the public service in a nation of freemen. Ambition

in this direction is a worthy ambition. It is the duty
of every man that he should be ready to meet the
obligation of such service if it comes to him; we should
train our children to this readiness as one of the most
imperative duties of manhood. But this ambition may
be a lamp to lighten the path of him who walks in it,
with lofty purposes, thorough preparations, righteous
scorn of every mean and low thing; or it may be a
snare and pitfall to his conscience, causing him to stumble
in winding and slippery ways,—if he reach the coveted
place only dragging down its honor to his own base level.
The one is a noble flame, kindling the spirit to climb the
hard

> "Steep, where Fame's proud temple shines afar,"

And to write one's name high among the benefactors of
the human race: the other is the degradation and often
the ruin of the nation which it plagues. But as the
public service is perhaps the highest, and certainly the
most shining, so is it also the most difficult way of duty.
I say nothing of the storms of obloquy from foes, or
the beclouding influence of flattery from false or unwise
friends. These may be hard to endure or to resist; but
the arduousness of high responsibility is not here, but
in the responsibility itself. For consider what various
qualifications—and how impossible to unite in a single
person—are demanded to meet all the exigencies of a
great place in the councils of a nation. What kind of
man should a great people desire to fulfil all the ideal
possibilities of high public service? He should be,
should he not, a combination of the recluse scholar and

of the practical man of affairs; wise with the wisdom of books and with the deeper wisdom of experience in human nature; reading the history of the past as an open page, and learning from it the lessons so easy for a nation to be taught by others' experience,—since all nations are made up of the same human nature,—so costly for a nation to be taught by its own mistakes; reading the characters of men by that trained instinct which cannot be deceived. He should be practised in the school of statesmanship, that highest and most diffi- cult of arts, which consists not in managing men by their low and base motives, for mere party success, but in shaping the policy, whether commercial or moral, of a great nation, with far-seeing perception of the causes that lead to prosperity or to decay. He should be kindled by the ardor of great convictions of truth and righteousness, ready to face unpopularity for the faith that is in him, yet never hasty or unjust; with a calm, deep comprehension of the views most opposed to his own, able to do justice to their convictions, and to find every ground of conciliation and mutual respect. Strong with a commanding personality, and with powers able to compel respectful recognition, he should fulfil that Eastern proverb which says, "A man that knoweth the just value of himself doth not perish," yet should have that respect for others' judgment which most surely wins their assent to the influence of a stronger nature, and should be untinged by that self-reference which centres the universe in itself. Eloquent with a manly strain, the power of his persuasion should never be embittered by words of personality or scorn. To bor-

38

row a figure from science, the spectrum of his speech should be rich in the rays of light, rather than in those of heat. He should be *before* his time in vision, yet *with* his time in comprehending sympathy; with forward-looking sight, but backward-reaching hand, to lift his people to his level. Must we say, in the Republic which Washington founded, in the State which sent the incorruptible Pickering to his counsels in war and peace, and has inscribed the names of John Adams and John Quincy Adams on the roll of his successors, that such a public servant must have an integrity above suspicion, with hands clean from money-getting and from office-seeking,—that he should have a lofty independence and a single eye to the public good? We live in a day when these plain dictates of honor and conscience are *distinctions* to be named with praise. He should be crystal pure from the vices of passion or of meanness, clad in an asbestos robe of principle to walk through the fires of the temptations which beset public life without so much as the smell of smoke upon his garments. He should sit at the feet of no human master, but he should have sat at the feet of Christ. The eternal principles of His Gospel of righteousness should glow in his heart, and the wisdom of his law of kindness should pervade his conduct with its fragrant breath, while in the lowly faith of a disciple he should be "as a little child." Of a public servant so endowed, it may well be said, in the words of the prophet, "I will make a man more precious than fine gold: even a man than the golden wedge of Ophir."

And now, if we look at the distinguished record of

that eminent servant of the nation whose finished life is close to our thoughts to-day,—not in the spirit of indiscriminate eulogy, but in the dispassionate attempt to anticipate the judgment of another generation, with that frank independence of judgment which he himself signally illustrated, we shall surely say, Some of these great qualities Senator SUMNER had in abounding measure; in others he was lacking. Perhaps no man ever lived so all-sided as to have them all: he who has the greater part of them must stand high in the remembrance of a grateful country, especially when the traits which distinguish him are those which the land needs to brace its conscience and renew the integrity of its will.

It has been the fortune of Mr. SUMNER to be associated more intimately than any other public man with the most agitating questions of our time. And this was no accident, but essential in the very nature of the man. From the very beginning, his character was a blending of two sides of character rarely united,—strenuous self-culture, and earnest, if not defiant, championship of the redress of wrongs. I do not need here to retrace the familiar story in detail, or to recapitulate what is in part so well known to his fellow-townsmen, and is in large part written on the history of the country itself. Of the years of study in our Boston schools, at the neighboring University (to which his noble bequest has testified to his enduring filial affection), in his close relation of pupil with master with Judge Story, of his studious years at foreign universities and in London, at a time when foreign study was comparatively rare, he might

truly have said, in the words of the English poet whom
he loved so well :—

> "When I was yet a child, no childish play
>   To me was pleasing; all my mind was set
>   Serious to learn and know, and thence to do
>   What might be public good; myself I thought
>   Born to that end, born to promote all truth,
>   All righteous things."

He returned here with marked distinction at the same
age at which Milton again wrote to his friend Diodati.
"Do you ask what I am thinking of? So may the good
God help me, of immortality." Or it might have been
the words of his own friend, De Tocqueville, in which
he might have said, "Life is neither a pleasure nor a
pain, but a serious business which it is our duty to
carry through and to terminate with honor." Eleven
intervening years were filled with various labors,—professional, literary, and philanthropic,—which I do not
need to enlarge on here. Meantime, the ominous cloud
which rose above the horizon with the annexation of
Texas spread and darkened more and more; the war
with Mexico followed; then came the dark days of
1850, when a call rang through the land, parting friend
from friend, brother from brother. The student of history finds in those years the seeds sown which were
harvested in civil war, and finds that Mr. SUMNER was
each year more prominent as one of the voices of the
ever-growing conviction against slavery in New England. He was a little more than forty years of age,—
that stage of life when, as he once said, "according to

a foreign proverb, a man has given to the world his
full measure,"—when he was chosen to succeed Mr.
Webster in the Senate of the United States. The
Quaker poet of New England tells me that at this time
he confessed to him that he had a great ambition, but
not for political life,—that his ambition was to become
a jurist, or to write history. In that desire he would
have satisfied the needs of half of his nature,—the con-
templative side; but the other half, the side of action,
could never have been content without a great field of
action and of power. And what a field it was on
which the Senator from Massachusetts entered in that
stormy time! As I have stood within the halls of the
old Senate-chamber, plain and bare, which shook with
the thunders of Webster's reply to Hayne, or within
the palatial new chamber, which saw the working out
of the drama of the civic side of the great war for the
Union, and the associations of the place have crowded
upon me, and I have remembered what echoes those
walls would give could they but speak what they had
heard, it has seemed to me that no place on earth was
such a sphere for worthy action or such a point of lev-
erage for the eloquence which would not end in words,
but shape the public will of a nation. Rufus Choate,
who knew it well, wrote to Mr. SUMNER, "How does
the Senate strike you? The best place this day on
earth for reasoned and thoughtful yet stimulant public
speech." "When I think what it requires," wrote Mr.
SUMNER himself, on his election, "I am obliged to say
that its honors are all eclipsed by its duties." To such
a sphere the Senator from Massachusetts came,—one of

the youngest of that august body, without experience
in public affairs, the bold and outspoken representative
of a small minority in Congress and of a growing fire
in the North. Ten days ago he was the senior member
of the body, trained by twenty-three years of its great
duties,—a longer sum of years than the office had been
held by any Massachusetts Senator since the foundation
of the Republic,—and he had seen the words, which
when he spoke them were deemed the enthusiasm of a
fanatic, surpassed by the stupendous reality of the history through which we have lived.   He might have
applied in his own case the words in which Mr. Mill,
in his autobiography, speaks of some matters in his
own parliamentary career : "My advocacy of" them was
"at the time looked upon by many as personal whims
of my own ; but the great progress since made by those
opinions, and especially the response made from almost
all parts of the kingdom to the demand, fully justified
the timeliness of those movements, and have made what
was undertaken as a moral and social duty a personal
success." The fiery heats of those years before the war
the next generation can never know ; for the battle
which they will have to fight has but one side,—the
fight of honesty against corruption : while the hardest
part of the struggle which preceded the downfall of
Slavery was that men at the North, equally good, equally
true, were on opposite sides, and each could hardly
avoid misjudging the other.   "The high contention" is
now "hidden by the little handful of earth"; but in its
record future generations will trace the manifest upheaval
of the tremendous forces which were to shake the nation

to its foundations. It was the fateful blow struck by a mad hand in answer to words spoken by him in his place as Senator which made Mr. SUMNER a *symbol* of the Northern idea. From that hour, the silence of his suffering spoke with a louder tongue than his most intense words. Then came the war, when the strife of tongues gave way to the strife of arms; and for ten years, as Chairman of the Senate Committee of Foreign Relations, he filled one of the most important posts in the Government so as to win the respect alike of enemies and friends; and then three years of loneliness as "a voice crying in a desert, Make the crooked straight and the rough places plain"; and the scarred warrior, who had been in the forefront of the battles of his time, passed from storm into rest. He had reached what he himself once called "the grand climacteric, that Cape of Storms in the sea of human existence."

He was buried with the mighty mourning of a sovereign State, as befitted the first Senator from Massachusetts (with one exception only) who ever died in office,—the Senator who had held office for nearly a generation of incorruptible life, the faithful voice of liberty and justice. Such is the barest outline of the external history of those tremendous years when "the fountains of the great deep were broken up," and that commanding presence was always where the storm was wildest.

And now, when we ask for the secret of his power, we find it, first, in that which was a weakness as well as a strength,—namely, the strong imperiousness of his convictions. He could not overstate them, they were so pronounced and positive; nor could he easily deal justly with opponents. Political charity is the

rarest of the virtues,—rarer, by a strange law, in proportion to the moral and philanthropic quality of the
opinions which one holds.　The very fact that conscience and the sense of right are so engaged makes it
well-nigh impossible to see how the conscience of honorable and good men may be engaged in adverse views.
O hard fate, when the sense of justice to an oppressed
race contended with the sense of duty to a bond whose
rupture might cause the sun of the Union to go down
in blood, and good men among us, both hating the
giant wrong, both loving the starry constellation of the
States, were sundered by an impassable gulf!　It was
in the nature of the man who swung what he called
"the great Northern hammer" to strike hard and stern
blows; and if in his record are found words which pass
the mutual respect of high debate, or which follow the
method of prophetic denunciation rather than that of
statesmanlike conciliation, we cannot doubt that now,
out of the wisdom of death, he would speak to us to
say that if he could live his life over, he would do
some things differently.

But other men have had convictions as strong and
imperious as his without becoming identified with them
as the acknowledged exponent and representative of a
principle.　His strength was in the identity of his principle with that of New England.　He was "a Puritan
idealist."　In all its differences of form, there lived
in him that most persistent type, which has impressed
its character on the civilization of our whole country,
which was strong enough to subdue granite and ice
and make a home for their children.　The Puritans
were impracticable men,—a projectile cast into Eng-

land, of such tremendous explosive force that when it burst, the fragments flew across three thousand miles of ocean. They were men of narrow conscience, and like some strong stream, the deeper and the more resistless in its flow because of the very narrowness. Their indomitable spirit is cast into a word by "Andrew Fletcher, whose heroical uprightness amid the trials of his time, has become immortal in the saying, that he 'would readily lose his life to *serve* his country, but would not do a base thing to *save* it.'" The children of the Puritans are still the same; and we, who are of them, can afford to acknowledge that the fathers would have been sometimes hard to live among, and that there is danger that even conscience and zeal for righteousness may be at times obstinate and one-sided. But one thing is certain,—that when these things are in the line of the ideas of justice, freedom, abstract right, they have irresistible power, over the mind of the race which has grown on our rocky soil. Men who are tempered with this spirit are better fitted to point a thunderbolt than to weld a nation; they belong in the time when controversy has passed beyond compromise. So far from sympathizing with that rule of practical statesmanship which old Hesiod sings,—

"Half is more than the whole,"

There can be for them nothing less than the ideal whole. The only rule of yielding or giving up what they know is in that saying of another Greek,—

"We must sacrifice to Truth alone."

39

It was the power of the Senator that he voiced this
intense Puritan strain in the ideas of the New England
conscience.   Said one of his most ardent friends of
him, in the heat of a political campaign :   He is "patient in labor, untiring in effort, boundless in resources,
terribly in earnest, . . .   the Stonewall Jackson of
the floor of the Senate, . . .   both ideologists, both
horsed on an idea."

Essentially characteristic of this moral intensity, which
makes the typical New England character like one of
those Iceland geysers, a boiling hot spring in the heart
of the glacier, is an elevated confidence in one's own
intentions, tending in small natures to self-absorption,
but in great natures to utter absorption in a great
cause, and giving an assurance of right which could
make the Senator choose for the motto to his collected
works, the proud appeal with which he would speak to
future generations, those words of Leibnitz : " Veniet
fortasse aliud tempus, dignius nostro, quo debellatis
odiis, veritas triumphabit. Hoc mecum opta, lector, et
vale."   One who knew and loved him well sums up
this characteristic in these words in a letter to me :
" He struck for the right and was sure he saw it. He
had a sublime confidence in his own moral sagacity,
greater than I have ever seen in any man ; and, let
me add, events usually justified such confidence."

And this zealous intensity in the man was served by
an indomitable power of work, such as has rarely been
equalled and probably never surpassed by any one in
the public service. I have the testimony of two of his
private secretaries to the fact that his strength and

fidelity in the unseen labors of his duty as Senator, and on the most responsible Committee of Foreign Relations, exceeded anything that can be imagined. He "toiled terribly." The key-note of his life is struck in an early lecture of his on "The Employment of Time," whose text is the famous exclamation of Titus, "I have lost a day!" and he might well leave as his legacy to those who would profit by his example the words of Seneca: "Vita, si scias uti, longa est." High office was to him no holiday perch, but an opportunity for more strenuous work, nor did anything so chafe him as enforced abstention therefrom. All the wide resources of a various learning were reinforced continually by special preparations, and he carried the student's habit of toil into the position where men are apt to think that they are officially infallible on all questions, from finance and diplomacy to the filling of the pettiest office.

And this is strikingly shown by that monument of labor, yet uncompleted,—the edition of his Works. As during the recent days I have read through the seven volumes, I have been impressed with many things, but with none more than this. From that oration on "The True Grandeur of Nations," which sounded again, in such rich and high-wrought strain, the note which Rufus Choate had struck the year before in the United States Senate, when he said, "War is the most ridiculous of blunders, the most tremendous of crimes, the most comprehensive of evils,"—an idea emphasized in these words, which form the key-note of Mr. SUMNER's oration: "War is known as the *Last*

Reason of Kings. Let it be no reason of our Republic;"—to his last speech in the Senate, there are the
same characteristics,—a labored affluence of illustration
from the widest sources of study, a style elaborate
even to excess, but, throughout, the sense that here is
one who has made thorough preparation for the great
office of advising the Elders of the Republic.

And one can hardly read these volumes without a
deeper realization how truly the Senator was not only
a prominent figure, but a powerful actor in the greatest
chapter of modern history. Friends will find nothing
save to admire; old enemies, much to differ in; and
those who have been independent from personal ties or
by-gone discords, both much to admire and something
to regret. But all must agree in reading the super-
scription of his name on page after page of most
eventful annals. If Abraham Lincoln shall stand forth
against the black background of the war as the Crom-
well of our great struggle, only far purer, more
unselfish than the Ironside Puritan was, the name of
the persistent friend of emancipation, who stood to him
in wellnigh as close a relation as did his Latin Secretary
to the Protector, will shine in the same constellation.
The future historian will perhaps picture the two in
scenes which are already recorded,—the Senator taking
his French friend with him to see the morning levee
which that kindly heart, all burdened with Presidential
cares, yet found time to give daily to the poor who
needed him most,—the sick soldier or the poor widow,
—with the invitation, "Come with me and see St.
Louis under the Oak of Vincennes"; or the President,

a week before his martyrdom, reading aloud to the
Senator, on the deck of the steamboat that carried
them to evacuated Richmond, those prophetic lines in
Macbeth : —

> " Duncan is in his grave:
> After life's fitful fever he sleeps well.
> Treason has done his worst; nor steel, nor poison.
> Malice domestic, foreign levy, nothing
> Can touch him farther!"

But no future historian will be able to describe in
all its dramatic intensity the struggle which involved
these men, so different, and the parts of the nation
which they represented,—the one eager always for the
highest and furthest thing, the other gauging the exact
mind of the people with that pre-eminent political
sagacity. He will try to describe the one "crying
aloud and sparing not," as the voice of the most
advanced conscience of the North, the other telling
him "You are only ahead of me a month or six
weeks,"—till at last the proclamation seals the policy
of the government. He will describe the growth of
the institution of Slavery on this continent, from the
time when the Mayflower, with its cargo of liberty, and
the first slave ship, with its cargo of human bondage,
were crossing the ocean at the same time in 1620, to
the time when, like the genie of Arabian fable, the
little cloud, released from the hold of that vessel,
darkened all the land, a giant in strength. He will
tell, too, how the man who spoke the intensest sentiment of the North was ever urging the principle of

absolute liberty, and would venture where it seemed wild to go, as the Douglas who bore the heart of Bruce to the Holy Land threw his sacred trust far before him into the hosts of the infidel, to witness that he would never give over his advance; and then he will tell how the great work was done by the hands of men differing widely in their sentiment even on the great question of universal liberty, but agreeing in being willing to die for their country,—that not the voice alone of eloquent oratory, but the deeds of devoted patriotism wrought the marvel of freedom. Let yonder marble speak, with its proud record of men who could be silent and give their lives; to testify how the great power of the land stood behind the Act of Emancipation, and made it, instead of a bit of paper, a reality! And then think of those long rows of colored faces, the representatives of four grateful millions, that on Monday last gleamed with hardly suppressed emotion, as of men parting with a mighty friend; and remember the coat-of-arms of Lord Exmouth, on which "was emblazoned a figure never before known in heraldry,—a *Christian slave holding aloft the cross, and dropping his broken fetters.*" Happy, indeed, is he whose name is forever linked with the eternal ideas of freedom and justice!

The lofty and permanent lesson which remains with us from the life of Senator SUMNER is one peculiarly needed in our time,—that of independent loyalty to the best conscience. Whatever else fails, that cannot fail. Not always does success come; not always do the wonderful forces of public awakening, the madness of

enemies, the awful arbitrament of war, justify the political seer with the attainment of his vision. "Prophets
and kings have died without the sight." But for fame,
as well as for one's own inward peace, the surest warrant is the boldest venture. Trust in the eternal truths
of conscience and duty and God! The sober wisdom
of that homely precept of one of our great poets,
"Hitch your wagon to a star," will be acknowledged in
the end.

Who now remembers, in his dispraise, that John
Milton staked his all on a losing cause, that he was an
extremist and a fanatic, that he spoke hot and bitter
words against the enemies of his party? But that
which shines in him is the pure and lofty spirit, the
consecration of great powers to his country's service in
a time of storm,—putting aside the plans of quiet study
and literary ease,—the great pleadings for liberty and
righteousness, the soul that "was like a star and dwelt
apart."

We learn, by contrast with those things which in the
presence of great death compel our reverence, what are
the dangers of the land. What kind of man is he
whose public service will prove the public servitude,
and will drag a nation towards its fall? We have
already described him by opposites. He will be one
educated enough to know the evil side of men, able
enough to compel their reluctant help, wise in the
secrets of corruption, who has grown rich from the
misfortunes of his country, who mounts to power over
heaps of blackened reputations, and uses every office

but as a round in the ladder of his ambition; who rules
by fear, yet whose friendship is even more blasting
than his hatred. Detected again and again in wiles
which would wreck the good name of better men, he
will almost persuade the multitude to believe his shame
to be a new form of virtue. If ever such a man should
come, woe to the nation which he tricks towards its
doom! for then, indeed, "Politics become a game, and
principles are the counters which are used."

But such men would have little power of evil in a
country, if there did not exist grave elements of danger
in the atmosphere of the time, in those murky disposi-
tions of the public mind to which they act as the light-
ning-rod on a lowering thunder-cloud, to draw the fatal
shock. First among these, we must name the worship
of money for money's own sake. So long as men and
women believe that this has any worth in itself, apart
from the question *how* it has been won, and will let
foul gains win a fair name, teaching their children by
precept to seek above all things to be honest, and by
practice to seek above all things to be rich; so long as
they fear the wholesome frugality of our incorrupt
ancestors more than they fear dishonor, and add a
double bribe to the temptation to get wealth in doubtful
ways, by respecting it after it is so got; when the
prizes of political preferment are gilded with unclean
perquisites, and leaders high in place sway the nation
through the purse-strings of their base tools and batten
on the spoils of industry; so long as a considerable
part of mankind look leniently on Judas, because he
carried the bag, we may well be thankful for one

example for lofty integrity, so pure and high that he could say, "People talk about the corruption of Washington: I have lived here all these years and have seen nothing of it,"—so true that no slander dared sully his reputation with the suspicion of a bribe.

And then there is the worship of power for power's own sake. Forgetting that ability, apart from moral gifts, is the sharpest cutting-tool, sure to turn in the hand that uses it unless it is grasped by firm principle, our people are tempted to idolize the very qualities by which the angels fell, and in which the chief of fallen angels is also chief. They count impudence and brazen audacity a sign of power; but do they think what power mere unscrupulousness may give a man? The moment he flings honor and decency to the winds, his power for evil in word and deed is multiplied tenfold. What then? Shall we straightway make the lack of scruple one of the cardinal virtues, and teach our children to take the "*Not*" out of the ten commandments? Or shall we turn again to the reassuring thought of a man of state who could hold high office for nearly a generation; whose motto was those words of Story, "No man ever stands in the way of another"; whom, having held such office, none accuse of turning it into an engine for private advantage; who sought sincerely to make the ends he aimed at in it his "country's, God's, and truth's"; who believed himself the servant, not the master, of the Commonwealth, whose honors sought him, and were unmarketed as they were unbought?

And yet again we are in danger of disbelief in the

honor of the honorable. In the hot and heavy fumes
of accusation and of proven failure to do clear duty
which befog the air, when great names are tarnished and
honors well earned are cheaply lost, the tempter whispers
that it is so the world over,—"There is none upright;
no, not one." Who shall measure the inspiration which
there is in such an hour in the unspotted example of a
great integrity towering above the mean rivalries and
small ambitions of petty greatness as a rocky New
England summit towers over the surrounding plain?

And if we are tempted to be discouraged, seeing a
wide distrust of educated skill; that the community is
prone to think that statecraft comes by nature or in flattering the mob; that it is often slow to seek the service
of the best-trained gifts, and hasty to condemn the
long-tried and upright public servant;—there is at least
the alleviation of seeing it wake to a sense of its loss
when one of its best-furnished and most faithful goes
out of the contumely and fickleness of these earthly
noises to where the silence is broken only by God's
"Well done!"

There is, I know, a theory which writes a new moral
law of party obligations, and makes infraction of those
behests one of the deadly sins. According to this view,
it is enough that men claim to represent the moral
sentiment of the country, to enable them to communicate
a sort of grace to any sinner whom they may sanctify
by a nomination for office. The Church of Rome is
sometimes accused of holding that a priest, though a bad
man, can equally administer the sacraments; and there
are those who hold that if duly named for the place,

the most corrupt man is fitted to become a high-priest in the nation's temple; there are those who hold that we elect men to keep the national conscience and are absolved from any public duty but doing as we are told. When we thus sell ourselves for nothing to the will of power, farewell indeed to the hope of our high heritage from God! If it were so, the free spirit might well say with Lacordaire, "I am forced to leave the scene by a secret instinct of my liberty, in presence of an age which had no longer all its own. I saw that in my ideas, in my language, and in my past, I also was at liberty, and that my time was come for disappearing like the rest."

But it is not so. Christian men and women, who have to do with forming the better mind of the Republic, see to it that you do your part to scatter these miasmatic vapors which threaten to stifle our best life, —and all will yet be well. Hold up afresh a higher standard of duty before others; hold to it those whom you place in power,—and test their claims by it; and that you may do so consistently, hold yourself to it. Enforce the Christian law of conscience, as personal in public as in private duty. Honor, as the great outburst of popular respect has honored, the man who tries to do his duty.

Ah, to what wholesome lessons does the event bring us back, whose shadow is still over us! I end as I began: death teaches us much that life could never teach;— the great and solemn lesson of charity, that searching spirit of love which will find the truth in a man and hold it fast, and help it in all its strong and radiant power; the faith in the ultimate victory of the truth, which will count all else loss if we can only lose ourselves in that triumphant, much-enduring service; the trust in character, in that rocky faithfulness to one's best and deepest convictions, which

> "Obeys the voice at eve
> Obeyed at prime."

And this is the meaning of that wonderful outpouring of the great heart of a Commonwealth which we ourselves have seen.

"And they buried him in the city of David among the kings, because he had done good in Israel, both toward God and toward his house;" "and all Israel mourned for him, according to the word of the Lord."

CHARLES SUMNER.

———

Born in Boston, January 6, 1811.

Entered Harvard College, 1826; Graduated, 1830.

Admitted to the Bar, 1834.

Elected United States Senator, 1851; Re-elected, 1857, 1863, 1869.

Died in Washington, March 11, 1874.

Buried in Mount Auburn,

March 16, 1874.

www.ingramcontent.com/pod-product-compliance
Lightning Source LLC
Chambersburg PA
CBHW020953030726
47496CB00005B/1483

* 9 7 8 3 3 3 7 0 9 3 0 9 9 *